The Holy Book of Ian

Kyle Vasarhely

Book Cover by CoverKitchen

First edition 2026

ISBN: 979-8-9931254-1-1

Contents

Chapter 1:

The Story of Rondithmuth

Thousands of years before this story occurred, freedom and prosperity rippled across the world. People could do what they pleased—within reason, of course—and were told that their individual rights and liberties would never die. I know, funny, right? It turns out they were lied to, and terrible consequences soon followed. The world was lured into being controlled, and as generations passed, people forgot what liberty was.

In the arid wasteland that was once the state of Delaware, the city of Rondithmuth stood majestically in the seemingly endless desert of the surrounding land. The layers upon layers of sand and dust surrounding the town might well be described as a blanket, except that blankets tend to feel comfortable. Large sandstone walls climbed to the heavens, protecting the land from the threats of the barren, untouched landscape, as well as from solicitors. Within the barriers stood small patches of vegetables that the farmers struggled to grow in the hot, dry air. As one approached, a strange smell wafted, and small structures made from the same stone as the city's walls appeared along the sandy, seemingly haphazardly laid roads. The windows were little more than open holes for looking out onto the street and an easy way to hand money over to the tax collector.

King Ron, for whom the city was named, ruled over it. A man of advancing years, he had a balding head and a bushy gray beard that gave him an aura of unearned wisdom. Ambitious but often stubborn to his own detriment, he enjoyed all the delicacies offered to a ruler of his stature—such as salad.

Ruling by his side was his wife, Gretchen. Of similar age to her husband, she sported short gray hair, narrow dark eyes, and a larger frame. She found joy in the little annoyances, such as complaining about the sun being too dark and the moon being too bright. Her favorite pastime, however, was belittling the servants.

Not that one really asked, but the story of Ron and Gretchen's union began 25 years ago at a protest demanding better conditions—and a reasonable 1,000% raise—for workers at the local Easily Breakable Plastic Goods Company.

As Ron held up his sign in the streets, his eyes were drawn to a beautiful woman being sprayed with a hose by the company's goons in what he perceived as a slow, seductive sort of motion. In his distraction, his sign accidentally smacked into another woman standing next to him—Gretchen.

Turning to apologize, he came face to face with her, which was not a very comfortable place to be, as her disgruntled face pierced through his eyes. "Oh, sorry about that. I was looking at that woman getting blasted by a hose for fighting for what she believes in. Inspiring stuff." He helped her up.

Gretchen's swift response was to smack Ron in the face with a pan she just happened to be carrying.

"Ow, what was that for?" Ron rubbed his cheek as the clang of the pan was still ringing.

"You irritate me."

At that moment, Ron saw something in this woman he had never seen before. "What is that dark spot behind your ear?" he asked, pointing.

"It's my birth mole. It showed up when I was eleven."

Realizing he had struck a nerve, he quickly tried to change the subject. "I'm Ron, son of the local pigeon feeder at the park downtown," he said, puffing out his chest as if this was some great accomplishment.

Gretchen snorted in a way that was reminiscent of a pig but responded in kind. "I'm Gretchen. My mother got rich after my father died from a freak accident involving a pillow and cardboard boxes."

Again unsure how to respond, Ron chose the sympathy angle. "I'm sorry to hear that. You must have been close to him."

Another snort by Gretchen, this time a little more like a horse. "Oh yeah, close as a daughter and an incompetent buffoon who dies from a pillow attack could be," she sneered.

Running out of conversation, Ron made one final attempt. "Would you like to have salad with me? I know a place that serves the best lettuce in miles."

Gretchen didn't make a noise this time. Instead, she studied him. "Would you call yourself a stand-up guy?"

Before Ron could answer, a shirtless man who, naturally, had a firecracker in hand, shoved into him and nearly knocked him over. "Watch where you're going," the man called back gruffly.

"Sorry, it won't happen again." Ron kept his head down.

To his surprise, when he looked back at Gretchen, she was smiling at him, which seemed to be something she was not used to doing. It didn't exactly look right. "It's a date," she said, her tone lighter than it had been through their entire interaction.

From that moment on, Ron and Gretchen were inseparable. Whether attending political rallies or throwing fake change at the homeless, they faced life's experiences together. Two years after their fateful meeting, they were married. Ron proposed during a hunger strike protesting the unethical killing of mosquitoes.

As the years passed, he became a high school chemistry teacher, while she found her calling as a professional food critic. It was at Ron's school where he met Artie Dimwit, an English teacher who invited the couple to secret political meetings. These meetings sought to overthrow the government, which was riddled with corruption.

It was the kind of corruption that Ron and his friends desperately wanted to be a part of. While he had eagerly joined these revolutionaries,

Gretchen chose to stay out of it, wisely saying politics was "just a tedious game of who's the more pathetic scum bucket."

The people in charge were indeed failing their people, though. Resources were being squandered, and crises were mismanaged. The final straw came when they failed to prevent the crippling of the phone book sector, the area's major service industry, which led to massive layoffs.

After months of street riots and terrorist—sorry—freedom fighter acts, Ron and the other revolutionaries stormed into the palace where the current government had taken shelter. They found the current government's leaders cowering in the corner of a secure room.

Ron stepped up with a new authority in his voice. "Oh, look what we have here. A bunch of leeches sucking our country dry. Well, boys, what do we do with leeches?"

The pompous Artie Dimwit answered him. "Well, I usually have my maid take care of it. They feel weird and icky."

Ron sighed at his compatriot's response. "We squash them like the vermin they are," he said sharply.

There was a collection of "ohs" from around the room before Ron turned his attention back to the leaders, who looked now more depressed than afraid. "Now, the keys to your government, please."

One of them handed over a nice-looking set of keys. Ron held them high, declaring, "Today brings the start of a better tomorrow. Today!" Everyone looked at him in confusion. Sighing again, he said, "Just get the handcuffs ready."

And so, the city's government fell. Ron and his comrades declared themselves the new leaders. Ron became the Minister of Health and Good Eating, where he would lead raids on individuals suspected of inadequate dietary practices.

"So, you thought you could hide chocolate under the floorboards and get away with it?" Ron sneered to a family whose home he had burst into without warning after getting a tip-off from an anonymous source. "Well, maybe a few months in solitary will teach you that we are a community and that community will do as we say." He threw the chocolate into the dirt and stomped on it. A little girl began crying and clung to her mother.

However, King Ron had ambitions beyond merely leading raids on people's pantries to ensure their nutritional adequacy. After a series of "accidents," Ron was the last remaining minister. The Minister of Control died from his toilet inexplicably collapsing into the ground. The Minister of House Temperature Regulation died from a tragic piano-from-the-sky incident. The Minister of Square and Rectangle Regulation was killed after being run over by a stampede of pigs from the community petting zoo. Even Artie Dimwit, the new Minister of Truth Language, was mysteriously killed by his book collection after tripping over it and falling out of an open window three stories in the air.

The day after the tragedies occurred, Ron addressed the crowd outside the city hall. Many gathered around in anticipation of what was happening, while others thought that a raffle was going on. Gretchen stood beside him, uneasy about the scene he was making.

"It is with great reluctance that I take on the responsibilities of my fallen brethren and assume the absolute power that is necessary to maintain the prosperity that is flowing through the veins of the city," he said to the crowd, garnering a mixed response as only a smattering of applause filled the air. "And the best is yet to come!"

Some seemed optimistic, while others looked worried. Others asked when the raffle was starting. Ron was officially crowned the city's king, with Gretchen as his queen. The area was formally renamed in honor of its new leader. No one knows where the end part of the city's name came from—it's rumored Ron wrote it down incorrectly when he was trying to write "Rontimore" but everyone decided not to question it.

The city suffered from this change in leadership. But King Ron thrived, getting all the good lettuce and premium channels the serfs could only dream of. He built a lovely new little palace in the center of town that oversaw the countless new bureaucratic busywork buildings.

Soon after King Ron took power, he also annexed the surrounding desert area, claiming roads and channels for trade in what he called "Operation Sandbox." People living outside the city's tyranny were now seeing the Rondithmuth soldiers with spears in hand—for whatever reason, Ron refused to allow his military to carry firearms—herding dissenters back into their homes or arresting them for "disturbing the peace."

"We have been free from your pathetic government grips for ten generations," said a man being chained in a carriage outside his bake shop. "You will never fully control us."

"Oh, really, is that why you're chained up?" responded the arrogant guard who was finishing his restraints while his steward was grabbing some cupcakes from the shop for him.

There seemed to be no hope. But Backwards Dog, a holy entity that helps oversee humanity—lovely guy, has a weakness for apple tarts—had plans for Ron and his city. He didn't like what he was seeing with the lack of liberty and insufferable South American-Asian hiring quotas. He decided something needed to happen to right the ship that had been wronged so it could be righted again, although he took his time to do it—eighteen years after King Ron took power, to be exact.

Chapter 2:

The Story of the Birth
of the Holy Ian

The day started like any other Thursday. Ron went to his throne room after having his breakfast salad and sat on his throne. The King's seat had red-leather arms and a gold-lined back etched in looping, unnecessary knots. No one knows where Ron had gotten the gold for his chair, and no one really had the enthusiasm to find out, either. Some suspected it was just paint, but they didn't usually live long enough to spread that rumor.

Ron sat with his queen next to him. Gretchen sulked in her chair like she would rather have been sentenced to prison. King Ron did not seem to notice or mind, though, as he smiled at his guards, oligarchs, and subjects scattered around the vast room. He clapped his hands together, much like that monkey with the cymbals.

"The King will now hold court. Who is first?" he called out to the room. A ragged-looking man in the front of the line, dressed in torn cloth that seemed to be stitched together to keep it whole, stepped forward. King Ron looked at him with disgust but hid his true feelings behind a light smile and greeting. "What troubles you today, good sir?"

The man looked up nervously and replied, "Well, Your Grace, I'm a farmer near the river channel on the outskirts of your kingdom. We haven't had a good harvest for years. The soil is dead. The plants are as brittle as needles."

Ron interjected. "And what does this have to do with me?" he asked mockingly. These sorts of people tended to be a common theme during court for the king. Nothing but complaints. Why couldn't someone just tell him his hairs were looking great today?

The man stuttered. "Well, Your Grace, if we can't grow at least an average crop of food, many of us farmers will be ruined and starved."

Ron shook his head, his beard lagging behind the rest of his face, and laughed in a condescending tone. "That is what our program for struggling farmers is for. Free money to keep your mouth shut."

The man sweated in his place but tried to reason with the king. What an idiot. He continued, "Your Grace, if we could just have some fertilizer so we can have some chance of growing food in a desert, we could—"

Ron stood up, irate as if someone had pulled his pants down, and interrupted. "I will not have my court subjected to these talks of toxic pollutants being put into my sacred ground," he cried. The man started to flee from him. "Get out of my sight before I make you one with your pathetic soil."

The man bolted out of the room. The large wooden door slammed behind him, leaving a quiet and anxious court. Ron smiled and sat down calmly as if nothing uncomfortable had just happened. Gretchen looked just as uninterested as she had before. She glared at her husband.

"Ron, I'm going to go back to our private quarters. You can take care of this unpleasant business with the commoners by yourself."

After standing up, she still wasn't as tall as her seated husband. Ron stared down at his queen and gave her a stern look. "It's a bad look to have the queen of the kingdom not seated with her king during his court. You will sit here until our business is done," he said firmly.

Gretchen, looking irate with a vein pulsating across her forehead, sat back in her chair, refusing to look at the rest of the court out of protest. The remainder of the court was relatively calm, as people didn't want to get the same treatment as the farmer from earlier. After it was done, Gretchen took her leave and went to her room, intending not to come out for some time.

That evening, after a very uneventful day of leaving Ron to his game of taxing the first occupation that came to mind (horse jockey, that day), Gretchen was in her room late, sewing by the fire. The night was as clear as ever. Bugs were yelling at each other, filling her room with white noise. She was sewing with generic needles that were about as useful as trying to cut a tree down with a feather. The queen became frustrated after two hours of dealing with this and threw whatever she was attempting to make onto the floor.

"Oh, Backwards Dog, why don't you just go to hell!" she shouted to the air.

Now, Backwards Dog is a simple divine figure. In general, he doesn't seek to intervene, unless he wants to pull some sort of prank like jamming all the toilets at the sports stadium, or he gets insulted and cursed at. In this instance, Backwards Dog had an important meeting scheduled with Gretchen anyway, but also didn't appreciate her cursing, and responded accordingly. His booming voice echoed and bounced around the room, shaking the shelves and fine china.

"What did you say?!" the voice of Backwards Dog boomed.

Lightning flashed outside on the clear summer evening. Gretchen started shaking and fell out of her chair. She tried to speak, but few words came out.

"Wha—what, I—I ..." was all she could muster.

"Sue," Backwards Dog boomed, ignoring the stuttering woman. They are always stuttering. As if that would make the conversation more enjoyable for both of them. Do you think Backwards Dog enjoys delivering divine intervention for the "good" of humanity? No, he just wants to relax and maybe catch whatever is on the odd channels you find on your antenna.

Anyway (sorry for the rant), Gretchen looked around the room, eyes panicking, which was weird since usually it was people's eyes panicking from her.

"My—my name's Gretchen," she cried.

There was the slightest of pauses from Backwards Dog.

"What did I say? Hmm '… anyway, I have a message for you," he said in a softer but still booming voice.

Gretchen continued to be dumbfounded at what was happening to her. This wasn't exactly how she had pictured this day going. Then again, her imagination wasn't the most extravagant.

"A-a—" she started.

"Stop that jittering! I'm trying to have a conversation here," he said more angrily. She stopped crawling around the room and sat down on the floor.

"Sorry," she said timidly.

Backwards Dog carried on without acknowledging her. "I have come to inform you that you are pregnant."

Gretchen scoffed at this and glared at the ceiling. "I find that hard to believe. How do you know that?" she said indignantly.

"Logistics aren't important," Backwards Dog continued. "What is important is that you understand that this child is the son of Backwards Dog, and he is to be me as I am to be him."

"That doesn't make any sense, and you know it. You're just trying to confuse me with complicated word phrasing so I get tricked into whatever weird cult thing you want me to do," she spat back more confidently than earlier. What was this talking ceiling even talking about?

"Hmm … I see I picked a mother with a fire in her," Backwards Dog responded with some surprise in his voice. "Good, you're going to need it. But all you need to do is keep him alive until it is time for him to lead a great rebellion and restore my word across the land."

"And what if I don't?" she asked. But Backwards Dog wasn't intimidated by this, obviously, because why exactly would he be?

"You don't want to know," he said coolly. There was an awkward silence. Gretchen finally broke it with a sarcastic sigh.

"Fine. You're lucky that you're an almighty deity and whatnot," she finally relented to the divine figure.

Backwards Dog seemed satisfied with this answer and said, "And don't you forget it. We'll be in touch."

And in a moment, there was nothing but the sound of bugs talking to each other in the summer air again. Gretchen looked down at her stomach, befuddled. She wondered how she would tell her husband that she was pregnant, given that he was clearly too busy raiding parties on the underground red meat market to have been the father.

She decided to keep it a secret. Over the next nine months, she attributed her growing belly to overeating at dinner parties and social gatherings.

"Oh, you know, we never run out of the peasants' chickens," she said once to an oligarch named Nancy who asked why she had gotten fat. Gretchen asked Ron to have her killed, but, unfortunately for her, Nancy and her husband were among the highest contributing oligarchs in the city.

Ron was also too busy with paperwork on Stick Control legislation to notice his growing wife, though he once asked why she wanted salmon and French fries splattered with taco sauce.

"Because if you don't get me it, you'll be the victim of stick assault violence where the desert sun never shines," she yelled at him, and he quickly sent a servant to fetch the classic food combination for her.

As months passed, it became more and more difficult to conceal her changing body. When Ron was in the area, she resorted to always having something, such as a laundry basket, in front of her belly.

One time, the child kicked hard while Ron told an oligarch how credit ratings were overrated, and she had to pretend that she was trying out a new dance that involved almost falling on her face.

It was likely that Ron wouldn't have noticed anything anyway, though. The Stick Control initiative had led to a thriving black market for twigs and other stick types, which were used to annoy and disrespect the Rondithmuth police force.

As the birth drew closer, Gretchen couldn't help but feel a mix of anxiety and anticipation for the incoming walking and talking bomb that was about to be dropped on her and the city. How would Ron react? Would he notice? How would this even play out? Was she about to give birth to some tentacled monster?

After nine months and many mornings of sickness, the day finally came. Gretchen was sitting through the musical "My Fender Gender Adventure" with her maids at Brecht Hall. Ron was busy at the office when the drawer that held all the tax receipts exploded from overuse. Suddenly, she felt her contractions begin. She demanded to be brought to the hospital but also that the king not be told, or they would find out what the true wrath of a pregnant woman could be.

After this thinly veiled threat, she was promptly rushed to the hospital. The hospital was just a hut with a faded Red Cross sign on the front, but it did the job.

There was screaming, names being called, and out came a holy gift. The doctor let out a gasp and took a step back. Gretchen then looked at what had departed from her. It was a boy, no tentacles in sight, but there were some abnormalities.

The baby sported a lush layer of black hair, seemed to have already formed some adult teeth, and had a rather big nose for a baby. Gretchen picked up the baby, dropped him, and picked him up again. She decided to name him Ian. This moment would be celebrated as the most holy of moments. She gazed at the child who was about to change her life and the fate of the entire world, and then caught the whiff of a stinky, and immediately handed him off to the nurse.

Ian was born on the fourth day of the fifth month, the Holy Sabbath Day. He was born on a full moon, even if we have no records of what moon it was—it's just assumed. Definitely makes it sound cooler. The world was not ready for what was coming for them, especially a certain balding king.

Chapter 3:

The Story of Ian Being Brought Home

Ian was one hour old, learning to make complicated facial expressions at 15 minutes and discovering how to read at 30 minutes, as Backwards Dog's prodigies tend to do.

"Do Not Enter: Toxic," the baby Ian babbled aloud, looking at a passing door as the nurse carried him. Earlier, the doctor had noticed Ian gesturing toward the glasses on the doctor's face, and after getting over the initial shock, he placed some glasses that were sitting on a nearby table on Ian's face. Immediately, Ian's face glowed with happiness, and he looked around the room in wonder and judgment.

Gretchen was in her room recovering from her birth, sitting in the makeshift bed they had set up there. She had a magazine in her hand titled *Rich Royals Weekly*, the magazine for the rich and powerful that talked about how great it was to be rich and powerful.

On the other side of the room, Ian was being bundled and clothed for the first time. Ian didn't like this and yelled and screamed about the whole affair. He calmed down, though, once the nurse slapped him with some baby powder, whereupon, she later swore to the other nurses, he had winked at her. When finished, she brought him over to Gretchen, who had put down her magazine and was now sitting in her bed practicing her frown.

"Here he is," the nurse said gently, handing the infant off to his mother, who took him warily. She was expecting something a little more from the son of a holy entity. The nurse awkwardly stared at Gretchen, not knowing what to say to her as Gretchen picked Ian up and checked under his armpits for anything unusual.

"We tried our best. The free towels haven't arrived yet, so he might be a little stinky," the nurse said with a little chuckle.

Gretchen put her practiced frown into action. "Yet another great program from my king husband," she said bitterly.

The nurse looked even more uncomfortable now, not knowing whether to disagree with the Queen or insult the king. "Of course, the king has been a blessing for our city," the nurse said with a scared smile, as one never knew when they were being tested.

"Oh yes, a blessing for all," Gretchen replied sarcastically. She put Ian in the little crib next to her and laid back down, exhausted from the eventful day. The nurse stood uncomfortably until someone began to scream for a pee bag in the other room. She took this opportunity to leave the more uncomfortable situation, leaving Gretchen to her thoughts.

Meanwhile, outside the hospital, three men in brightly colored thawbs entered and started creeping up and down the hallways, looking in and out of rooms. They all wore long gray beards that went down to their chests. To match it, they had long gray hair that went down to their backs, making them look like walking mops. The man in the bright red thawb seemed to be the leader. He grabbed the arms of the man in the yellow thawb, who was doing something next to the wall.

"No, my friend. That is a breaker switch. Don't stick your screwdriver in there," the man in red said, pulling the man in yellow away. The man in yellow smiled at the man in red, putting his screwdriver down to his side.

"Thank you, my friend. You are much wiser than me. I always make the stupidest mistakes," he said, looking to the ground sullenly.

The one in red lifted the man's chin and smiled at him. "We all have our faults, my friend. It's our intentions that matter. And those intentions are nothing but good from you," he said gently. This seemed to cheer the man in yellow up.

They eventually looked into Gretchen's room and enthusiastically entered. Gretchen looked up maliciously at what she thought was some hallucination from the hardcore narcotic drugs she was on.

"The children's room is down the way. That's where you can do your clown show," she said bitterly.

The man in the green thawb looked around the room as if he had dropped his keys somewhere, which he did, but that was 30 minutes ago. "I see no clowns. Are you okay, woman? Do I need to perform surgery?" he said, stepping toward her before the man in red held him back. The man in red then looked at Gretchen and smiled, arms still clamped to the other's chest.

"Hello, my dear. We are the Three Ill-Advised men. I am Ill-Advised," he said, pointing to himself. "This is More Ill-Advised," he said, pointing to the man in yellow. "And this fine gentleman here is Very Ill-Advised," he said as he pointed to the man in green.

Gretchen did not look amused. "Like I said, clowns. Go bother someone else," she said coldly. Ill-Advised hesitated for a moment.

"Is this the room of an Ian?" Ill-Advised asked, not seeming to care about, or even notice, her tone.

Gretchen glanced at the baby lying in the crib, who had managed to sit up and seemed to be listening intently to what was happening. She then looked at the men suspiciously.

"Yes, what's it to you?"

Ill-Advised smiled gleefully. "Wonderful," he exclaimed, face brightening. "We have come to congratulate you. You see, we were walking down a dark alley earlier after someone called us over from the shadows. Naturally, we followed the voice. But before we got there, a sticky note came out of nowhere and smacked into the face of Very Ill-Advised."

Very Ill-Advised waved his hand at Gretchen, who did not return the gesture.

Ill-Advised continued. "We looked at the note while the nice man from the alleyway handled our baggage. The note told us to come to the hospital in Rondithmuth and look for a newborn named Ian. It had the address, a map, and the hospital's number in case we got lost," he said, beginning to trail off.

"That was a stupid and pointless story," Gretchen said.

"Would you say that it was ill-advised?" Ill-Advised asked.

"Very," she said curtly.

"Yes?" Very Ill-Advised responded.

Ill-Advised tried to keep the conversation moving, though. "Our apologies, madam, for any inconvenience caused by our actions."

Gretchen shifted in her chair like she wanted something to throw. She glanced briefly at Ian, then resumed glaring at the scene in front of her.

"What are you going to do now?" she asked.

The Three Ill-Advised Men looked uncomfortably at one another. Clearly, they did not do this sort of thing often.

"Well, we are not sure. We only got one note," More Ill-Advised finally answered.

A sticky note flew through the room's open window and slapped Very Ill-Advised in the face.

Ill-Advised smiled, peeled the note slowly off his face, and read it out loud to the room. "Hmm, it tells us to look for a sign that Ian is the true son of Backwards Dog alluded to in the previous sticky note," he said before looking up blankly for an awkwardly long time.

After some amount of time in uncomfortable silence, a pigeon suddenly slammed into the window, startling them, but mostly Very Ill-Advised, who threw his screwdriver at the window in self-defense.

Ill-Advised glanced up from his note and then looked back at it again. "Hmm, interesting," he said as if he had just been told some trivia about girdles. "Now it says if step 1 is complete, tell Gretchen that this boy, indeed, is the Holy Ian, son of Backwards Dog. If no sign occurred, walk to the next room and repeat step 1." He put the note somewhere where apparently a pocket was hiding amongst the chaos of his garments. He then looked down at Gretchen's irritable face.

"Gretchen, your son is indeed the son of Backwards Dog," he said proudly.

Gretchen huffed. "Good, great, now get out of here before I take away whatever manhood you still have left." She gave the three men death stares that, to her increasing annoyance, weren't working on them.

Ill-Advised held out his hand for pause, unfazed by Gretchen's threats. "Hold on. It says to wait for the next holy message," he said, and then went back to staring forward blankly in awkward silence. Luckily for Gretchen, a sticky note soon flew in from the hallway and smacked Very Ill-Advised again.

"Ah yes, there it is," Ill-Advised said as if this was part of his daily routine. He ripped the note off the face and read it out loud again. "Now we must pick up Ian and raise him in the air and say, 'Here is Ian, the son of Backwards Dog,' then await further instruction."

Gretchen was looking more irritated by the second. "Don't you have a role-playing convention to go to?" she snarled.

"Yes," said More Ill-Advised, but Ill-Advised ignored him.

"I'm just reading what the note says, ma'am," he said, with a tone like his hands had actually been tied. He picked up Ian—who'd been doing cartwheels on the bed—and raised him in the air.

"This is Ian, the son of Backwards Dog," Ill-Advised proclaimed. Ian surveyed the room from his new height. More Ill-Advised tapped Ill-Advised on the shoulder.

"Uh, Ill-Advised, I think it's supposed to be 'Here is Ian, the son of Backwards Dog' instead of what you said," More Ill-Advised said. Ill-Advised smiled childishly.

"Thank you, More Ill-Advised, how silly of me. Here is Ian, the son of Backwards Dog."

"Ill-Advised, you forgot to raise him," Very Ill-Advised pointed out. Gretchen yanked Ian out of his hand.

"That's it. Leave now and never annoy me with your presence again!" she yelled furiously.

Ill-Advised ripped Ian back, as if Gretchen had stolen his chocolate bar, and frowned. "We will leave, older wrinkly woman, but only after we are told to. We let the notes guide our way," he said indignantly. A note slapped him in the face. He took it off and read it.

"Now, I am to remind Gretchen that she must protect Ian as a child, or she will lose the taste for oats forever," he said.

He looked down at Gretchen. "Gretchen, you must protect Ian as a child, or she will lose the taste for oats forever," he said as if this was new news. His two companions looked at him in slight confusion.

Gretchen fumed in her place, smoke starting to become visible from her head. "You are horrible people!" she cried, but Ill-Advised shook his head.

"Just reading what the note says, ma'am," he replied.

Another note flew in but missed them and slammed into the wall. Ill-Advised approached it and read it.

"It says to back out of the room slowly and say ominously, 'Remember.' Then, go back into the alley and wait for further instructions," he said. He looked at Gretchen, and then the Three Ill-Advised Men all backed up.

"Remember," they said in unison. They backed out of the room, though Very Ill-Advised accidentally slammed into the wall next to the door before they were all out of sight. Soon after, a young boy enthusiastically walked by the doorway, shaking some maracas, beads rattling violently with the boy's enthusiastic whip of his arms. Gretchen threw a tray at him, and he ran off in terror. The sound of the frantically shaking beads trailed off in the distance.

The nurse came in right after. "Oh, I see you met our little maraca boy. He said he wanted to play a song for your child," the nurse said cheerfully. "Isn't that wonderful?"

Gretchen was done with this hospital and got up to leave. Ten minutes later, she came back and got Ian, who was still sleeping in the crib. She held him and went out of the hut, making sure nobody was watching. Then she headed back toward the palace.

However, with her view obstructed by Ian, Gretchen failed to notice a young girl, probably around five, who was observing her and what she possessed. The girl quickly darted away across the town and eventually came up to a dirty-looking shack, mold dripping down its sides, a visit from a health inspector just waiting to happen. She went up to it and knocked three times in a rhythmic tap, pause, tap tap. The door cracked open, and she was let in.

Inside was a single musky room with tables and chairs laid out haphazardly. Many people were scattered throughout different corners, performing various tasks such as writing notes, instructing others to write notes, and ordering materials used to write notes. The girl approached a large and beefy man with a dark, thick mustache. He wore a suit with various buttons, pins, and other artifacts that looked like they had been found in a junkyard. He turned around and looked down to see the little girl.

"Margaret, what is it? What have you found out? Are the rumors true?" he questioned her.

"The queen have baby," the girl named Margaret answered. The room stopped cold and everyone dropped what they were doing to see what was happening. The man with the mustache had a look of triumph and fear in his eyes.

"Are you absolutely sure?" he asked Margaret again, bending down to her level. She nodded.

"Simon, is it the one who we were told of?" a woman in the corner asked him. "Has the Maud'Ian come?"

The man named Simon bristled his mustache in annoyance. "How many times have I told you?" he replied gruffly. "That is nothing more than a superstition. And we can't bet our lives on a superstition." A restless mutter ensued, which annoyed Simon even more. "No, he is just another brat that will lead the terror and tyranny of King Ron for another generation. He will be dealt with in time."

"We're going to, you know? Kill him?" a man near him asked.

"War is dirty, and the Coffee Party will not exit this world clean," Simon said, and he left the shack, still muttering to himself. Many of the rest of the people in the room glanced at each other warily.

"The Maud'Ian will come. Have faith," the woman in the back said to the room, and this seemed to calm them down.

Meanwhile, Gretchen returned home, and Ron awaited her at the door. "Where have you been?" he asked with worry and a hint of anger.

Gretchen wasn't in the mood, though, and wasn't intimidated. "Oh, you know. Speaking to the serfs, having a baby," she said after clicking her teeth.

Ron spat out the radish that was in his mouth. "What?" he yelled.

Gretchen looked annoyed at this reaction. "Oh yeah, here. Look at this," she said, taking Ian out of her purse and holding him up. Ron gaped at him, and she scowled at him.

"You're acting like you've never seen one before," she said.

"But how did this happen?" Ron asked, still in shock.

Gretchen rolled her eyes. "How do you think it happened, Ron?"

Ron thought for a moment, then shook his head, looking even more confused.

"Of course, how silly of me to think of alternative ways. Well, Ian it is, then," he said finally.

Gretchen had already moved on from the conversation, though. "Fine, here. I've been with him all day," she said. Then she tossed Ian over to Ron and walked by them, out of sight.

Ron barely caught Ian and looked at him curiously as if he were looking at some weird rock. "You weren't what I expected today," he told the child.

Ian shrugged in Ron's arms. Ron raised his eyebrows, and Ian followed suit. Ron handed him a Karl Marx doll. Ian took it and threw it on the ground, which then caught on fire. Ron frowned at him.

"Ian, that was very naughty. We don't harm depictions of prophets," he said, wagging a finger. Ian giggled, but Ron continued. "Now, if we're going to make this work, you have a lot to learn, and you'll have to change your attitude. And this Backwards Dog-forsaken dry air needs to stop causing things to spontaneously catch on fire."

Ian coughed up an application for a charter school into Ron's hands and frowned again.

"No, Ian, we don't hack up applications from evil institutions, and I'm going to find out who let you eat this. But now we're going to get you to bed. Daddy's got a meeting with the Teachers' Union," he said, and he put down Ian, who began to crawl away.

Ron stared at the child in wonder. He had always wanted an heir. I mean, any king who seeks to have their great legacy last for an eternity knows that the easiest way is to have a mini version of themselves. But he had given up hope after so many years. Maybe this was a blessing and a sign that he was doing the right thing with his rule. This thought comforted him, and he smiled at his new son. What a blessed day.

Chapter 4:

The Story of Ian and Ron's Big Desert Adventure

I an was the age of two, having learned at one to talk in sentences, and at one and a half, how to discuss politics at the dinner table, much to Ron's chagrin. Ian seemed not to grasp the ideals that Ron had tried to bestow upon him at a young age. While Ron would stay up late reading *Chucky the Cheetah's Class Struggle*, Ian would not pay attention, or worse, point out theoretical flaws in the picture book depicting Chucky's secret union meeting getting interrupted by the evil hired-goon elephants.

His mother wasn't much better, as she left most of the upbringing to Ron while she invested in her programs on television. "You're the one who wanted the child, Ron. Remember?" she gaslit Ron one evening when Ian wrote a particularly troubling picture book depicting a boy operating a lemonade stand and becoming the CEO of a multimedia lemonade empire. So, in light of all this, Ron decided it was time to steer his son in the right direction. He decided to take Ian with him to find the element that kept his kingdom operating.

"Ian, it's time to go. Pack up your fishing equipment, shovel, and bucket," Ron called up to Ian, who was in his room. It was another unremarkable Tuesday morning. People were hurrying along to their morning jobs for the day, and kids were yawning over to the bus stop to wait for the electric bus.

Little Ian hopped down the stairs dressed in his fancy royal uniform and ran to Ron. Ian's glasses, rather large for his size, bounced on his face. His lush black hair had only gotten lusher since he was born, so much so that Ron had trouble keeping it at least passably straight.

"Put on your coat, Ian. Yesterday, the temperature was 92 degrees. Today, it is 90. The world is cooling," Ron said as he grabbed a thick jacket off the rack by the front door.

"It was 87 three days ago. It's warmer now," Ian said, holding the little coat up.

Ron rolled his eyes at this remark, all too common from Ian lately. "Never you mind, global cooling doesn't necessarily mean that it has to be cooler." Ron grinned, happy with his answer.

"That's a paradox," Ian replied quickly in his squeaky voice.

"Yes, but it makes it easy to say whatever I want. So, coat up." He grabbed the coat out of Ian's hands and pulled it on him, then ruffled his lush black hair. Then, putting on his own jacket, he called out to Gretchen, who was in the living room watching *Spirit Hunters*.

"Honey, we're leaving. We'll be gone for a couple of days. Can you make dinner for when we get back?"

"No, I do everything around here. You can make dinner yourself. Or have your son do it. He'd probably be better at it anyway."

"He can't even reach up to the counter yet," Ron said, which was supposedly true, though he wasn't sure how exactly he'd found him on top of a shelf eating a cookie one night. The main question was where had he found a cookie in the first place?

"That's the King's problem," she said, and that was the end of it.

Ron sighed and led Ian out the door. They walked down the dirt roads crowded with people wearing clothes that were not in any way close to the quality the two royals were wearing, making Ian and Ron stick out like sore thumbs. Eventually, they made their way to the edge of the city.

Ian suddenly looked up at Ron, who seemed deep in thought. Or he was drifting off. Either was possible. "Ron, what are we wasting our time for when it could be used for earning money?" Ian asked.

Ron seemed to get back to reality. He looked down at little Ian and smiled at him. "Ah, my young biological son, for generations, our ancestors have used the great element Pla-toh as a means to our power and wealth," he said, smiling up at the sky in wonder. Ian also looked up, though he didn't know what he was looking at.

"Aren't you a first-generation ruler?" Ian asked.

Ron ignored this and continued his exposition. "It makes our whole system of government function, Ian. That's what you need to know."

"So, for socialism to work, a magical element is needed?"

"I, uh, yes. Yes. So, we go out and fish for the worms that hold Pla-toh," Ron said, growing wary of the fact that he was being one-upped by someone younger than a toddler.

"Some of that made sense. How do we get there?" Ian continued to press.

Ron went up to a rusty metal rack that stood alone near what seemed to be a street of run-down buildings. "Why, with the community bikes from the community bike racks, of course," he answered.

There were only two rusted bikes, both of which seemed to have flat tires, with one bike missing its handlebars.

"Ah, I see everyone is enjoying and using our community bikes. That's good," Ron said proudly.

An old man chained to the rack sat up, startling Ron, who instinctively got out the disinfectant. One might've taken great exception to what the man was wearing, but one probably would've passed out from the stench coming off of him before being able to see him. It smelled like a stadium bathroom on free beer night, possibly even worse.

"There haven't been more than these two bikes here for five years. Kids steal them and don't bring them back. I was the last to use one before they mugged me. Been tied up here ever since," the old man croaked.

Ron looked at Ian. "Now, Ian, one of the first things to know while being a king is to keep the people happy and tell them what they want to hear," he whispered so the old man couldn't hear him. He then turned to the chained man. "Do not fear, young citizen. I will get someone to get you out," he said, his chest out like a stuck-up rooster.

"Well, the key's down there. It's just out of reach," the old man said, pointing to a rusty key that looked weathered and rotten.

"Come, Ian. We've done all we can," Ron said, leading Ian away. Ian didn't seem like he wanted to go, though.

As they walked away, Ian looked back and waved at the old man. At that moment, the lock on the chain suddenly broke off, freeing him. The old man quickly stood up, wobbled in place before gaining his balance, and ran out of sight, exhilarated that his luck had finally turned.

Ian and Ron grabbed their bikes, began leaving the city behind, and entered the empty desert. They stopped for the night when the sun began to drift below the horizon and the moon rose, illuminating the sand in a silvery glow.

"Why are we stopping?" Ian questioned.

Ron was getting really annoyed at all these questions but gave Ian a hearty smile. "Well, Ian, the desert is very cold at night. Plus there may or may not be monsters," he said, the last part being said as an afterthought.

"Monsters?" Ian again asked. Ron sighed, realizing he couldn't avoid Ian's probing.

"The great worm king, Ian—they say the spirit of George Bush roams these sand dunes in the form of a slithery beast, searching for things that may or may not exist," Ron said uneasily.

"Which Bush?"

"Eh, either one works," Ron shrugged.

Ian nodded as if this cleared things up. "Well, thanks, Dad, for that nice information that will certainly not come up later."

"Sure thing, son," Ron replied, happy to end the conversation.

The following morning, the two royals headed to the perfect fishing spot. After a mile or two, Ron started teaching Ian proper fishing techniques.

"When finding a good spot, Ian, you must kick the sand on a hill," Ron said to his son. "If it only blows back and burns your eyes slightly, you're in the right place."

Ron kicked up some sand and yelled in pain for a minute, then stopped and shook his head. "Not quite yet. Let's keep going," he said through the pain coming from his eyeballs, and they kept on moving.

After more kicking and subsequent screaming, they finally found the supposed right patch of sand, and Ron got ready to cast with his rod.

"Where's the bait?" Ian asked, perplexed.

Ron chuckled heartily. "Oh, Ian, har har har, we operate under socialist fishing," Ron stated.

Ian's eyebrows did a loop around his head. "Socialist fishing?" he echoed.

Ron nodded sagely. "Yes, we wait for the worms to surrender themselves to us for the greater good of the community."

Ron swung the rod over his shoulder. The empty line buried its head in the sand and sat motionless as Ron waited patiently.

Hours passed as Ron sat in the sand, his robes getting dirtier by the minute, while Ian sat playing a tune on his knees, bored out of his mind. The only interesting thing that occasionally happened was a gust of wind that spat sand in Ron's face, which Ian thought was pretty funny.

Eventually, Ian got a rod out of his backpack himself, and when Ron wasn't looking, he attached some worm bait to the line and swung it in the sand next to Ron. Ron looked behind him and smiled. His son was starting to get it. Those happy thoughts were short-lived, though, as suddenly the ground began to shake.

Ron jumped up in surprise. "What, the Koch brothers?!" Ron yelled as he stood on the now uneven ground.

A giant worm burst out of the sand and hovered over Ian, who looked up in awe, and Ron, who cowered behind him.

"Ooh, big wormy," Ian said in wonder as this got his attention more than the sand kicking into his father's face.

The worm made a loud noise that started sounding like words in a low Texas accent. "He has come," it said, its voice rumbling the sand and causing waves.

Ron stood back up, shaking. He peeked out from behind Ian. "What did you say?" he asked, his voice trembling.

"He has come, the Maud'Ian has come." The sand shook under the worm's voice.

Ron frowned at the worm. "You are just a worm. What do you know?" he questioned.

"Do not misunderestimate me," the worm rumbled back.

Ian looked back and forth from the worm to Ron curiously, unsure if this was supposed to be unusual.

"I can and will, no matter the detriment," Ron replied stubbornly.

"Worms and people can live together peacefully," the worm responded.

"Not if you keep talking nonsense and dangerous lies in front of my son Ian," Ron spat back.

"The Maud'Ian has come," the worm said again.

"Come on, Ian, let's go." Ron dragged Ian, who was still mesmerized, away from the worm.

"But what about the Pla-toh?" Ian asked his father as his legs were dragged quickly through the sand.

"Oh, that crap doesn't exist," Ron said quickly, and they sped away back toward the city.

"What?" Ian blinked, more confused than ever.

"It's just a way to keep the people happy," Ron said. "It's important to keep the people happy or you may end up with your head not where you want it to be."

"Wait, come back. I have more wormisms to say," the worm called out to them. "Gosh, I get so lonely out here." The worm then put its massive head down on the ground in disappointment.

When Ron and Ian had made a considerable distance, they slowed down. Ron's hand was still shaking slightly.

"What was that about?" Ian asked him, and Ron hesitated.

"What was what about?" he answered, playing dumb.

"Big wormy," Ian said, but Ron waved him off.

"That was just a figment of your imagination, Ian. Don't worry about that," Ron said.

"But?" Ian tried to press, but Ron wasn't having it anymore.

"Ian, rule number two of being a king: What I say goes, so if I say you saw nothing, you saw nothing, got it?" Ron said more harshly than he intended. It had been a long couple of days.

Ian pondered this sentence in his head for a moment, then decided to nod.

When they returned to the palace, Ian ran past Gretchen, who was still watching TV. It was unclear if she had actually gotten up after all this time.

"It was great. Dad says nothing happened, and apparently, what goes, he says," Ian said excitedly as he ran by her feet.

"I don't recall asking how your day was," Gretchen said, eyes not leaving the screen. Ian went into his room, almost jogging in excitement.

"Go to sleep! I don't want to hear you thinking up there!"

That night, Gretchen woke from her dreams of the maids stealing her dignity. When she looked over, she saw Ron was not there. She got up and went to find him. She found him in his study, surrounded by many paintings of his idols scattered around the room, with a giant wooden hammer and sickle hanging over a large fireplace. Ron sat in a cushioned chair, with a single lamp shining over him. He was silently sniffing and swirling a glass of wine in his hand.

"Ron, the TV's still on. Turn it off so I can go to bed."

"You were the one watching it," Ron tried to say confidently, but his attempt at a confident tone left much to be desired.

"So lazy. What are you even doing?" She crossed her arms.

"Ian lied. Something did happen out there," he said flatly.

"Who? Oh, right, *Ian*," Gretchen replied after some confusion.

"A worm sounded like the old recordings of Bush," Ron continued.

"Which heretic?" she asked.

"Eh, either one works," he shrugged. "It said something that I thought I would never hear. He spoke of the Maud'Ian, the one who will change the course we've been set on. Those Coffee Party loonies have been waiting for him for years."

He turned to Gretchen suddenly, a thought entering his head, startling him.

"You don't know anything about this, do you?" he asked her.

Gretchen's face went pale briefly before she frowned at him defiantly, grabbed his wine glass, and threw it in his face.

"I don't need this accusatory tone, Ron," she snapped.

A wet Ron sat up, very much over this day. "All I know is that something is different. Things are changing in ways that will probably make things at least inconvenient," he said worriedly.

"TV, Ron," Gretchen said, ignoring her husband's downer attitude.

Ron didn't respond. He just sighed and started walking back up to his room, with the voices of his wife and one of the Bushes in his head.

Chapter 5:

The Story of Ron's Dinner Party

I an was now three. It had become clear to Gretchen and even Ron that Ian was, at minimum, adventurous and, at worst, a sociopath. Wandering around the backyard to rip out some of Ron's plants in the royal garden was a favorite pastime for him. He would also sometimes stroll out of the house when nobody was looking, to say hello to the local butcher or set a trip-wire trap for one of the patrol guards.

Ron set aside his concerns about the mysterious Maud'Ian and continued cracking down on illegal laundry detergent operations considered harmful to the environment. To mark this achievement and the anniversary of the debut of the Gorbachev pizza commercial, Ron decided to host a grand oligarch dinner at his palace.

This would be the first time the oligarchs got a good look at Ian, whom for obvious reasons he had been hiding from them for the last three years. He had tried to delay this meeting until he had "fixed" him, but time was growing restless, as were the oligarchs.

"Now, Ian, this dinner is very important. It will shape how the people who actually fund this place think of the potential next ruler after I'm gone," Ron said to Ian before the party.

"I'm three," said little Ian.

"Yes, well, you act like a ten-year-old," Ron muttered, rubbing his temple, which was bothering him more and more.

"Eleven-year-old," corrected Ian, as was now more common than not. Ron sighed and pointed upstairs.

"Just go and get your fancy suit on for the party and be down here in one hour," he said. Little Ian stormed off as dramatically as a three-year-old with an intellectual attitude could and went to his room. He began throwing his clothes around the room angrily, hitting the walls with such force that his underwear knocked a dent into his old hammer-and-sickle mobile that Ron had hung up over his old crib. "We have to get him while he's young and gullible. I mean, impressionable," Ron had said to Gretchen, who had been oddly against it.

"Stupid Ron. Always telling me what to do. If I had a bodyguard who would listen to my every word, this wouldn't be a problem," said Ian to no one in particular, and not exactly in the intimidating tone he thought he had achieved.

Ian suddenly heard a popping sound behind him, like a small balloon had burst. He looked around and saw a tall man in a black suit, staring down at him. He had a serious and fairly intimidating expression, his shades covering his eyes.

"The area is secure, Mr. Ian. What are your further instructions?" His hand was on the wireless earphones wrapped around his ear.

Ian blinked, raised an eyebrow, and decided it was probably just some weird coincidence. Either way, he should take advantage of it. He sent the bodyguard to the door. It was opened a moment later by Ron, who had come up after hearing multiple voices.

"Ian, I heard thoughts that sounded independent. What are you …" he said before noticing the large bodyguard standing inches from him. "Oh, sorry. I didn't realize you had company."

Ron's brain then caught up with the situation. He realized this scene didn't make any sense, and he glared at the man suspiciously, then glared at Ian, who had his arms wrapped behind his back, smiling at the scene in front of him.

"Ian, who is this man, and how did he get into my palace?" he asked his toddler son. Ian simply shrugged ignorantly.

The security guard stepped forward and grabbed Ron's arm. "Please step away, sir," he growled.

Ron ripped his hand away and wiped it on a cloth he had for such an emergency.

"Who do you think you are? No one touches the royal wrist," Ron snapped.

The guard promptly shoved Ron out of the room, and the door slammed behind him.

Ron yelled from the other side of the door, "Ian, we're having a talk later."

Ian grumbled as he put on his little red-and-yellow palace robes, emblazoned with the symbol of Rondithmuth: a donkey eating from a giant salad bowl while a herd of sheep watched behind.

"Have a talk, have a talk. Well, how would he feel talking with no pants on?" he wondered out loud.

"What the?" cried out Ron from another room. Ian blinked like a typewriter.

"Gretchen, have you seen my pants?" Ian heard Ron yell.

"How the hell should I know?" Gretchen yelled back from another room.

Ian paused. Was he able to conjure whatever he wanted? He started to think about a giant roast beef sandwich.

In his hand popped a ten-pound sandwich smoking with meaty goodness. He took it from the air.

He then realized, as he took massive bites of his sandwich and his bodyguard got some bear spray ready, that he could conjure whatever he wanted. This was going to make things much more interesting.

Meanwhile, Ron, now with some new pants, had come down to meet Peter Handson, the oligarch who funded the windmills. Handson was dressed in a posh suit that was only befitting for the out-of-touch and arrogant.

"Ah, King Ron, what a wonderful dinner you have provided. And I just wanted to tell you that I'm looking into that pesky turbine that just isn't, you know, functioning," Handson said, glossing over the last part. King Ron was happy to gloss with him, though. Donors were important, after all, and a wealthy oligarch was a happy oligarch.

"I'm sure everything will be all right," Ron said, helping himself to a massive plate of chives.

Handson continued, "And I think I speak for everyone here when I say we're looking forward to meeting your legitimate heir and son."

With the mention of his son, Ron realized that Ian was missing. "Uh, yes, he was just getting ready. He should be down shortly," he replied, only half paying attention now.

Gretchen, meanwhile, was across the room, having to listen to the oligarchs' wives and husbands talk about their interesting lives. "So I had ordered one of the art pieces from that artist from the artsy side of town," one old, pampered woman was spelling out to the crowd around her. "You know the one, Figaro, not Harmenado, Harmenada. I prefer Harmenada. They are better at conveying the plight of working people through the thickness of the lines." Everyone but Gretchen nodded around her. "Waiter, I'm out of the uh, what is this again?"

"Foie gras macarons," Gretchen replied coldly. The woman smiled.

"Ah, yes. Waiter, more of that," she said. Gretchen was desperate to leave but needed some kind of distraction. Suddenly, without warning, a large procession of tuba players came thundering down the massive staircase, playing a sweet tuba tune.

The oligarch who owned the Sandstone Low-Quality Housing Company, Carol Galantene, clapped her hand on the top of her other hand on the beat and went up to Ron, who was picking up his limp bottom lip.

"Oh, splendid, absolutely splendid. Ron, you've done it again," she beamed, still clapping along to the beat. "First that light show with the fluorescent bulbs flickering like a dance floor, and now this. You've got a knack for the art."

Ron, whose eyes were still glazed in shock, was too confused to answer her. He had ordered a parade of people carrying salad dressing, not tubas. This had to be the bureaucracy's fault. He would need to have the department investigate themselves to see what was happening, then create more positions to ensure everything was running smoothly.

But before he could figure out what was happening, he received his answer when he saw his son Ian on the back of his new bodyguard, coming down the stairs majestically. Handson, who had joined Galantene with the clapping, looked excitedly at Ron.

"Ah, this must be Ian," Handson said, and he looked at the boy who had finally reached them.

"That is so," Ian replied from the top of his bodyguard mountain. He hopped down and went up to the oligarch, shaking his hand.

"Hello, Mr. Handson. Your mind certainly seems to be spinning more than your wind turbines," Ian said, smirking.

Ron went up to Ian and a now red-faced Handson and laughed. "Oh, Ian, you have such a quick wit," he said. "Now get over here." He dragged Ian over to a corner next to a fountain of Rosa Luxemburg, which had water flowing out of the feather on top of her hat. He glared down at Ian, who stared back at him innocently.

"Ian, what are you doing? Don't insult the people who paid for that gold jacket you're wearing," Ron said, holding the sleeve of Ian's shiny attire.

"He's wasting our money on electricity that doesn't even work. He's making you look like a fool," said Ian sharply.

Ron frowned at being called a fool by the very toddler who, the other day, had been caught eating cereal with his hands. "Nobody is making me look like a fool!" he snapped. "Now, take these complimentary smallest violins and hand them out to everybody," he added, pulling a handful of tiny violins out of nowhere and dumping them in Ian's hands.

After Ron had walked away, Ian took the violins and shoved them into the fountain. When Ron came back and saw Ian's empty hands, he patted Ian on the back. "Well done, Ian. You're a good follower," he said proudly. Then he walked away and started talking to Tommy Weiner, the owner of the city's only solar company. "Ah, Weiner, the solar panels are looking good on the houses. And when they start working, they'll be even better."

Ian's eyes narrowed. He was no follower, especially not at some stupid oligarch tickle party. Looking around him, he shook his head. The pompous stuck-up snobs almost made one want to vomit from the overwhelming stench. These people needed to be taught a lesson in humility. It was time to act. Ian left, disappearing from sight.

Five minutes later, the cooks came out with salad glistening on gold plates. Ron saw the procession and smiled at it. "Ah, dinner, ladies and gentlemen, should you choose to be referred to in that manner, is served," he announced.

Suddenly, though, the cooks began to run around in panic. Ron rushed over, then immediately rushed back when he saw what the chaos was about. The lettuce, tomatoes, and all the other main course goodies were dancing around the plates and jumping on some of the guests. Peter Handson ran over to him, slices of onions ripping at his toupee. "Ron, if this is some kind of sick passing for a joke," Handson yelled.

"Oh, this is just some of the many entertainments we have planned for tonight," Ron lied, sweat beginning to fall down all four of his cheeks.

A piece of lettuce attacked the obese oligarch, John Nackey, who owned the Community Fitness Zone. He ran around the room, lettuce glued to his face, refusing to let go. Ron looked helplessly at his party unraveling. He heard more screams from the kitchen and went to see what food had come alive this time.

However, when he got near the door, the chefs and assistants burst through in a panic. Ron peeked in and then ran away from the door. It was not insane animated food. A tornado had formed from the kitchen and burst through the door; it whipped furniture—chairs, tables, and the sofa—around the room in the shape of a fist. Carol's wig had flown off and narrowly missed Ron's head.

He ran to comfort the oligarch, who was screaming in a panic. "Well, those windmills seem to be working now," he said, trying to chuckle.

They ducked as the oligarch who owned the Red Tape Corporation flew by them, tied to his chair with his own product. Ron noticed

Ian was sitting in the corner drinking from a giant tavern mug with Gretchen, who was happily making fun of the wigless oligarchs.

"I told him I should've planned this party," she complained to Ian. Ian laughed. "You may have something there, Mother." They toasted their mugs together and each took a gulp.

After the tornado had blown out of the mansion and into the streets, the oligarchs who were still in the room angrily left, muttering things like "What a waste of my time that I could have spent counting my bribes" and "That son of his is so strange. The king should be ashamed." Okay, that last sentence Ron had possibly made up in his head.

When everyone had left, Ron stood in his dining room, which was now covered in dishes and the lettuce that had declared war on the tomatoes. He went over to Ian, who was still sipping his drink through a silly straw.

"Ian, what was that?" asked Ron.

"What was what?" asked Ian blankly.

Ron shook his head and closed his eyes. "I shouldn't have introduced you so early. You clearly were not ready for this," he growled.

Ian sat up, though. "Oh, I've never been more ready."

Ron got right in Ian's face, though Ian held his ground. "I don't know where this attitude has come from, but I'm sick of it, and I'm going to fix you before it's too late."

"Maybe fix the kingdom you've overseen first before you worry about me," Ian replied, causing Gretchen to choke on her drink from laughing.

Ron ignored her. "Things are going to be changing around here right now," he said, although he had obviously lost the room.

Ian's bodyguard came over, and Ron backed away from Ian with his hands up. "All right, all right, I'm leaving," Ron said, annoyed, and he stormed off, wondering how someone like Ian could have come from the seeds of him. Ian smiled at Gretchen, who was still laughing and, for the first time that Ian could remember, was looking at him with pride.

Chapter 6:

The Story of Ian vs. Beans

Ian was in the palace office of Dr. Fakeci, the royal quack doctor. He was sitting on a medical table surrounded by medical propaganda posters that said things like "Your care is free, so what did you expect?" and "I am the science," which Ian found tacky even for this city.

"Where is my lollipop?" he whined to the old doctor with deep glasses and a smile that was simultaneously warming and deranged.

"You'll get your lollipop when you put on your mask," Dr. Fakeci said, somehow sounding both like a kindly old man and a serial killer. He went to grab a mask from his desk drawer, but when he tried to pull one out, it was stuck in the box and refused to leave.

"Hmm, that is odd," he said, continuing to yank on the masks as if something different would happen.

"Having some trouble, doc? Maybe try using one of your PhDs to help you out," Ian said, grinning.

After the rest of the examination, Dr. Fakeci came out to consult Ron, who was waiting in a chair outside, doodling ideas for new government departments.

When he saw the doc, he went up to him, looking worried. "So, what's wrong with him, doctor?" he whispered as if someone was spying on them. He wasn't exactly keen on the idea of his only son being insane. People might start talking.

"Physically, nothing. In fact, he's about as healthy as Hercules himself," Dr. Fakeci said, voice muffled through the masks he was still wearing.

"The town shepherd?" Ron asked in surprise.

"Yes, that's the one." It was hard for Ron to tell, but Dr. Fakeci looked dumbfounded and very distracted.

"So what is wrong, then?" Ron pressed.

Dr. Fakeci put on another mask layer. "Ian seems to be suffering from what we call Roark Syndrome," Dr. Fakeci said.

Ron closed his eyes in disappointment. "Oh, I feared it was that bad."

"Yes, it's when someone, usually a child, garners more than average independent and selfish thoughts."

"Yes, I was a high school chemist," Ron said, annoyed. "I think I know my political and psychological terms."

"Well, then, you know the best treatment is usually lecturing and belittlement. People usually respond well to that," Ron thought he heard Fakeci say.

"Yes, I think that's the route we'll take," Ron said, returning to some of his senses. "The queen is already very adept at it."

Suddenly, there was a scream, and the nurse in Ian's room came out in a bikini, ran off into the bathroom near them, and slammed the door. Ron was no prude—he approved the nude beach oligarch parties regularly, though he never went himself—but even he thought that this woman was being very unprofessional.

"Huh, that's never happened before," Dr. Fakeci said, his bushy eyebrows raised.

Ian came out of the room humming a satisfied tune. "Okay, Ron, we can go home now," he said, grinning to his father.

"First off, we are home," Ron said. "Second, I will tell you when we can go. Now, let's go home."

"Oh, one more thing, Your Grace," Fakeci said, and Ron turned back around.

"What?"

"Has your son ever done anything, what's the word? Abnormal?"

Ron frowned. "No, and I don't appreciate you implying that something is wrong with my son."

Dr. Fakeci retracted. "Oh, I wasn't implying anything. We ask all the patients that right before they leave. It's standard procedure," he said, then ducked back into his office. Ron led Ian out of the office. As they were leaving, Ian smirked back at the door Dr. Fakeci was hiding behind.

That night, Ron was in his bedroom pacing around while Gretchen was sitting on the bed reading "Jingles of a Mad Woman."

"He can't keep getting away with this rebelliousness," Ron told the room that was ignoring him.

"Why are you worried, Ron? Just leave well enough alone," Gretchen said, eyes not leaving her book.

Ron turned to her. "This is the kingdom at stake, Gretchen," he said, raising his voice. "Why do you seem to be ignoring this issue?"

Gretchen took a side glance at the oats on the nightstand. Now was definitely not the time to explain prophecies and such to him. He was always cranky when the lettuce from the salad was uneven. "It takes away the uniform texture of the leaf," he had said numerous times to the vendor, who always looked like he was questioning his life decisions.

She sighed after probably too long of a pause. "Fine, if you want to waste your time on him, I want no part of it," she said. "Now quit interrupting me with your footsteps." She went back to her book and didn't say another word.

"All right, here's what we'll do," Ron continued to himself. "We'll hold an intervention tonight at dinner and show him the error of his ways. Yes, that'll do marvelously." Gretchen rolled her eyes at her hopelessly conniving husband, who always had a stupid grin when he thought he was being clever.

Later that evening, they all gathered in the dining room, which had been cleaned up from the party a few nights ago. Gretchen was cooking dinner.

"Mmm, mmm, mmm, that smells delicious. What are we having, dear?" Ron said, rubbing his stomach in circles.

Gretchen angrily banged the pots around on the counter. "We're having beans and salad, Ron. I already told you this, so stop calling me gang slang."

"I don't want beans. I want spinach," Ian complained from across the table.

"Well, we're having beans because that is what the community wants, and Gretchen is making food for the betterment of the community," Ron replied. *Ah, well said, Ron,* he thought to himself.

"I'm making it because there's a food shortage," Gretchen corrected him.

Ron ignored her, though, and continued on his crusade. "So, do you understand what I'm trying to say?" he asked Ian.

"Yes, I just beg to differ," Ian said.

Ron couldn't think of a response and decided to sit silently for a moment. Gretchen then served dinner to a pleased Ron and a disgruntled little Ian.

Ron cleared his throat. "So, hon, do you want to know how my day was?" he asked her.

Gretchen loudly made a noise under her breath, sat down at the end of the table, and grabbed a plate for herself. "Fine," she grunted.

Ron smiled and sat up in his chair. "Well, we finally banned private delivery services—bunch of weirdos with cargo shorts and good delivery times due to consumer competition. Well, the Rondithmuth Post Office will never go bankrupt now. Picking winners and losers? Hah, in my opinion, we're all winners now," he said, taking a sip of wine from the glass next to him. He sat back in his chair, quite proud of himself.

Let's see Ian squirm out of that one, he thought.

"I saw that stamp prices quadrupled in cost," Ian said, squirming in his chair majestically after Ron's rant.

"Ian, eat your beans," Ron said. After a moment, he spoke up again, and Gretchen put her face through her hands. "Well, the good news is my economic consultants told me that money does indeed grow on trees, so I think we'll be fine."

Ron grinned smugly, and Gretchen put her index finger on her temple while shoving a carrot in her mouth. Ian stabbed the beans on his plate like he was a maniac.

Hah, I got him now, Ron thought again.

"I think that's the craziest theory of currency I've ever heard. If money did grow on trees, the cost of living would go up exponentially, causing a depression the likes of which hasn't been seen since the great wine episode 120 years ago," Ian said before taking a drink from his sippy cup.

"Ian, eat your beans," Ron said again. *This child*, he thought.

"I don't want beans. I want spinach," Ian said, slamming his fork on the table and turning the beans into spinach.

Gretchen angrily yanked the bowl off the table. "Ian, how many times have I told you no powers at the dinner table?" she yelled at him.

"Six," replied Ian, counting on his fingers.

"Well, now I have to get up and get you more. You know, in most countries, you would be doing this for me," she said, getting up and furiously grabbing the pot of beans off the counter.

As she attempted to scoop them onto Ian's plate, the beans disappeared before touching the plate and reappeared in the pot. It took Gretchen a few minutes to figure out what was happening. Ron just watched the beans do their loop, looking defeated.

"Ian!" Gretchen yelled finally.

"It wasn't me," Ian said.

"It's not okay to lie, Ian," scolded Ron, seeing an opening.

The phone rang, startling all three of them. Ian caused the beans to explode out the window, and Ron got up and picked up the receiver. "Yes, what is it? Of course public post services with more regulations are more efficient. Don't be silly," Ron said, then hung up and turned back to Ian.

"I will not have this rebelliousness in this house. Ian, go to your room," Ron said.

Ian sprang up defiantly. "No, you want beans so bad? Here's your beans," he yelled, raising his arms in the air. The ground began to shake, and thunder cracked through the house.

Ron's face immediately went from anger to concern. They were surrounded by the sound of something pattering on the side of the house. "Gretchen, what's going on?" he asked, his heart beating very quickly now.

Gretchen frowned at him. "You got schooled by a three-year-old."

Beans were falling from the sky, as plentiful as rain and as heavy as hail. The room also began to fill up quickly, and it looked as if the walls and floor had been painted an ugly green. They all ran out of the dining room and the palace. When they went outside, they saw that the sky was pouring beans, which were now piling up on the ground.

Many people were also standing outside and looking at the sky, perplexed by what they saw. Others were panicking and flipping over the local lettuce carts for no reason.

Ron looked down in both anger and fear at Ian, who seemed quite pleased with himself.

"Ian, whatever you're doing, please make it stop," Ron begged. He didn't exactly have the infrastructure in place to clean this up quickly.

"No, not until you leave me alone and I can have spinach," Ian cried over the sound of the falling beans splattering against the ground and palace.

"Ron, just give him the damn spinach," Gretchen yelled at him.

Ron shook his head fiercely and stared down his toddler. "No, you're doing this just to hurt me. You will not bully me and get whatever you want," he said. "You will do what the community needs."

"Well, it appears we've reached a bean impasse," Ian replied, arms crossed.

"You don't scare me, Ian," Ron said defiantly. "I like beans."

"For now," Ian warned. He went to his room, leaving his parents, who had beans in their hair.

For three days, beans fell from the sky nonstop, clogging the sewers and causing many bean-related head injuries.

"The weather forecast looks cloudy with a 100% chance of beans," the local weatherman said. He pointed to a radar map. "You can see here that there is a particularly heavy system of string beans north of the city, while the south seems to be getting a heavy dose of lima."

The road crews could not keep up with the flow, since the roads were covered with what looked like green-dyed snow. Plows were getting stuck before they could clear the way and the workers could only shovel so fast. It turned out that a city overloaded with beans didn't exactly smell good, either—there was a ubiquitous odor of earthy rot, with a hint of spoiled casserole.

Ron had called a town hall to address concerns after he had gotten tired of constantly having to get off the toilet to answer the phone. He stood at the podium, looking at several angry citizens.

"People, people, let's not look at this as a negative. Beans are a healthy vegetable that provides vitamins and nutrients for us all," he pleaded.

"I've had diarrhea for four straight days," a man yelled from the crowd.

"Beans have only been falling for three," he answered, questioning him. The man crossed his arms.

"I stand by what I said."

An older, plump woman stood up with three young boys next to her. Ron wondered whether he could arrange a trade.

"My kids are now obsessed with taking beans and flinging them off of spoons all over the house," she cried.

"Children are a blessing. Cherish them while you can," Ron responded, trying to sound stoic and reasonable.

Another angry woman stood up. "I had to make a bean-flavored cake for my husband's birthday," she said in disgust. "He's filing for divorce now."

"A good, healthy use of resources," Ron said.

After the event, Ron went out through the back of the town hall and was escorted to his bean-ridden palace. He came in and found Gretchen in the kitchen.

"Hey, what's for dinner today?" he asked her.

Gretchen turned around and gave him a death frown.

Ron groaned, frustrated. "Fine, I'll talk to him," he said. "This is the thanks I get for trying to be a competent father."

"Ron, priorities, please," Gretchen said as she swept some beans into a corner so she could open a drawer.

Ron marched off and went to find his son. He found Ian outside playing with a bunch of dolls that resembled various Federal Reserve chairmen, not seeming bothered by the river of beans passing by him from the road.

"Okay, the meeting over the raising of interest rates has commenced. Mr. Powell, what is your opinion?" Ian said, moving a doll up and down.

"Ian, can we talk?" Ron said, trying to sound gentle.

"I'm a little busy with something important," Ian said, not looking up. He picked up a doll with gray hair and glasses.

"Yes, we should be cautious about the effects on mortgage rates before taking any drastic action," Ian said in a low voice that was meant to sound like an adult but ultimately sounded more like a high-pitched windup toy that was running out of batteries.

Ron couldn't take it anymore. "All right, Ian. You win. If you want to be an independent thinker for now, be my guest, but this is not done."

Ian put down his doll and looked up at him suspiciously. "Can I have spinach when I want?"

"Yes," Ron relented, and Ian smiled.

"Alrighty, then," Ian said, and suddenly, Ron looked up at the sky and saw the sun peeking through the green clouds. He looked down at Ian, who didn't even seem to notice or to have broken a sweat.

"Thank you, Ian," he said.

"Sure, Ron," Ian replied as if he had given him a tool to borrow.

"Do you still respect me?" Ron asked, and Ian again smiled up at him.

"Ron," Gretchen demanded from inside the house, "get in here and clear this house of your royal handiwork."

"I respect you just as much as I ever have, Dad," he said.

Ron smiled and turned around. There was still some hope. *It's not over yet,* he thought, oblivious to the "Kick Me, I'm a donkey" sign that had been taped to his back.

Chapter 7:

The Story of Ian's First (and Last) Day of School

Ian was now four. He seemed to be growing more intelligent and rebellious, but now arrogance had been added to the list of things that bothered Ron. Ian knew he was smarter than most adults, and he wasn't shy about showing it.

On one particular day, for example, Ron had to calm Earl Butockz during the oligarch's visit to discuss increasing ethanol-powered fuel for electricity. After the negotiations over salad, Ian told him his plan would cripple the grid if there was an overreliance on a crop for energy. Needless to say, a deal was postponed until later, and the price of maize mysteriously tripled every time Ron tried to buy some.

Ron's promise to leave Ian to his conservative enlightenment didn't last long. After walking in on Ian dressed in a suit, bowtie, and big round glasses like Murray Rothbard, Ron decided enough was enough.

"It's not what it looks like!" Ian had cried out, covering himself up.

"Oh, my son! My own son!" Ron had yelled, shaking his head and putting his hands on his ever-shinier dome. With all this in mind, Ron decided it was time for Ian to start school early.

"He's four years old, Ron," Gretchen pointed out, picking up Ron's hair off the bed. It was another dry morning, and the poor ventilation in the bedroom was making it even drier.

Ron's face turned dark. "Oh, he's ready." There was only so much one could take of a young Ian. Passing him off to some poor, unfortunate teacher might at least help a little.

"Mom, where do we keep the dry ice?" Ian called from his room.

Gretchen groaned and relented. "Fine, Ron, but it's your problem when this blows up in your face," she warned.

"Oh, Ian will be ecstatic," Ron replied. He put on the baseball cap that he used (unsuccessfully) to cover his head and left the room.

However, when Ron told Ian the news at dinner, Ian was not ecstatic.

"Why can't I go to a charter school for a real education?" he protested.

Ron winced at the mention of the C-word before answering him.

"Because, Ian, those, uh, schools don't teach anything good, and we can't tell them what to teach. This makes their teachers underpaid compared to our great public Rondithmuth education system. That's why they are banned in this city," Ron stated.

"But these higher salaries are being paid to teachers who aren't incentivized to earn them," Ian replied. "And charter schools are usually better-quality facilities, so that amounts to higher expenses."

"Ian, eat your beans," said Ron, having had enough of the back talk.

"Wrong story," Ian corrected.

"Oh, yeah," Ron muttered.

Gretchen interjected. "Ron, did they fix that roof on the school that collapsed a few years ago?" she asked, in what Ron thought sounded like a mocking tone.

Ron turned defensive. "Government contracts take time, dear." He turned to Ian to shift topics. "Ian, go to bed. You have a long day ahead of you."

Ian thought for a moment, then smiled. "Yeah, I'm going to be the smartest one there, so I'll also be the most popular, logically," he said, jumping out of his chair.

Ron thought this was one of the stupid things Ian had said—which to him was saying something—but he replied, "Uh, yeah, good night, Ian."

Ian ran to his room and went to bed, jubilant for the day when he would finally be among his peers—poor kid.

He had lovely dreams that night. In his dream, Ian waltzed into the school while everyone cheered him on near their lockers. Ian waved in appreciation.

Next, he was in the classroom, answering questions to great applause. "The second derivative determines the increasing or decreasing rate of inflation," he had answered to the nice, attractive teacher, who smiled at him.

"Well done, Ian, you're so smart," she had said. "And handsome."

The class cheered him on, and he stood up and took a bow. Two girls simultaneously kissed him on both cheeks out of nowhere.

Unfortunately, his dream abruptly ended, but he woke up grinning with excitement. He came down the stairs in his Rothbard outfit and a briefcase to accompany it. Ron, in the middle of eating his morning salad, looked up from his Communist Times newspaper and its articles about how everything was great. Upon seeing Ian's getup, he held in his anger and exasperation and forced a smirk.

"Well, someone has had a change in attitude," he said, putting his paper down.

Ian sat down and took a salad for himself. "Yeah, it'll be fun. What's the worst that could happen?" he said, taking a bite of a deviled egg. "I'm not going to get bullied or anything."

Ron choked on his eggplant but tried to hold it in and said, "Oh, of course not. Kids are usually pretty nice."

Gretchen, who was smacking the coffee maker that wasn't working, turned around and frowned. "Oh, come on, Ron, look at him," she exclaimed as Ian adjusted his bowtie.

"Kids like other kids who express themselves differently. My city values equity and inclusion," Ron said, somehow with a straight face.

Gretchen rolled her eyes and went back to her coffee. Ian finished his salad and headed out the door. He arrived at a small bus stop filled with children waiting for the electric bus to come. A small boy with red, curly hair approached Ian, who was trying to pose next to his briefcase like he was a model for a late-night commercial.

"Hello, I'm a boy whose name no one can pronounce," the boy said, shaking Ian's hand.

Ian waved him off. "Oh, I'm a brilliant prodigy. I think I can handle it," he bragged. After five minutes, though, Ian gave up and decided to just refer to him as the boy whose name he couldn't pronounce. "Well, I am Ian, son of the king."

Everyone at the bus stop immediately turned around toward them. A large boy with a mole that seemed to be moving around his face as if trying to find a home went up to him, fists clenched. "So, you're the little prince?" the boy grunted at him.

"Well, technically speaking, I'm the crown prince, so when my dad dies, I'll be able to tell you what to do," Ian corrected him.

"Are you the ruler now?" the boy asked.

Ian hesitated. "Well, technically, no, but—"

The large boy shoved Ian to the ground into a muddy patch of grass, ruining his bowtie. The boy whose name Ian couldn't pronounce attempted to help him up, but Ian shrugged him off and glared at the large boy, who was chuckling down at him.

"Aw, poor little prince go boom," the boy cackled.

Ian bit the top of his lip and then grinned at him. The boy stopped laughing. Everyone at the bus stop was silent. Suddenly, the large boy started screaming. The mole on his face was multiplying and dancing around his nose, ears, and anywhere else it could find. Panicked, the boy ran off into the distance and out of sight.

Ian got up. The boy whose name he couldn't pronounce slid sideways on his heels, away from Ian, who was both furious and embarrassed at the eyes that kept staring at him.

The bus never arrived that day because it ran out of charge after one minute of driving, so the students had to walk three miles to the school, passing through the plastic-burning plant and the homeless camp that King Ron and the government didn't officially recognize.

"They're campers, Ian, who enjoy the outdoors," Ron had told him one night after he saw one crapping on the front porch.

Ian walked with the boy whose name he couldn't pronounce, who was still a little nervous about getting too close to him. Ian discussed his recent studies into why weeds aren't flowers grown for their beauty while his new friend talked about the new toy truck he had gotten.

They arrived at the run-down school, which, as Gretchen had pointed out, didn't have a functioning roof. The hallways were dirty, and the bathrooms were so disgusting that a description couldn't be clearly given. Water from the lack of a roof was causing puddles so frequently that the janitors had run out of Wet Floor signs after lining them up and down the corridor.

Ian entered his classroom and placed his briefcase into his cubby. He tore the butterfly sticker name tag off the front of the cubby and replaced it with his business card. After grabbing some coloring supplies from his briefcase, he chose a desk in between two girls. He flashed them a slick smile and adjusted his bowtie. Pointing at him, they started laughing, their giggles piercing his heart.

"Haha, what a dork," laughed one of the girls, whom Ian only described with a word that isn't appropriate, but it started with a B.

Ian put his head onto his desk but then immediately lifted it back up when he saw mold on it. First, he spread his hand over the mold, which then disappeared under his hand, making the desk sparkle clean. Then he glanced at the two still-laughing witches. He put away his markers and stared at them intensely, causing them to halt their cackling in their throats.

Suddenly, both were screaming, similar to the boy from earlier. The same pitch, actually. Their lovely, straight black hair was now falling out, revealing large bald spots on each head. They got up and ran out the door, where an old, plump woman had just entered, looking confused.

She shrugged, gathered herself, and looked at her classroom, contemptuous. Her beady little eyes, barely visible through her oversized glasses, scanned the room like radar. After she was done scanning, she shook her head in dismay.

"Another year of pathetic excuses for children," she sighed and took a swish of some caffeinated drink, though Ian thought he had smelled the hint of wine that he had grown accustomed to smelling at his house. Ron was, after all, a connoisseur that had made his own wine since before he had even met Gretchen.

"Good morning, class. My name is Ms. Betch, and I will be your teacher and authority for the next 12 months due to school now being year-long."

The class groaned. "Yes, nobody is more annoyed than me," she agreed. "Do you think I want to spend a summer with you brats while I could be vacationing in Gaza?"

Ms. Betch looked around the room again and, for a moment, locked eyes with Ian, who was fixated on her.

"Anyway, you will learn, and you will learn well, and you will have minimal fun," she demanded. She got out a notebook and started reading from it.

"The first assignment I have for you all is to draw who you think is the biggest oppressor. I will grade you on whether I agree with you and how well you color within the lines," she said, reading off the sheet. "You have one hour." They all got their supplies out to get to work.

After an hour, the students presented their pictures on the board. Ms. Betch took out a red pen and a clipboard and began looking at the pictures.

"Let's see. Excellent. I see a big skyscraper, so this must be big business. Well done. That is also a nice choice on the color palette," she said, smiling at a boy with a polo and combover hairstyle. "Well done, Mr. Sucup."

She continued down the line. "All right, here's a picture of what looks like a white male with a hard hat. Excellent. I see white male supremacy here. I think you could've included a Star of David, though, too, but it's okay," she said to a girl with short pink hair, who waved back at her. "Well done, Ms. Femmunt."

Ms. Betch moved on down the line. "Now, let's move on. Here is—ugh," she said with disgust. "What is this trash?"

She ripped a picture of a crudely drawn stick figure with a crown on his head. "This is unacceptable. Who did this?" she growled, her eyes red, looking furiously around the room. She looked at the name in the corner, which was written in perfect cursive.

"Ah yes, Mr. Ian," she hissed at the smirking boy in the glasses. Ian, who was leaning back in his seat in satisfaction, sat up at attention.

"You know who I am?" Ian asked, surprised.

"Oh yes, your father warned us about you. You sniveling, convoluted, conniving klutz of conservative catastrophe," she yelled, out of breath.

"Fatherly love at its best," Ian quipped, causing a little giggle from some of his classmates.

Ms. Betch noticed the snickering and decided to set an example. "In K-12 classrooms, the punishment for insulting the government through various forms of expression is to be beaten with a bat," she snarled. She took a wooden bat out of the closet near the door.

The classroom gasped—except for Ian, who gazed at her stoically.

"Mr. Ian, come up here," she demanded. Ian obliged, went up to the front of the class, and turned around. She raised the bat high into the air, and with a sudden whooshing sound swung hard at Ian.

It took her several swings before she realized that her bat had turned into a feather duster. The class was laughing hysterically, and Ms. Betch threw the duster aside.

"Enough of this," she shrieked. "Class, every day, I want you to make Ian's time here as a student as miserable as possible. Get in his face, set his pants on fire—I don't care. If you're in a bathroom stall while he's waiting in line behind you, I want you to use up all the toilet paper."

A young girl in the back raised her hand. "Yes, do we have to? I mean, I think he's kind of cute, like a dorky rebel," the girl said.

Ian waved at her, and she waved back. Ms. Betch slammed the desk of the boy whose name Ian couldn't pronounce so hard that he fell out of his chair.

"Enough. Mr. Ian, go to the principal's office," she yelled.

Ian stormed out of the classroom and went to the office of the principal, Mr. Fuzz. Mr. Fuzz was a middle-aged man with a goatee and graying short hair. He was at his desk inspecting the records of the students' parents.

"Ah, complained that the books are falling apart and said that sections in the books aren't true," he said, writing down some notes. "The RSS (Rondithmuth State Security) will be very interested in this."

Ian came in and sat down in front of him. Mr. Fuzz looked up and grinned, reminding Ian of Dr. Fakeci. Apparently, all highly educated shills had that maniacal smile.

"Ah, Ian, I didn't expect to see you so soon. I was just filing these security reports for your father."

The folder with the files suddenly caught on fire. Mr. Fuzz panicked, threw it into the trashcan, and stomped on it until it subsided.

"Huh, that doesn't happen often," Mr. Fuzz said as Ian tried to hide a smile. "So, Ian, why do you like attention so much?"

"I don't know," Ian said with a smirk.

"Well, you must know that we here at this school will not tolerate the desecration of our values, and as long as this school is standing, I will defend that," he pronounced.

"Values, huh," Ian mocked.

"Yes, values that are worth fighting for. And you better believe that I would do that."

"Do those values also include having my friend slip in puddles?" Ian interrogated.

"We have Wet Floor signs for a reason," Mr. Fuzz defended. "And what is the name of this friend of yours?"

"I can't pronounce it," Ian admitted.

"Oh, you can't pronounce it?" Mr. Fuzz mocked, leaning back in his chair. "What a great friend who can't even pronounce their own friend's name. Honestly, Ian, I expected better. I really did."

Ian pointed to the trashcan, which was starting to smoke again. "Uh, Fuzzy," Ian said.

"Ian, do not interrupt me while I'm soapboxing," Mr. Fuzz said patronizingly. "The son of the king is supposed to set an example, and you seem to be doing the opposite. That won't do. No, that won't do at all. And don't break wind in my office."

Mr. Fuzz's coat was now smoking. "Um, Mr. Fuzz? Fuzzman? Sir Fuzzalot?" Ian tried to warn.

"What, you sniveling … ah, holy Leningrad!" he yelled, and jumped up in a panic.

The fire spread from the trashcan quickly. Everyone got out safely, but the fire lasted seven days because the judge was on vacation and couldn't issue a fire warrant for the fire department. The school was destroyed and plans to rebuild it had an estimated completion date of 60 years.

Ron was shocked to hear about the fire and the rumors that some dorky kid may have started it. That night, the skyline was tinted red from the still burning public institution. Ron was again in his bedroom pacing around, much to the irritation of Gretchen, who was trying to watch *Finding Bigfoot's Killer*.

"I'm at the end of my rope, Gretch," Ron said, pacing.

"Never call me that again," she spat from her side of the bed.

"I think we need to start to think about what to do with this kingdom," Ron continued.

Gretchen looked up from her show and sat up. "Well, it was a good run, Ron. I'll pack the 'escape into the night' bag," she said, and she tried to get off the bed but gave up and plopped back down to her show.

"No, this is about Ian," Ron said sharply, a little irritated at her quickness to flee.

"We don't have time to bring him."

Ron sighed again, still more frustrated. "No, I will have to think about our options with him, however drastic they may be."

"*And the killer was found to have killed something that may or may not have been furry,*" said the narrator on the TV.

"Wrap it up, Ron," Gretchen said, turning the TV's volume up.

Ron slumped into bed. "No, I'm done now. I'll think of something later."

"*And the DNA was ... inconclusive ... after the machine broke,*" the narrator proclaimed dramatically.

Chapter 8:

The Story of the Arrival of Kimmith

Ian was now the age of six, which was two years older than four. At four, he had finally figured out how to float in the air. This had scared the crap out of Ron when he had woken up to Ian floating over his bed asking for a glass of strawberry milk (Ron had rightfully pointed out that Ian could obviously get it himself, and that he was just trying to annoy him).

At age five, Ian had figured out how to fly around the palace, where he was now even more of a nuisance to everyone else, especially the poor old butler Stan. Until now, he had avoided Ian's shenanigans by cleaning wherever Ian wasn't. Now that Ian was more mobile, though, he could no longer escape his torment.

In particular, Ian liked to fly past Stan's head and pick at his wiry black mustache that curled in a loop. He would also do a fly-by and wax his head, causing it to shine so bright that one time, the reflection of the sun's rays blinded one of the housekeepers, causing her to crash into Ron's wine shelf.

Ron, meanwhile, had finished raising the funds to build The Land of Windmills, a massive project that would become the city's primary energy source. The project would not be completed for ten years, five of which would be used to put up signs and close roads. Nevertheless, he was very proud of his wind farm, and he would find every opportunity to bring it up, even if it made no sense in the context of the conversation.

"The wind farms will be just as white, I think. Or maybe they'll be gray," Ron told the maid proudly.

"Your Grace, I asked if you want a load of whites or darks done," she said. Ron immediately began bragging about how the windmills would glow in the dark and could be seen at least a hundred miles away.

"It's a desert, Ron. Of course you can see it from a distance," Gretchen had said irritably as she passed by.

On this particular day, King Ron was in the palace's backyard, dressed in royal gardening attire. He was on his knees, tending to his desert garden, which was always a sad sight to look at. Ian was outside with him, swirling the sand before him like a top not too far away.

Ron hummed, *"I'm just a poor old soul on the company's dime."*

Ian looked up from his sand top and saw his father. He then saw the garden and smiled with devilish intent. Ron continued to brush. Suddenly, though, he leaned back in surprise, his eyes wide. Purple flowers had sprouted out of the ground, waving to a shocked Ron, who tentatively waved back. He also heard high-pitched voices coming from the flowers, and swore they were trying to say hi.

"Ian, come here, they're coming up," he called over to him. "And you said that growing deciduous flowers in the desert couldn't work."

Ian strolled up behind him and looked over Ron's shoulder. Noticing the flowers, which were continuing to grow, he said calmly, "Yep, you showed me, Dad."

Ron smiled at the sound of Ian's words. "Yes. Yes, I did," he said to himself more than anyone else.

As Ron was boasting, though, he failed to notice the flowers had begun to wrap around his legs like a vine.

"So, maybe next time you'll listen when I tell you taxes boost economic growth," Ron continued.

The flower stems tightened around his legs, causing him to yell and fall over. He tugged at the plants, but they seemed to tighten the more he messed with them.

"These flowers are, like, demented or something!" he shouted.

The plants dragged Ron around the garden, slamming him into the cacti and the fountain that used fifty percent of the city's water. Ian smiled and giggled while he watched.

Eventually, Ron grabbed some weed cutters and frantically snipped at the flowers. Two minutes later, he finally freed himself from the flowers' death grip. He stumbled upward, kicked them, and stepped back. Then he turned to Ian, who was trying to hide a wide grin. Ron's face and legs were purple, and he roared, "Ian!"

That night, Ron was angrily scribbling on his desk an order banning all electrical plugs to address kicking plug violence in the city after an accident involving a boy on life support. Gretchen came in, looking exhausted from her day of belittling the gardener for ruining her flowers in the garden. She lay on the bed and turned the TV to *The Curse of Murder Plateau*. Ron turned around in his chair and looked at Gretchen.

"Gretchen, we need to talk."

"*If we poke another hole in it, all the answers might be solved this time,*" a man said on the TV, pointing at the side of a hill. She looked up at her husband and turned down the volume.

"So, you're finally admitting to throwing away my book on identifying animal poop," she said.

Ron stared at her in confusion. "I don't even know what you're talking about," he said.

"Sure, Ron," she sneered, and turned the volume back up.

"*Whoa, whoa, whoa, the hole is getting deeper,*" the man on TV said in a panic.

"I wasn't finished," Ron continued.

"*Was the hole in the plateau proof that something wasn't right about this natural landscape? Who's to say?*" the man on the TV asked no one in particular before the show went dramatically to a commercial.

Gretchen snorted, sighed, turned down the volume again, and looked at Ron as if he had dumped paint on her poetry book.

"Look, I love Ian, but—" Ron said before he was interrupted by her.

"We should banish him," she said, attempting to guess what he was about to say. This took Ron aback. What an awful thing to say! In general, this was actually pretty standard for her, but still.

"What? No," he replied. "I was going to say we should have another heir who accepts our principles and will do what we want them to."

Gretchen's eyes darted to the side of the room. "Yes, that's what I was going to say," she claimed. Ron decided not to linger on this.

"So, let's have another child," he said, slightly hesitant, knowing how she felt about the subject. She had always talked about why children were such a terrible idea, which was part of the reason Ian had been such a shock.

Gretchen frowned at Ron as if he had just said her shoes were fake. "I can't have children, Ron," she said bitterly.

Ron looked at her confusedly and glanced at a picture of Ian pulling down his pants during the opening ceremony of the Museum of the Disadvantaged.

"But what about Ian?" Ron questioned.

Gretchen waved him off. "Eh, he was just a fluke," she replied.

Ron didn't understand what this meant—he was pretty sure that's not how it worked—but he accepted this answer. He thought for a moment while Gretchen turned the TV back up.

"What if we drilled another hole?" asked the TV person to his colleagues.

Ron then had an idea. "We can always adopt," he said, expecting an answer, but Gretchen appeared not to be listening anymore.

"Whatever, Ron, quit bothering me," she said indifferently.

Ron tried to keep the conversation going, though—his mind was actively thinking, which was a weird sensation for him. "Do you think Ian will be jealous?" he asked.

Gretchen seemed to be annoyed that the subject of Ian was now disrupting her program. "Ian, Ian, Ian. Everything's about Ian," she complained.

"Yes, maybe this will finally put him in his place," Ron said, defeated.

Gretchen didn't answer, so Ron decided it was time to wrap it up. "I'll pick one up on my way back from tonight's raid on those Coffee Party people. Can you tell Ian tomorrow?"

Gretchen looked up from her show again and looked like she was imagining Ron being attacked by a rabid chicken. She answered through gritted teeth, "Fine."

King Ron clapped his hands together, quite satisfied with the night's progress. "Well, good. Good night, honey."

There was no answer again, and Ron slid into bed and went to sleep.

"*Our drill suddenly stopped mysteriously. The technician said it was out of gas, but I'm not so sure,*" the man on TV said skeptically in the background of Ron's dreams.

The following day came, and when Ron had left for work, Gretchen reluctantly took Ian to Joseph's Average Vegetarian Bar & Grill for lunch.

When they had finished, Ian rubbed his tummy. "My tummy is so good, which is surprising given the lack of calories, but this has been a great day that can't be ruined," he said.

Gretchen thought that Ian talked like an alien who had learned English from a dog but smiled half-heartedly and said, "Ian, I have something to tell you. Your father went to the adoption center today."

Ian perked up and got excited. "Are we getting a dog? I've always wanted a dog to ride through the streets," he said. Gretchen often questioned if Backwards Dog was just a sick exiled deity that was banished from the holy land, because how could this child possibly be the son of a divine power?

"More like a little girl or boy who will be taking over your succession," she finally said.

Ian stared at his mother in shock and dropped his bowl of plum soup onto his lap. "I'm getting a what?" he asked blankly.

"A new brother or sister, a person about your age who lives with you, takes your room and goes to the bathroom when you need to," she said.

Ian clutched his faceless doll on the table. "They sound scary!"

"Ian, they're not scary," she said, talking down to him.

"How do you know? You have no siblings," Ian retorted.

Gretchen exhaled angrily. "This is happening, Ian, so just get used to it."

Ian pouted and didn't speak the rest of the time at the restaurant and during the ride back home, which was just fine with Gretchen. She wasn't sure why Ian thought she was being punished.

When they got to the door, Gretchen opened it. On the other side, Ron was kneeling behind a little girl about three years old. She had bushy brown hair and round brown eyes to match. She smiled at Ian and Gretchen, showing her missing baby teeth. Ron scooted the girl toward Ian, and she shuffled before his hand.

"Say hello, Ian," Ron said gently.

Ian crept forward carefully and nervously squeaked, "Hello."

"BOO!" the girl screamed, jumping at him. Ian screamed and leaped behind Gretchen, who immediately shoved him back in front of her. Ian ran to the windowless hole where a window probably should've been and hid behind the satin drapes.

Gretchen glared at the girl and then at Ron. "Ian took the news well, as you can see. So, what's its name?" she said, looking at the girl with disinterest.

Ron was a little irked at her tone. "Her name is Kimmith, and she's a she, I think, but you're right, we shouldn't assume," he said, beaming at the little girl.

"What kind of name is Kimmith? No first name has an 'ith' at the end," she shot back.

Kimmith waddled over to Ian, who was still hiding behind the drapes. She ripped the drapes off him. "Found you!" she yelled, and Ian screamed again. He ran into his room and locked the door. He then magically put an airlock seal on the door, snapping it shut.

"Is this a good idea?" Gretchen asked, looking at Ron.

Ron waved her off. "Oh, what's he going to do? Sell her on the black market? Throw her down that open well near the town center over there?" he said, then laughed at himself oddly.

"I meant, what is he going to do to *us*?" Gretchen pressed, but Ron only chuckled again.

"Oh, Ian's harmless."

"He flooded the town with beans," she pointed out, which briefly gave Ron flashbacks, but he again waved her off.

"Oh, that was only once."

Meanwhile, Kimmith had somehow unlocked the sealed door and wandered into Ian's room, prompting another scream from Ian.

The next six months were the worst of Ian's life. For this amount of time, he would not touch Kimmith.

"Go, shoo," he said as he poked her with a two-foot stick to reroute her away from him when she got too close. She happily rerouted away and went into the other room.

After a while, though, Ian's fear turned into resentment. Since Ron refused to get rid of his second wine cellar, Kimmith was given Ian's old room. Ian, in turn, was forced to conjure a tent to live in outside, since Ron refused to give up materials for his future windmill project.

"You can't have a tent, Ian, if the world is a chilly frozen wasteland of snow bombs," Ron told him.

"I think a tent would be ideal for that situation," Ian countered. "But this is pointless because she doesn't even need that big of a room."

Ron ignored him, though, and ordered his "workers who choose to work for free" to put up a bouncy castle waterbed that was filled with water from the reserves for droughts.

"Bouncy, bouncy," Kimmith cheered as she jumped up and down on her new bed.

Ron smiled down at her and shook his head at Ian. "Oh, Ian, quit being so needy. Think of yourself as an outside cat," he said as Kimmith broke the bed, spraying the room with water. "It's okay, honey. We'll just get some more from the reserve."

"But, but—" Ian tried to say, but Ron declared that his decision was final.

The treacherous acts didn't end there, though. There was also that time at the dinner table. All four of them had sat at dinner, with Kimmith in a highchair with a big bib on her lap that had Lenin's face on it. Kimmith whipped the mashed potatoes on her plate at Ian, hitting him in the face and creaming his glasses. Gretchen and Ron smiled at her.

"Oh, Kimmith, did you throw your mashed potatoes at Ian?" Ron asked in a condescending tone, and he yanked the plate out from under Ian's nose. "Here, you can have Ian's." He took Ian's plate and plopped the taters in front of Kimmith, who dug in.

"I object!" Ian protested, but Ron turned to Ian.

"Ian, you know full well this is not a democracy," he said, frowning.

There was also the incident with the doll. Ian had a doll that he called "Milton," which he liked to cuddle and have philosophical discussions with under the covers at night. One day, Ian was in the living room playing with it.

"Oh, so you think the Great Depression was caused by the banks not acting fast enough?" Ian said to the doll, which didn't respond, though Ian had tried to make it magically speak.

Kimmith came wandering in, wearing her little green royal dress. When Ian set the doll down to look at his data for rebuttal, Kimmith picked the doll up and then, with a sound like a hook-and-loop fastener (legally can't say Velcro), ripped the head off. When Ian turned back, he saw a smiling Kimmith holding Milton's head while the body lay lifeless on the floor. He promptly screamed in terror, and Ron and a displeased Gretchen came into the room. They saw the remains of Ian's doll and smiled.

"Look, Ron, she's getting stronger every day," Gretchen said to Ron and then turned to Ian. "Ian, quit leaving your crap all over the floor."

Now, wherever Kimmith wandered around the mansion, she carried the head of Ian's former fully-headed doll. She also liked hiding it around the palace. Ian would find it under his pillow, in the shower, and in his dinner.

Finally, there was a time when the power went out due to an eclipse. They were outside in the backyard building a fire because Kimmith was cold. The fire was lit, but Kimmith was still freezing.

"Ian, get your blankets." Ron told him. Ian got up and went to his tent to retrieve his blankets, including his favorite, which had squares of his favorite Founding Fathers on them. When he came back with them, he handed them to Ron. Ron took the wad and threw it into the fire, much to Ian's shock, and Ian fell to his knees as Samuel Adams's face disintegrated into ash.

"There, honey, is that better?" Ron asked Kimmith, who bounced on his lap.

"More blankets!" she demanded excitedly.

Ian stood up and stomped his foot, which sank into the sand, limiting the dramatic effect. "That's it!" he yelled. "That's the last straw!"

He stormed off twenty feet away into his tent. Ron smirked at Gretchen, who was trying to roast a sugar-free marshmallow and didn't seem to notice anything had happened.

"Kids, they can be so overdramatic," Ron said, though she didn't answer. Kimmith poked the ruins of Ian's blankets for entertainment.

From this point forward, Ian declared war on Kimmith. The next day, after spending all night in his tent strategizing, he set his first trap. His first idea was to use another of his faceless dolls as bait. He went into the living room, gently set the doll down, then hid behind the pumpkin-colored couch and waited anxiously. He then saw Kimmith waddling in from the kitchen looking like she was up to something. Ian saw her catch a glimpse of the doll, and he clenched his fist, chuckling to himself, as she started walking toward it.

"Like a fish to a worm," he hissed.

She picked it up without hesitation and smiled gleefully when she reached it. She then grabbed the top of the head, ripped it off, threw the body on the ground, and walked away. Ian then realized he had forgotten to set a trap for after she grabbed it. He came out from behind the couch and looked at his doll, which had sacrificed itself for no reason.

His next plan was to have her float away and never return. He chose balloons as his weapon of choice. Late one evening, Ian bought five green balloons from a stand outside his mansion, though the recently passed air tax meant spending most of his money. He found Kimmith in the backyard juggling his doll heads. He called her over. "Kimmith, come," he barked, and she jolted up, looked behind her, and smiled at him. She got up and waddled up to Ian. He then took her arm and tied the balloons around her little wrist. She laughed happily as Ian stepped back, and then she began to float into the air. Ian watched in awe.

However, as she drifted up, she stopped about five feet in the air and floated gently around the yard, giggling the whole time. "Wheee!" she cheered.

She then drifted over to Ian's tent and knocked it over. Ian ran over to his crumpled tent and looked down at the rubble of his own making. Clearly, he needed to up his game.

He decided to drop her down a sewer grate and leave her there. On a crisp, dry Tuesday morning, Ian made his move. He told Gretchen that he was taking Kimmith for a walk and to go and laugh at the homeless. Gretchen acknowledged them from the kitchen.

"All right, you two have fun and get out of my sight," Gretchen said. "Don't drop her down any sewer grates."

Ian heard this and hurried out the door with Kimmith, who thought it was a game and started hooting excitedly. Once they were outside, Ian put a harness on her and began to head into town, ignoring the passing glances of bystanders.

He searched for a sewer grate anywhere, looking up and down the sandy dirt road. Kimmith skipped around him as if she was frolicking through a pumpkin patch. After three hours, though, Ian realized that, after the bean incident, there were no sewer grates anywhere in the city. Ron hadn't been able to repair the damage and decided sewers were a luxury they couldn't afford. Ian got so frustrated that he took a rock off the ground and threw it. Kimmith went up to the rock and stared at it. She then picked it up and threw it at Ian, knocking his glasses off. When he picked them up and put them back on, he saw Kimmith looking up at him, smiling. He frowned down at her.

"I know your game. You look all cute and innocent on the outside, but I know what foul beast of the jungle, roamer of the night, hides within your stomach just waiting to explode with excrement and bad breath," Ian said, panting and taking a long-winded breath afterward.

Kimmith tried to repeat what Ian said, but it came out as a jumbled babble. Ian wasn't moved, though. "You see, you're evil. I know the serpent trying to slither its tongue out of you," Ian said, pointing at her accusingly.

Kimmith stuck her tongue out at him and snickered. Right at that moment, though, Ian saw three figures approaching from the vast emptiness of the desert outside the city. As they came closer, he realized that they were dressed in colorful robes and riding three cows, one for each man. They came up to Ian and reined in their cattle. The frontman spoke.

"Hello, young sir. We are the Three Ill-Advised Men. We are looking for the forbidden dust bunny. Can you be of assistance?" Ill-Advised said. They smiled at Ian, who was slightly put off by what he saw.

Eventually, though, he regathered himself. "Well, I don't know about a forbidden dust bunny, but we do have a forbidden umbrella, a forbidden record, and a forbidden 99-cent store," Ian said, and they all looked at him, rather pleased.

"Thank you, my small friend," Ill-Advised replied solemnly. "We will see these anomalies. Is there anything the Three Ill-Advised Men can do for you?"

Ian shook his head. "No, I don't think so." Then he saw Kimmith at his side, looking at the clouds in the sky.

"Blel-ola-bo-llama," Kimmith said incomprehensibly.

Ian's brain began racing, and he turned to the men again. "No, my friends, there is no price," Ian said before he picked up Kimmith and held her up. "But, as a token to recognize and welcome you to our fair dystopia, we bring you this."

Kimmith giggled, and the men squinted in, eyes wide.

"A baby!?" Very Ill-Advised exclaimed from the back.

"Yes, she can be your slave," Ian said, nodding. "She does the dishes very well, though you do have to make sure to soak her bottom before you dip her in the dish soap."

Ian made a scrubbing motion with Kimmith.

Ill-Advised put his hand upon his chin, contemplating this offer. He finally beamed down at Ian. "An intriguing offer, young sir. We are in need of another slave after the last one ran away," he said and then glared at the man in the middle of their group. "More Ill-Advised, over here, thought it would be a good idea to let him go and stretch his legs outside before returning to work. Needless to say, we never saw Ruffbacah again."

He looked down in disappointment for a moment, then looked back at Ian. "Are you the child's father?" he asked, and Ian's pupils dilated.

"Uh, yeah, of course I am," Ian said after a pause. "Why would you think otherwise?"

"Take no offense. I, too, was a late bloomer," Ill-Advised said, looking relieved. "But you see, we don't bargain with children anymore, especially since Very Ill-Advised lost our life savings when a child said to him, 'Whoa, look over there.' He turned, and the kid ran away with our bag of money."

Ian wasn't following whatever the man was saying, but he took his tone as a good sign. "So, we have a deal then?" Ian asked him, and Ill-Advised smiled and shook Ian's hand.

"Yes, we have a deal, Mr. um …"

"Ian, son of Ron," Ian clarified, and they released their grips.

"Ian, son of Ron, good day, and good luck with whatever meets your way," Ill-Advised said, and he gestured to Very Ill-Advised, who was trying to touch a rope on the ground that just happened to be hissing and rattling its tail.

"Put the child in front of me on my cow. And let's ride!" Ill-Advised ordered, and Very Ill-Advised placed Kimmith on the lap of Ill-Advised. After the cow let out an earth-shaking *Moo,* they began to slowly stroll away into the sunset until their silhouettes disappeared over the horizon and Kimmith rode with them out of sight.

Ian smiled, feeling good about himself—like a small weight had just been lifted off him. He headed back home, almost skipping past the people now staring at him in judgment for a different reason than earlier. When he got home and opened the front door, Ron and Gretchen were waiting for him on the other side.

"Ian, where is Kimmith?" Ron asked, eyeing Ian and the lack of Kimmith.

Ian halted in his tracks, his happiness flying out the nearest window. "Um, she was mauled by a, uh, goat," he said hesitantly.

"A goat?" Ron asked, raising his bushy gray eyebrows.

"Yeah, it was a nasty sight," Ian said, playing with his fingers. "I had a colorless cloth to prove the incident happened, but I dropped it somewhere along the way back here."

"You don't look sad," Gretchen cut in while Ron continued to stare at him.

Ian quickly tried to tear up and said, "I am sad! Boo hoo hoo. Boo hoo."

"Why didn't you bring her back?" Ron continued to interrogate.

"Well, there wasn't really anything left to bring back, you see," Ian mumbled.

"A goat?" Ron repeated, blinking, looking at him as skeptically as he did Catholics.

"It was a big goat," Ian replied.

"Well, this is a somber day," Ron finally relented, much to Ian's relief. "I think we'll have salad today. Ian, get ready for dinner."

Ian decided to press his luck. "Can I have my old room back?"

Gretchen moved her face around for a moment. "Well, I suppose since we won't be having her back, you can have it back for now," she finally said, and there was obvious resentment in her tone. Ian caught a little relief, too, though.

Ian brightened up and got ready for dinner, more than happy to put up with salad. About an hour later, the three of them sat silently at the dinner table, munching on lettuce, onions, and the like.

"So, Gretchen, what do you think of my concoction today?" Ron said, attempting to break the silence.

Gretchen, who was thinking about all the laundry and dishes she would now have to do, came back from her daydream and said, "What? It tastes like vegetables. What do you want me to say?"

"It tastes great, Dad. I can really taste the green in the lettuce," Ian interjected.

"Thank you, Ian, that's a good boy," Ron said, rubbing the top of Ian's head. Ian grinned happily at how his day was going.

Suddenly, though, a loud knock on the door startled them all. Gretchen jumped so much that she slid out of her chair. Ian flung his tomato in the air, which landed on Ron's head. Ron jumped up and yelled, "What the Reagan!"

He walked over to the door and opened it. On the other side stood the Three Ill-Advised Men. Ill-Advised held Kimmith out in front of him, as if she were a pamphlet. The three cows were grazing on the front lawn. Ron looked at them with disbelief. Though not as bad as having the religious people come to his door, this was almost just as bad.

"Uh, yes, is Ian here? We have his kid," Ill-Advised said.

Ron, looking dumbstruck, turned around and yelled behind him, "Ian, get in here!" He then turned back to the men and said, "That is my child!"

The men looked at Ron embarrassedly. "Oh, uh, then, here you go then," Ill-Advised said. "We realized that we don't take young girls as slaves anymore. Bad press usually follows."

"What, just because she's a girl, you think she's worthless and can't be a slave? So sexist. I can't believe what I'm hearing," Ron said, scowling at them.

"Ron!" Gretchen yelled from the other room.

"I mean, give me her," Ron said quickly, taking Kimmith out of his hands.

Ian arrived at the doorway and glanced at Ron, Kimmith, and the men. He looked utterly dejected.

"Ian, did you sell Kimmith to three men on cows?" Ron asked Ian darkly.

"No, I did not sell her to three men on cows," Ian said, putting his hands on his hips. "I gave her away to three men on cows."

Ron's face turned red. "Ian, go to your tent!" he barked, pointing toward the backyard. Ian stormed off in a fit, and Ron turned back to the men, who seemed not to know what to do with themselves.

"And as for you three," Ron said, his tone judgmental. "What is wrong with you? Allowing a child to give away his sister to you. That was very ill-advised."

They all lowered their heads in shame. "Well, it is part of our reputation. We apologize, though, for any inconvenience we may have caused you," Ill-Advised said.

Ron wasn't listening, though. "Get out of my city," he said, and they all turned around and got back onto their cows.

"Come, my friends, the dust of a bunny awaits!" Ill-Advised proclaimed. They rode off again until they were out of sight.

Ron looked down at Kimmith, who looked around like nothing had happened. He put her down, and she began collecting the heads of Ian's dolls, scattered on the floor, and putting them in a trash bag she was carrying around with her.

Ian, meanwhile, was stewing in his tent, angrily ricocheting a tennis ball off the sides of the tent with his mind. He was done with Kimmith and knew he had to get rid of her before he became an outcast forever.

He came out of his tent and looked up at the sky. "Oh, whatever is out there, I need your help," Ian said, kicking the ground angrily. "I need answers!"

At that moment, the moon emerged from behind the clouds, and its silvery white light shone down to the Earth, highlighting far off into the distance. Ian followed it almost in a trancelike state. When he reached where it was shining, he saw a rusty old well near the city's center. A decaying sign hung on the side of it, reading, "Very deep, hard to get out of, perfect for throwing children down."

Ian smiled as a dark, wonderful, awful idea formed in his mind.

Chapter 9:

The Story of Ian, Kimmith, and the Well

Ian came out of his tent early the following day. The sky was tinted green, and a storm seemed to be on the horizon. He went up to the palace's back door and banged the door knocker in the shape of a sickle. Ron came out and looked down at Ian, who seemed slightly frustrated and uncomfortable.

"Oh, it's you," Ron said as if Ian was an ex-girlfriend.

But Ian gave a sarcastic smirk. "I want to say that I am so very sorry for what I did," he said, putting his arms behind his back. "I will never give Kimmith away before asking you first."

Ron stroked his chin with his hand, which disappeared into his beard. He studied Ian carefully. Finally, he said, "All right, Ian, but it's not me you should apologize to."

Over Ron's shoulder, Ian saw Kimmith on the floor, spinning his doll's body around like a top and throwing it in the air like she was flipping flapjacks. He nodded, hurried past Ron, and approached her despite his legs trying to go in the opposite direction. When he finally got to her, he couldn't help but look at her and feel sorry for her. It wasn't her fault that she was so annoying and terrible. He knelt down to her level.

"Kimmith, I'm sorry we have had our differences. I hope we can both learn from this and grow up to make each other better." Ian dug his toe into the ground, and now red in the face, he waited for her response. Kimmith got up and ran off after seeing a speck of dust and deciding to chase it. Ian's face remained red, but for a different reason. *That's it, that's the end. Nobody betrays me by chasing dust,* he said to himself. The time had come to implement his plan.

In the darkness of the next night, Ian slipped into the house and went into the kitchen. He opened the cabinet with his mind and grabbed a jar of peanut butter from the top shelf. He then took a butcher knife from the drawer near him and admired it maniacally.

With that, his long night began. Sticking the butcher knife in the jar more times than he could count, he slowly made a trail of peanut butter that dragged and wove its way to the well he had found the previous night. Peanut butter was Kimmith's favorite food. Ian often found her with her head stuck in one of the jars or sticking her hand in to take a scoop. One time, Ian found her upside down with her legs in the air and her head in the jar. When he was finally finished, he tossed the jar aside, returned home to his tent and prepared for the next day.

When the night had ended and the day had broken, Ian again came into the back door of the palace to find Kimmith in his old room, chewing on one of his research papers. He swallowed hard and went up to her.

Ian pointed at the sticky mess on the floor that he'd stepped in. "Kimmith, look, peanut butter on the ground."

Kimmith looked up from her activity and saw the shiny gleam of her favorite delight. "Peb-nit-bubbler!" she babbled excitedly. She started sniffing the ground and following the trail out of the room. Ian followed behind her, rubbing his hands together.

She continued through the palace. When she approached the front door, Gretchen came in from the kitchen and looked at Kimmith, whose face was buried on the floor.

"What is going on here?" she asked, trying to feign some interest.

"A scavenger hunt." Ian was barely looking up from what he was doing.

Gretchen pressed her lips together as if she had accidentally swallowed a whole lemon before saying, "Well, that's pretty stupid, but I'm glad you two are at least getting along."

Ian was barely listening, though, and just said, "Yes, it's great now. Kimmith, say goodbye to your mother."

Kimmith looked up with peanut butter on her chin and said, "Bye-bye." Ian tapped her with his two-foot-long stick, leading her back onto the trail and out the door.

The trip was long and tedious, as it turned out that it took a long time for a child to crawl across a town. Ian also had to ignore the townsfolk who were eyeing them suspiciously and judgmentally.

"It's for your own good, people," Ian said like he was a health inspector.

It was late afternoon when they finally made their way to the well. Ian was starving, but Kimmith was bloated by all the peanut butter she had eaten. She perched herself on the side of the well and began to sway back and forth. Standing up, she started hopping across the hole on the adjacent stones.

Now, the events that transpired next have been debated and are murky.

Here is Ian's account of what happened:

Ian looked at his sister, who seemed to be frolicking in slow motion, playing on the side of the well. He was then possessed by a massive wave of warmth and love that flowed through him like the rays of the sun on a hot day at the beach. He dropped his stick, which bounced onto the ground, and ran up to the well. He momentarily picked up his sister and held her in the air, then embraced her. Then setting her down gently, he smiled down on her.

"I'm sorry," he said. "I'll be the best brother that ever was to you. You'll never be neglected again." He patted her on the head.

Kimmith glared up at him for a moment. She then kicked Ian in the shin, which made him buckle. She blew raspberries at him, hit him on the head, then bent down and jumped into the well, happily cheering as her voice got fainter into the darkness of the surprisingly deep chasm.

Ian collapsed to his knees and pounded his fist into the ground. He reached for the sky and screamed, "Nooooo!"

According to a random artichoke merchant, this is what happened: He was set up on the street corner across from the well. Business was particularly slow that day, mainly due to the new tax on artichokes. It was a risky business to get into, but someone had to do it.

Anyway, his eyes caught sight of a little girl doing a jig on the old well. Puzzled by this, he went up for a closer look. When he got closer, he saw the girl swaying back and forth on the wall, but she kept her balance. He then heard a voice yell from somewhere.

"Oh, just do it already!" it yelled.

He saw the girl get startled by this, begin to lose her balance, and eventually fall backward down the well. Her cries disappeared down the hole. The horrified man saw a kid sneak up to the well and peer down it. The child then tripped and slammed his shin into the side of the well, losing control of his stick, which flew in the air and hit him on the head. After this, the artichoke vendor saw him look around suspiciously before darting away out of sight.

No matter what actually happened, it did not change the fact that Kimmith had fallen down the well. Ian got home panting out of breath, and then coolly strode up to Ron, who was playing with the artichoke tax money at his desk.

Ian cleared his throat. "Father, something terrible has happened!" he cried.

"What has happened, Ian?" Ron asked, looking up from his coins. "Don't tell me those nude free-will advocates are out expressing themselves again."

"No, it's Kimmith," Ian said. "She fell down the well."

Ron jumped up. "What? How could this have happened?"

Ian clicked the back of his mouth with his tongue. "She just jumped down before I could stop her. You know how insane she is," he answered.

Gretchen came in holding a wooden tunic decoration. "What is all this ruckus?" she asked.

"Kimmith has fallen down the well," Ron said, and Gretchen immediately glared at Ian.

"Did you even try to stop it?" she questioned Ian, who immediately put his hands on his hips.

"Of course," Ian said resentfully. "What kind of monster do you think I am?" He then began to "cry," and Ron patted him on the shoulder.

"It's okay, Ian," Ron said. "You did all that you could."

"No, I could've done more," Ian cried, wiping his eyes.

"Well, if you want to help, Kimmith needs to be fed," Ron said as if he was talking about a bear at a roadside zoo. "Now, all we have are canned coconuts, but you can open them up and toss them down to her."

Ian nodded his head sullenly. Gretchen looked suspiciously at Ian but then took her glare to Ron. "Ron, why can't you get the firefighters to get her out?"

Ron seemed to take exception to the ridiculousness of this question. "Because, my dear, in the budget, we had to choose between getting the windmill project going or continuing to fund a fire department. And since wind happens more than fires here in the desert, we had to make sacrifices."

Gretchen took in her husband's stupidity but decided it wasn't worth continuing the argument. She scoffed and marched away. Though she was happy about the return of the status quo of Ian being in a better position, she also didn't know if Ron's reign would last long enough for Ian to take over.

So, ever since that fateful day, one of them has gone down to the old well to feed Kimmith her canned coconuts. Ian took down his tent and returned to his room, looking at it with a smile across his face.

"And they say karma will come back to bite someone," he said. "Well, obviously, they haven't heard of me."

He then heard a knock on the door. After heading down the stairs, he opened the door. On the other side stood a young boy, probably slightly younger than him, though not by much. He had thin brown hair that seemed already in the early receding stages. He was on the larger side of boys his age, but Ian wouldn't consider him overweight. The boy stared nervously at Ian with his wide blue eyes and round, freckled nose.

"Can I help you?" Ian asked, attempting to feign interest like his mother. He was having such a good day and wanted that to continue.

The boy seemed startled by this question. "Uh, yes, is this the home of the king?" he asked.

Ian gave him a side-eye. "Maybe, what do you want?"

The boy clutched his wrist. "Well, I'm here to have you sample some lovely soaps my family has made and would be honored to take some of your time to have you try them out."

Ian gave the boy another skeptical glance. "We don't need any free stuff. Enough of that is already done in this city."

The boy smiled slightly. "As Ayn Sand says: 'I will never live for the sake of another man, nor ask another man to live for mine,' at least that's what I think it is."

Ian's face brightened, and he had to do a double take with his ears because he couldn't believe what he had just heard.

"Did you just quote Ayn Sand?"

The boy shrugged. "Yeah, you know what I was quoting from?"

"Of course I do," Ian said, smiling. "Please come in. We can have a little chat about soaps and stuff. Who are you again?"

The boy beamed at him. "I'm John." Ian nodded and led him into the mansion.

"John, nice to meet you. I'm Ian," he said, and John dropped the soaps on the floor, detonating into a cloud of lavender-scented shrapnel.

Chapter 10

The Story of John

Seven years before the events that just transpired at the well, the small fishing village of Bolshevik Bay stood on the city's outskirts. Most made their living off the deformed fish that were in the radioactive stream that flowed through the village. Another major trade in the village was fishing for the lost belongings that people had dropped in the river closer to the big city after spending time at the beach.

However, around this time, King Ron announced that all fishing had been nationalized and the government was now in charge of all fishing permits and quotas in the town. The townsfolk were infuriated by this. So far, during King Ron's rule, they had avoided what was called the "Red Ron Fist." But now, some people's livelihoods were at stake, and something had to be done.

A group of men and women held a secret meeting late one night in one of the bed and breakfasts, Breakfast & Bed. The man who called the meeting, George Tucker, stood up and held up a mug. His ragged beard swayed with his animated movements.

"Men and women," he hollered across the room. "We have gathered here today to call for an end to this tyranny that has gone on for long enough."

The crowd gave an enthusiastic cheer. George rode the wave of excitement. "I hereby declare our independence from Rondithmuth and disown our blessed king and his meddling queen," he said, which was followed by another cheer ringing through the crowd.

"And we should be known as, uh … what are we drinking here?" he asked a woman from the back of the crowd.

"Coffee!" she shouted, and George toasted his mug.

"The Coffee Party it is, then," he said, satisfied. "To freedom and happiness!"

"To freedom and happiness!" the crowd barked back.

For the next two years, the Coffee Party ran guerrilla tactics and sabotage throughout King Ron's land. But as hard as King Ron tried, he could never figure out where they were hiding.

"These damn rebels," Ron said as he slammed the desk in his bedroom one particularly frustrating night.

"Weren't you a rebel, Ron?" Gretchen piped in from her seat on the bed, but Ron scoffed at this notion.

"That was different," he replied indignantly. "We actually had something to complain about."

Two years after the rebellion started, King Ron received a tip-off that the rebels were hiding in the fishing village of Bolshevik Bay and dispatched a raiding party to arrest them.

The rebels, though, were informed ahead of time of the troop dispatch and were evacuating their homes and fleeing into hiding. George Tucker and his wife Martha were packing their things frantically after George got a call on his paper cup phone.

"Why do we have to flee now?" Martha asked. "We're so close. We were just about to implement our plan to throw his son down a well."

George continued to pack his rebellious T-shirts. "There's no time," he said. "Take everything valuable, and let's get out of here."

"But what about John?" Martha asked, pointing to a crib in a corner holding a little baby. George stared at it for a moment, then shook his head.

"We don't have time, and the place we'll be going is not suitable for a child."

"We can't just leave him!" Martha's voice cracked, but George shook his head.

"No, we can't," he said, and he began to frantically look around until he spotted a pile of blankets in the corner. "Wrap him in the blanket over there and put him in that bucket outside, then send him down the river."

Martha recoiled. "I'm not sending my son down a river!" she cried.

"He'll be fine," George replied. "People do it all the time. We have to go, and this is our only option."

Martha reluctantly went to the crib and picked up John, who was sleeping. She gently wrapped him in a salmon-colored blanket and went outside to find the bucket next to the door. She laid him in and made sure he was snug. She then went to the river a few feet from the house and took one last look at her son.

"Be safe, John," she said to her child. "Never forget that no matter what they tell you, you're your own person." She kissed his forehead and then threw him into the rapid flow of the water. John was off down the river.

The bucket traveled far and wide through fields, forests, waterfalls, and water parks. Finally, after two days, the river took him in front of a giant mansion with large windows, a large garden, and whatever other rich stereotypes you wish to add.

An old lady with a put-together wrinkly face and brown-dyed hair came over to the bucket and looked inside. She then turned toward the mansion. "Chuck! I found another baby in a bucket!" she yelled in a harsh, raspy voice.

"Dammit, Nancy, not another one!" a balding old man with a big nose and crooked glasses called back as he came out. "We already have nine. We can't take in any more right now."

Nancy put the bucket on the shore and went up to him. "But Chuck, think of the tax write-off if we have another orphan," she pleaded with him. "I can finally get that facelift I've needed for a month now."

"Yes, you do need it," he said after considering her and nodding in approval. "All right, then, but this is the last one."

So, Chuck and Nancy took in their tenth child and welcomed him to The Baby Bucket Orphanage. By pure coincidence, they decided to name him John.

John's early childhood was not very notable. Chuck and Nancy, who were both prominent oligarchs for King Ron, acted like they were generous in accepting orphans, but they mainly used them as an excuse for free labor.

John's job was usually to try to make Nancy look as passable a human as possible, typically an all-day affair. From a very young age, John was a bright boy, a quick learner, and an avid reader.

One day, when he was around four years old, John was reading a beauty magazine on the floor in the living room, desperately trying to find some ideas he could use for Nancy. However, a knock at the door interrupted him. He waited for a moment for someone else to answer it, but after a few minutes, he couldn't take the anxiety of the situation and opened the door.

He jumped back when he saw what was on the other side. Standing in front of him was a hooded figure about seven feet tall and dressed from head to toe in black. John eventually regained his composure and was able to muster a squeak.

"Gosh, mister, you scared me," John said in his nice voice that was also slightly off-putting.

The figure didn't answer and just faced John, motionless. The young John nervously tapped his foot. He wasn't used to this kind of human interaction—or whatever kind of interaction this was. He tried again to get the conversation going.

"So, are you one of those religious types?" he asked. No answer.

"Are you trying to sell me something that'll break after a few days?" he asked again, but there was still no answer.

"Well, you're wasting my time," John said, giving up. He began to close the door, but the hooded figure suddenly reached out and offered him something before he could shut it. John took it carefully and examined it. It was a small book, titled *Makes Sense to Me*, by a man named Tommy Pain. John looked up, confused.

"Yes, it's a book, but what do you want me to do with it?" John asked, somehow getting more bewildered as time went by. The figure floated backward without turning around, and the door slammed shut on its own. John took in all the weirdness of what had just happened for a second and then stared at the book again. The thing that people usually do with books is read them, so he figured that's what he should probably accomplish with it. What harm could it do?

Over the next week or so, John read the small book cover to cover. It was about why it was okay and even necessary to rebel against tyranny. John found it a good read but didn't really get why he needed to be skimming it in the first place. For the next few months, nothing else weird happened, and John returned to his dull life as Nancy's caregiver, though it was getting harder every day to find a way to make her look right.

On a hot summer afternoon, though, John was in the dining room, trying to bend Chuck's glasses so they pointed down, when he again heard a knock on the front door. He paused, hoping that someone else would open it this time, but quickly realized everyone around him sucked, and went up and opened it himself again. The hooded figure was back in front of him, and again, John was startled and fell backward.

He got up and scowled at the figure. "You again," he cried. "No, can't you wear different attire besides the black hood? You have 'I'm going to kill you' written all over you."

The figure did not answer, much to John's annoyance, but not his surprise. He really didn't have time for this. He needed to put skin bleach on Nancy.

"So, I read your book and burned it as the note in the back asked me to," John said, trying to sound casual although one could only get so casual with a weird hooded being. "But I don't get it. Why are you bugging me?"

The figure handed him another item. John took it. It was another book, this one almost as thick as him, titled *Atlas Doesn't Care Anymore* by Ayn Sand. John gulped and looked up at the figure.

"How am I supposed to finish this?" John asked, getting a ruler out of his pocket to measure the book's thickness. "It's literally bigger than me. You realize I'm only about four, right?"

Just then, Chuck walked by, and John quickly stuffed the book down his pants. "Jim, go play with your friend somewhere else where my glasses can't see you," Chuck said as he passed by. He left the room. John sighed and, turning back to see the figure almost face to face with him, gave an internal squeal.

"Don't do that!" John yelped, staggering backward. "What's wrong with you?"

But the figure floated backward without turning around, and the door slammed shut on its own, again leaving John with his disorienting thoughts.

For the next six months, John worked hard to finish his new book, which was extremely difficult not just because it was bigger than him but also because crows kept landing on Nancy, as she tanned by the pool before John could scare them off.

When he finished, though, John was a changed kid. He now understood exactly what Rondithmuth's problem was and was also convinced that the king needed to go. However, he couldn't bring this up to his adopted parents or siblings, poster children for King Ron's kingdom. So, John waited for his moment.

That moment came on a foggy morning. The sky was green, which meant a storm was likely on the horizon. John was in the kitchen taking inventory of Nancy's ice cream when he heard a knock at the front door. Not even bothering to wait for someone else, he went to the door and opened it. The hooded figure was there, but standing next to him this time was a tall, lanky man with thick glasses on his stubby nose. His messy red hair was mismatched with the green sky. The man smiled at John.

"Good morning, young sir. I am the Translator, and I'm here to help you talk to my friend here," he said, smiling at both John and the black mass next to him. "He was concerned that his point wasn't getting across."

"Well, not saying anything will do that!" John said, standing there bitterly.

The Translator looked uncomfortable but continued on and looked at the figure. "He says that you, John, have become quite the handsome, bright young man." John smiled.

"Why, thank you! I try my best to look my best. It's important to …" John said, but the Translator cut him off, looked at the figure again, and then turned to John.

"He says that he knew your mother and father and that they would be quite proud," he said, and John was taken aback.

"You knew my mom and dad?" John asked, more softly this time.

The Translator looked at the figure again. "He says that he did, and that they were members of a secret organization to overthrow the king and restore freedom across the land and wait for the coming of our Maud'Ian," he said.

John stood there, head spinning. "This is insane!" he cried, putting his hands on top of his head, but the Translator kept going.

"He says that now is the time for you to join us and start with a special mission."

"A mission?"

The hooded figure handed John a flask with crossbones on it.

"He says that it is your job to use this to poison the son of the king," the Translator continued.

"Poison," John said, again taken aback. "Isn't that, like, wrong?"

The Translator looked at the figure and looked back at John and said, "He says that who's to say?"

"All right, I guess war is always ugly," John said, scratching his head. "I'll do it. For the good of my people."

The Translator smiled, looked at the figure, and quickly turned back to John. "You have two hours," he said.

"Two hours!" John cried, his eyes widening, but the Translator continued without missing a beat.

"Yes, you better get going. If they find you out, we'll deny that any of this ever happened," he said, again looking at the figure and then back at John. "Good luck, John. The fate of everything is in your hands, but there's no pressure. Now it's time we leave."

The Translator looked at the figure and frowned. "No, I'm not doing that," he said. The figure continued to glare at him. "Fine," he sighed, and he got on the back of the figure. They floated backward without turning around, and the door slammed shut on its own.

John sat in a chair nearby, thinking hard. How was he supposed to get to the prince in two hours, much less get him to drink poison? Just then, Nancy came in.

"Jack, I need you to get these documents to the king as soon as possible," she said, dyeing her hair as she walked. "So, get going."

John's eyes almost shot out of his head, and his face went white. "Um, okay, Nancy, I'll get going right now," he said.

He scurried out the door, ensuring the flask was safe in his pocket. As his mind raced, he passed by an old, abandoned factory and many other structures that had long been empty. Things had escalated very quickly. One minute, he was trying to invent a new lotion that would work on Nancy's skin but also not cause the house to become chemically contaminated, and the next, he was supposed to murder a fellow child. As he got more into the town, he noticed people walking in groups quickly by him.

"Excuse me, where are you all going?" he asked a dirty man with socks for a hat as he passed by.

"Some girl fell down the old well in the center of town," the man said quickly in an almost folksy manner. "We're all going to go and look at her."

And without further discussion, he was gone, and John hastily moved toward the enormous palace, hovering over all the run-down shops and dirty streets. When he was younger, he would've seen the palace as a bright beacon of hope amongst the depressing surroundings. Now that he was a wiser five-year-old, he saw it more as a vacuum that was sucking up all the light and leaving a dark wasteland in its path.

When he got to the doorstep, he rang the bell near the door. The chime, an old Russian hymn, could be heard before the door opened, and a young boy stood before him, glasses shining on his face, his black hair sparkling with the rest of the gold around the house.

John gulped.

Chapter 11:

The Story of the Poisoning of the Holy Ian

"Ian?" John said blankly. Soap was still foaming everywhere as Ian quickly grabbed some towels from nearby.

"Yes, Ian," Ian said as he wiped up the mess on the floor, much faster than John thought possible.

"Son of the king?" John asked, instinctively grabbing the flask hidden under his clothes.

"I wonder sometimes, but yeah," Ian said, smirking. "Come in."

John took a seat in a lime green chair, visibly sweating. Ian sat on the pumpkin-colored couch across from him and put his feet up on the coffee table between them.

"Are you okay?" Ian asked, eyeing John, who looked like his mind was in another book. "You look a bit pale."

"Oh, yes," John said, jolting up from his thoughts. "I just need to use your restroom."

"That makes sense," Ian said, nodding in approval. "There's one in the corner over there."

John saw the small bathroom that seemed to have been installed at the last moment. He got up and walked a few feet before entering the room. John looked at himself in the mirror after shutting the door behind him, gleaming and seeming like he had aged in the last half hour. Suddenly remembering he was on a timer, he took out the poison flask and looked at it.

How could he kill the son of the king now? Ian seemed to be just the kind of person the Coffee Party would like. There must be some mistake. Then again, second-guessing a giant, hooded black figure probably wasn't a good idea either. If it has to be done, it has to be done.

A knock came from the other side, causing John to almost drop the flask.

"Are you okay in there?" Ian asked from the other side. "I find being emotionally flustered can get things moving faster."

"I'm fine, thanks," John answered, quickly flushed the toilet, and washed his hands.

"I'll be in the other room," Ian continued on the other side of the door. "We can discuss our favorite theories of free will."

John ran his hands through his hair, took a deep breath, then stepped out. Ian was still where John had last left him, and John sat across and stared nervously at the king's son.

Ian seemed to notice the tension and smiled at him. "Don't worry, you don't need to call me Prince or anything," he said. "We can figure that all out later."

John didn't answer, seeming to just be admiring Ian's ear hair.

Ian took his feet off the table. "How about a drink? What do you want?" he asked.

"Some poiso—I mean nitro gle—I mean cyani—I mean water would be fine," John said as if he was having a stroke.

Ian glared at John with some concern then got up. "I'll get you some nonalcoholic beer. That usually calms me down." John bolted up from his chair.

"No, no, I'm the guest. I'll get it," John said. He ran by Ian and went into the kitchen.

"Shaken, not stirred," Ian called after him.

"You got it," John yelled back nervously as he tapped his fingers on the counter.

He went to the refrigerator, grabbed their drinks, carried them back to the nearby counter, and started pouring. After filling the two glasses, he took out the flask with the skull and crossbones on it. He took a deep breath and then poured about half of it into one of the cups. Picking up the two drinks, and making sure he knew which was which, he went back into the living room and set them down in front of a smiling Ian, who sat up straight.

"Here you go. This one is mine," John said, quickly pointing to the one he had kept track of as the non-killing one. Ian looked at the glasses, put his hand on them, and then smiled at him.

"Hey, I've got an idea," Ian said, mind visually spinning. John stood still, a single line of sweat running away from his face.

"Let's play a little game," Ian said excitedly. "I'm going to take both glasses and switch them really fast. Then you pick up which one you think is yours, take a sip, and I'll tell you if you're right or not."

"Ho-how will you tell which one is which?" John stuttered, face as pale as a dead ghost. Ian touched his chin, pondering his new friend's question. Finally, he smiled, grabbed a grape from the table, and squeezed the juice into one of the glasses. The color didn't really seem to change in John's eyes, but Ian seemed satisfied.

"Here, I put the grape into yours, so we'll know," Ian said.

John pressed his lips together and then plopped down into his chair, annoyed at how his day was going. "All right then, let's do it," he said, and he locked his eyes onto his glasses. Ian smiled and grabbed the glasses.

"Here we go," Ian said, and he whipped the glasses around with such speed that John's eyes seemed to keep going when Ian finally slowed down the spinning glasses as they shimmered to a graceful halt.

"Guest first," Ian said, smirking.

It seemed John's eyes were doing somersaults and complicated math equations. He had no idea which one was which. Ian seemed to notice this and smiled again, this time more softly.

"It's okay," Ian said. "I'll go first, then. I know which is which any-way." He grabbed what he thought was his glass and raised it in the air.

"To life and not dying," he toasted, and looked to John. "And new friends."

He began to take his glass to his lips. John watched in what seemed like slow motion. His mind was working on overdrive, flip-flopping, then flipping back, then flipping on the flip-flop. At the last second, when the liquid was about to touch Ian's tongue, John jumped across the table and slapped the drink out of Ian's hand and across the room.

Ian looked at John, put his hands up, and cried, "John, what the heck was that?"

John quickly thought of something, anything. "Uh, I have muscle spasms," he said uncertainly.

Ian stared at him briefly, causing John to squirm in his chair uncomfortably. "Well, it's okay. These things happen. I'll go and get some more this time," Ian said happily, and he began to sit before John jumped up once again.

"It's okay, it's my mess. I'll get some more," John said, quickly returning to the kitchen. On the wall, he saw a picture of a toddler, Ian, throwing darts at a picture of Mao, with what appeared to be King Ron sprinting at him in the corner of the picture.

He then saw an image in his head of the hooded figure throwing a dart at him while he was tied to a rotating board. It had to be done. It just had to. John made two more glasses. This time, after putting the poison into one glass, he taped a piece of paper to the one that was poisoned and, with a pen, wrote on it "Do not give to John. Equals death." He took another deep breath, returned to the living room, and handed Ian his glass.

"Thanks, John, you're all right," Ian said brightly. He raised his glass again and began to take it to his mouth. Again, John looked at the glass and at Ian, his thoughts racing again. He was going to have a heart attack, stroke, and an asthma attack if this went on. At the last second, John's hands instinctively knocked the glass out of Ian's hand again, smashing it into the corner.

Ian glared at him. "John, I think you have a problem."

Finally, John couldn't help himself. "That was poison, Ian!" he blurted out, before covering his mouth as if that would do anything. Ian looked at him for a moment, eyes slightly wider than John had thought they were. But then, he casually laid back in his seat.

"I knew that," Ian said, causing John's heart to try to run away from him. He had been caught.

"You did?" John asked, panicking.

"Yes, of course," Ian said, looking to the side of the wall. "I was just testing you."

"How did you know?"

"Well, John, when you get to be my age, you learn a thing or two about people's reactions and states of mind," Ian said as if he was in theory class. "You looked like you wanted to poison me from the moment I first laid eyes on you."

"Wow!" he said, looking at Ian in amazement. John's thoughts went to the hooded figure. He immediately told Ian everything: his upbringing, the mission, the Translator. When he was done, Ian was smiling.

"That's quite the origin story, John," Ian said, impressed.

John still wasn't calm, though. "They're going to kill me, Ian," he said. "What am I going to do?"

At that moment, Ron came in from the front door carrying bags of lettuce over his shoulder like Lettuce Claus.

Ian got up and ran over to him. "Dad, can I get your help with something?" Ian asked, feeling a little disgusted with himself.

"Yes, Ian, the government is always here to help," Ron said, though he couldn't see Ian past the bags. "But put these in the refrigerator first." Ian stuffed the lettuce away and then went back to his father.

"Dad, the Coffee Party just tried to assassinate me and is now threatening my friend John here," Ian said, and Ron finally noticed there was someone else in the house. He stared at the two of them and then frowned.

"Those heartless savages," he said furiously. "I've had enough of them. Don't worry, Ian, I'll help protect your friend here. Where does he live?"

"At Nancy and Chuck's orphan house, Your Grace," John said, speaking up and then bowing. King Ron liked this and patted John on the head, causing some hairs to fall out from the day's stress.

"All right, my lad, I'll station several men at Nancy and Chuck's place. They've always been loyal supporters," Ron said. "Watch your back, though. You never know when a free-thinking conservative can come out and get you. They're like snakes in the grass. They could be hiding anywhere." Ron looked around the room like he was expecting one to come out of the cabinet or something.

John nodded at the king's words. "Yes, Your Grace," he repeated again, making Ian want to vomit.

"Good, come join us for dinner, lad," Ron said, clapping his hands together like he had just solved some sort of riddle. "We're having salad."

"Thank you, Your Grace," John said graciously, and he bowed again, which Ian was again repulsed by.

Ron left the room, leaving Ian and John to their own accord. John finally was able to sigh and take a breath. It had indeed been a long day, but when he looked at Ian, who was talking about the time he changed Ron's wine into water just to piss him off, he knew it had been worth it. They smiled at each other and went to the dining table for dinner. And thus began Ian and John's friendship, which went on for decades, minus a few speed bumps—but that's for another day.

Chapter 12:

The Story of Ian's Vision

Ian was now the age of eleven. For the last five years, he had been hard at work hanging out with his new friend John and being as much of a pain in the butt to Ron as possible, like that time at the parade.

"Ian, were you the one that changed my name on the side of my chariot to 'King Ronnoying?'" Ron asked him accusingly. Ian smirked at the side of the chariot, proud that he had gotten the "y" to curl majestically.

"Why, Father, I'm not clever enough to come up with a funny thing like that," Ian said, not really hiding the crap coming out of his mouth. But all Ron could do was sulk away, as he had no proof it was Ian, and he had other important matters to take care of.

During this period, the Coffee Party became bolder in their rebellion, attacking shipping and trade lanes from which Ron got his salad ingredients.

"I'll kill them all for this!" Ron shrieked after finding out that the rebels had targeted his lettuce supplies, which might not be fixed for two years. "All I have is iceberg lettuce now. And I'll have to raise taxes to pay for the markup." He rubbed his wrist. "And that always hurts when I'm writing the order." Gretchen looked at Ron, slightly amused by his troubles but also annoyed at all the complaining she was about to hear about how bland his salad was now.

Ian, though, was more than happy to let Ron deal with a rebellion because it amused him and kept Ron off his back. He didn't need any more problems with Ron than necessary, especially with how his mother had been on his butt.

Gretchen had gotten into a habit of constantly scolding Ian for not being professional enough—for instance, when he wore a hat backward at the dinner table, which, as Ian pointed out, Ron did all the time. She also nagged him to stand straight when talking and not to slouch. It was more appealing to people.

Ian assumed that she must be just going through the change or something and tended to take these "suggestions" with the enthusiasm of a kid watching a documentary on the history of gravel. He did actually like that one, though, so maybe not the best example. Anyway, Ian had gotten comfortable, which was always a bad plan, as this would be followed by insane and annoying stuff happening, and this time would be no different.

One cold but also hot winter day, Ian was in his bathtub, simulating a medieval battle with his rubber ducks. He lay back in the tub and relaxed, the water gently waving halfway across his face as his ears were filled and unfilled with liquid. He closed his eyes in tranquility, wishing this feeling could last forever without all the consequent skin issues.

Suddenly, the hundred rubber ducks drifted over to him and pressed him under the water. Opening his eyes with a start, he tried to lift his head out, but the ducks blocked his way. He flailed his arms wildly, which surprisingly did nothing.

Then, everything went dark.

Ian awoke in a blinding light. Blinking feverishly, he saw nothing except the endless white that reminded him of a clean gas station bathroom, if anybody had ever seen one. Scrambling to his feet, he began walking around, searching for something significant. He then banged his head against something hard and fell backward. He looked up and saw a high ladder floating in midair. He couldn't determine where it led. Ian was used to weird stuff happening around him, but this certainly took the cake. Suddenly, a booming voice came from the top of the ladder and knocked Ian down.

"Ian!" the voice said.

Ian, eyes wide and hands shaking, stood up and looked up the ladder. "And who are you?" he asked, concerned but also curious.

"I am Backwards Dog," the booming voice replied, and Ian immediately stumbled to his knees.

"Thanks for the kneeling, but we do not have that kind of time," Backwards Dog said. Ian imagined him looking at his watch. "Ian, it is time you were told who you really are."

"Who am I? I'm Ian," Ian said, not understanding what the big booming voice was talking about.

"Yes, you are indeed Ian," Backwards Dog confirmed. "But, uh, climb up the ladder. Let's talk face to face."

Ian squinted at the never-ending ladder. "That looks like a lot of work, though." Backwards Dog sighed, knocking Ian back a bit.

"Ugh, kids these days," Backwards Dog complained. "Fine. Take the elevator next to it, then."

Just then, Ian noticed, next to the ladder, an elevator with a halo on the door. He pressed the button after 'Purgatory'—labeled the 'The Top'—and the elevator shook and creaked before slowly moving upwards. While it clattered and clanged, Ian tried to process his thoughts, but his mind wasn't working with him.

Right when Ian was about to have a realization, the elevator ground to a sudden halt, knocking him down on the clear floor. Backwards Dog's voice came through on the intercom overhead.

"Darn blasted piece of junk," he said. "All right, we'll just talk here, then, if that's okay."

"I don't really have a choice, do I?" Ian said, shrugging.

"No, I guess you don't. Alrighty then," Backwards Dog went on. "Ian, I am your father."

"Aren't you supposed to be everyone's father?" Ian replied, unfazed by this revelation.

"I, well, yes, technically, but I mean, like, more than usual," the voice tried to clarify.

"Ah, that makes more sense," Ian said, nodding like he knew what Backwards Dog was talking about.

"Of course it does. Ian, haven't you wondered where all those weird things you can do came from?"

Ian thought for a moment and then replied, "I thought Ron just had a weird great-grandfather or something, and the gene skips about three generations."

"Well, he doesn't," Backwards Dog grumbled, not sounding amused. "He is not your father, though your mother is still true."

"What did you do to my mother?" Ian demanded, pointing to the elevator's ceiling.

"Nothing weird, if that's what you're getting at," Backwards Dog boomed quickly. "I'm not Zeus. Now *that* dude's a weirdo. Always makes passes at Hathor at the dances."

"Wait. There's more than one divine figure?" Ian asked, realizing the implications of what Backwards Dog was talking about.

"Um, well, it's a little complicated," Backwards Dog muttered in a thunderous overtone, regretting the can of worms he had opened. "Just drop it for now."

"Well, okay then. Is that it?" Ian asked, a little disappointed at the lore he was missing out on.

"Not quite. You haven't heard your destiny yet."

"Will this take long?" Ian asked. "I'm currently drowning."

"For too long, the grips of tyranny and the destruction of free will have cursed your land with its foul stench," Backwards Dog exclaimed, disgust in his voice. "I have decided that you, Ian, are the one destined to lead an uprising and found the holy city that values freedom, justice, and free will."

"So, in order to restore free will, you set a preplanned destiny for me?" Ian asked, tilting his head to the side in mocking confusion.

Backwards Dog didn't answer for a moment but eventually said, "You can't make an omelet without breaking a few eggs."

"I do not wish to be an egg that is broken," Ian snarked, not liking this answer.

Backwards Dog made a low sound that vibrated the elevator and made Ian grab his behind. "Come on, Ian, work with me here," he said. "Do what you've always wanted to do. Rise up to your authority figures."

"But how?" Ian asked, grabbing the back of his head.

"First, you're going to need followers. Gather your close allies and friends to your cause. Then, try to get as many people to know you as possible and, more importantly, spread your message," Backwards Dog said.

"Then what?"

"All in good time, young Ian," Backwards Dog stated. "Oh, one more thing you should know. You must be wary of—"

Ian awoke to the sound of splashing water and felt the cold air as he was dragged out of the tub and onto the hard floor of the bathroom. His eyes darted to the picture of Trotsky staring at him from across the toilet. He looked up to see Gretchen glaring down at him, her stern brow firm and unyielding.

"What is wrong with you? Are you stupid?" she asked furiously.

Ian then remembered the vision he had. He stared up at his mother. "I had a vision from Backwards Dog," Ian said, unsure of how else to put it.

Gretchen's stern look suddenly turned into fear. She stepped back.

Ian stared at her in wonder, then suddenly realized what was going on. "You know what I'm talking about. It's true, then. It's all true. Ron isn't my father," Ian said, but Gretchen hushed him quickly and leaned in.

"Keep your voice down. The last thing that needs to happen is for your father to find an excuse to get rid of both of us," she said, but Ian didn't respond. "You need to watch yourself. If you do what I was told you are meant to do, do you really think that the powers that be will so easily throw their control down a well?"

Ian made a slight motion with his mouth at the mention of that place.

"Poor choice of words," she admitted. "It's my job though to keep you alive, but I can, and want to, only do so much."

Ian nodded silently and, as Gretchen got up to leave the room, spoke suddenly. "Did you always know?" he asked, and she stopped, turned around, and stared at him.

"Thirteen years ago, I was told my young life was to be forfeited so that I could raise a child who would change the world," she said. "I've always wondered why me. Why am I being punished? I'm still asking that question." And then she left, leaving Ian wet and deep in thought. He got dressed, angrily hit the rubber ducks that had nearly killed him, and went toward his room, where he bumped into Ron, who was carrying his to-kill list. He looked down at Ian, who almost looked sickly.

"Ian, are you all right?"

"Yeah, it must have been something I ate," Ian said, hesitating.

Ron clenched his fists. "That abominable iceberg lettuce. Don't worry, Ian. Soon, those conservative rebels will rue the day they rebelled against the kingdom. Get some rest now."

He walked away, humming an old Soviet tune. Ian went into his room and closed the door. He lay on his bed for hours, going over his conversation with Backwards Dog again and again in his head, and thought about his mother and what she had said. Changing the world, now there's some pressure. How could anybody meet those expectations? The world had always been the same since he had remembered. What did a different world even look like?

At last, after hours of circling his thoughts, he realized what he had to do. He sat up and dialed the phone next to him. Waiting for what seemed like forever, someone finally picked up.

"John, this is Ian," he said. "Meet me in the usual spot in an hour. I have something to tell you."

Chapter 13:

The Story of the Birth of Ian's Rebellion

"**Y**ou're the son of a who and need to do a what?" John asked an increasingly agitated Ian, who had tried explaining the situation to John five times already. They were behind the old burned-down school, throwing rocks at the rubble. Ian threw a rock in frustration that blew up a window.

"I said, I'm the son of Backwards Dog and need to lead a rebellion to overthrow my father," Ian said as if this was a typical conversation to have with a friend. John threw a rock, but it didn't make it to the wall he was aiming at.

"Whoa, that's some heavy stuff. How are you doing with that?"

Ian threw a rock so hard that it smashed a hole into the wall. "As well as you'd suspect," he said. A fat RSS officer came around the corner and stopped in his tracks when he saw them.

"Hey, you punks, get out of here. Do you want a firm talking to?" he said, and Ian and John took off and went down an alleyway. After taking a minute to catch their breath—well, for John to catch his breath—they resumed their conversation.

"So, what is the timeframe for this rebellion?"

"Not sure. I was dragged out of the tub before I could get more answers," Ian said. "Probably best to gather everyone sooner than later."

"Well, I'm in, but I'm not sure if others will be as receptive," John said, a little worried.

"Are you sure you want to join me?" Ian asked. "It could get dicey."

"I'm not a communist supporter, and the only other rebellion group wants me dead," John said. "You are my only option, Ian." Ian couldn't decide if he was more touched or saddened by this.

"You could've put that nicer, but I'll take it," Ian said. "We'll go recruiting later this evening."

"It's a date," John said, now getting excited.

"No, door knocking. No date," Ian corrected.

"Right," John muttered, avoiding Ian's gaze.

That evening, Ian and John met up and began going from house to house, trying to spread the word about Ian's movement. Their first stop was a nice little house on the corner of the main street. Ian went up to the door and knocked three times. An old woman opened it. She balanced a crying baby in one arm while stirring potato salad with the other.

Ian, who was dressed in a light blue tunic with royal attachments, stepped up and bowed his head. "Hello, ma'am. Have you heard the terrible news?" he asked her.

The woman rolled her eyes and put her baby down next to her. "Oh, what has he done this time?" she asked contemptuously.

"Excuse me?" Ian asked, not knowing what to do with this question.

The woman held up the pot of potato salad like a baseball bat and stormed past Ian and John toward a man with a suitcase who was approaching the house from the road.

"So, Tom, what little damsel in distress were you just helping change their wagon tire this time?" she interrogated.

The man, whose name was apparently Tom, backed up and dodged the pot that the woman had just thrown at him.

"Look, Agnes, if you're going to get jealous here, how about you explain what is happening with those two men you got over there? Did something else in the house conveniently break while I was away?" he spat back.

Ian and John exchanged uncomfortable glances.

"Um, we're twelve, sir," John tried to pipe in, but the man named Tom just grinned like he was holding in a fart.

"Ah, so it's sicker than I thought, you old hag," Tom said to Agnes, who Ian thought was old, but not a hag.

He stepped between the feuding couple. "Now, this is just silly. Sir, have you heard the terrible news?" he asked him, sensing his sale slipping away. "Are you happy with your misery and meaningless life?"

Tom glared at Ian, who took a step away from him. "Do you want to see how strong your hair is when I tie it under a tree to watch you swing?" Tom asked, and John shook his head feverishly. Ian, though, just smiled.

"Have a good day, sir," Ian said, resisting the strong urge to turn Tom into a Tom Cat. "John, let's get out of here."

He quickly turned to the woman and handed her a pamphlet and bolted after John. Only once they thought they were safe did they slow down.

"Well, that could've gone better," John said, panting.

"That's just the first one. Every salesman knows it's a numbers game," Ian said optimistically.

However, a salesman would have also told Ian to get to know his audience, as the rest of his night didn't improve. At one house, a man with a bun in his hair and no shirt pressed Ian, skeptically asking him, "What are you selling?"

Ian handed the pamphlet to the man. He looked at it briefly before crumpling it up and tossing it behind him.

"A bold new way of life," Ian said, ignoring the crumpled state of the pamphlet he had spent three hours trying to figure out how to fold. "Have you ever heard of supply-side economics?"

"No," the man said, frowning. John, who was behind Ian, looked slightly embarrassed and winced.

"Well, you have to have heard of Milton Friedman's natural rate of unemployment theory," Ian said, his voice going unnaturally high.

The man crossed his arms. "Are you trying to sell me on some cult?" he asked, more aggressively.

Ian closed his mouth briefly before opening it again, annoyed that people kept asking him this question. "No, just a new economic and political structure with me leading the way," he deflected, but the man again looked skeptically at Ian.

"Do I get my free stuff?"

Ian smiled a jolly, almost sincere smile. "Even better. You get to work hard and be rewarded with free market prices and wages, which maximize benefits for producers and consumers," Ian said, but he saw he was losing him.

"But I still get my free stuff?"

Ian tried to keep smiling. "Well, um, no, not technically," he said before the door was shut in his face. He turned to John. "I told you I should get a nice hat and a colorful suit. Then people will see I'm being authentic."

John, still a little frightened of Ian as if he were some sort of god, just nodded in agreement.

At another house, a frail, cranky woman glared up at Ian from her wheelchair. "So let me get this straight," she said after hearing Ian make his thirty-minute whiteboard presentation, during which he had run out of markers three times. "You want me to give up my daily rations so the rich can buy a new house for their exotic animals?"

"Well, I wouldn't put it like that," Ian said as he nervously crossed his marker-smudged fingers. The door slammed in his face, this time on John's foot. He turned around angrily. He walked over to a bench on the broken sidewalk, stomped at the crack, then sat down. John sat next to him gingerly.

"How am I supposed to change the world if the world doesn't want to change?" Ian asked John, but also himself. "If they're content with their mediocrity?"

"Maybe it was all just a dream?" John said, secretly hoping that this was the case. He liked the nerdy, quirky Ian much more than the divine figure Ian, but his friend just shook his head.

"No, my mother told me it was true. And trust me, if she was going to lie, that's not what she would've said," Ian replied, thinking back to that conversation with her. They sat in silence, both deep in thought.

"Maybe we should just walk around and see what happens?" John finally suggested, and Ian looked at him.

"Well, it's better than just sitting around," Ian said, now regaining some of his confidence. "We'll try again tomorrow."

The next day, they walked along the dirt roads, looking for anything or anybody who might be interested in what they had to sell. After about an hour of walking, Ian saw two young boys playing baseball with a rock and a stick, quite unsuccessfully. Ian recognized one of them. He approached the boy with the stick and tapped his shoulder. The boy turned around and looked at him.

"Hey, I know you," the boy said, recognizing Ian.

"Yes, I know you too," Ian said, smiling. "You're that boy whose name I can't pronounce. How are you?"

"Can't complain," answered the boy. "Although I could use a bat instead of this stick."

"Well, what if I told you there was a way to have all the bats you could want?" Ian asked him.

"Sorry, I'm not interested in whatever you're selling," the boy replied. "I've already been scammed by things that were too good to be true. Some peddler promised me a potion would make me grow, but it just gave me constipation."

"What if I proved it?" Ian asked, getting a little desperate.

But before he could answer, a rock hit the boy on the side of the head and knocked him to the ground. Ian went down and raised his head.

The kid who threw the rock, a large redhead whose curly hair matched his freckles, lumbered over to them. "Sorry, it was an accident," he said.

"What were you doing? They were talking for like a minute?" John asked in disbelief.

"Don't worry, I'll help him," Ian said, placing his hand over the boy's bruised head. The gash disappeared into thin air before John's and the other kid's eyes. He came to and sat up and rubbed his head, eyes widening with astonishment. Squinting, he looked up at Ian.

"How did you do that?" he asked.

"I'll explain in a minute. But what have you been up to?" Ian asked, attempting to change the subject.

"Since the school burned down, I've been homeschooled, which is not very much fun when both parents work all day, so nothing gets done. The only fun I get is with my friend here. Ian, this is Moofapafadapolis."

Ian again stared at the large boy, who seemed to be interested in the sand on the ground. "Okay, that's a little too much of a mouthful. I'm going to call you Moof," Ian said, and the kid nodded.

"I like that. I'm now Moof," Moof said. Ian looked at the boy whose name he couldn't pronounce.

"Um, what's up with Moof?" Ian whispered to him.

"He's a little slow, but he's cool, and big," he whispered back.

"Who are you? And how did you make his head better?" Moof interjected.

"Yeah, it's just like what you did to me at that bus stop," added the boy whose name Ian couldn't pronounce.

Ian laid out all that had happened so far in the story in a montage-like aesthetic. After he was done, they were staring at him with awe.

"Wow!" Moof said, gawking at Ian. "We're in the presence of a holy man."

"You believe me?" Ian asked in surprise. He may have been slow, but so far Moof was the first to take him seriously.

"Well, you did just make me better. Hard to argue with that," said the boy whose name Ian couldn't pronounce.

Moof grinned widely. "We're with you, Ian. What has the king done for me?"

"Nothing," said the boy whose name Ian couldn't pronounce. "Moof's the son of a carpet maker. One day, the queen wanted a new carpet for her demeaning balcony. When he put it in after two months of work, she said it was *too carpety* and refused to pay him for his labor."

"Yeah, that sounds about right," Ian said, rolling his eyes.

"Then the price on the pills I take went up," Moof said. "So yeah, I'd love to get back at the king and queen. And I can get my friend Mark or Judas to join up."

"Just bring Mark," Ian said, hesitating. "Judas can stay home and not know about any of this." Moof nodded in agreement. Ian smiled for the first time in at least a week. "Well, it's not a lot, but it's a start. The first meeting will be at John's place next weekend."

They all agreed to this, though John was surprised by this development. He would have to arrange to get the twenty-plus people out of the house. He told them about the competition celebrating the best-looking plastic surgery in the city. He also told them that the competition for the most condescending voices was happening in the same place. Needless to say, Chuck and Nancy were excited about this and entered, saying they were going to take the whole family. John got out of it by claiming he had an internship with King Ron where he would design wigs for the queen, which Ian found amusing, since Gretchen hadn't gone longer than a week without a haircut in twenty years.

Thus began Ian's religion and rebellion. However, other entities had also found out about Ian's mission. Forces that were more sinister than Ian could possibly imagine.

Chapter 12:

The Story of Ian's First Temptation

I an was sitting on the floor of the abandoned warehouse with his followers in a circle around him like they were about to play spin the bottle.

"And the pigeons then saw what was there and the consequences of not getting to their nest sooner," Ian said, finishing one of the meeting's parables. Everyone around him looked around in confusion.

John raised his hand. "Yes, Ian, uh, what were you actually talking about?" he asked.

Ian looked at his followers in annoyance, as this was the third time he had been asked this question today. "It's a lesson about the dangers of a central banking group not taking action quick enough when an economic downturn occurs," Ian answered as if this had been obvious from the beginning.

"Sorry, Ian, it's just that your parables aren't exactly clear, and they tend to go all over the place. Like what was with that seal and sea lion love story?" asked Mark, a ten-year-old boy with brown, curly hair.

"It's a lesson about, uh ... Okay, even I'm not sure about that one, but all the others make sense if you're smart enough to pay attention," Ian exclaimed.

"But Ian, some of us are just ten years old," Moof said from behind him.

Ian, having had enough of the meeting for the day, stood up. "This meeting is adjourned. We'll have another one next week when we discuss the dangers of walking into places without looking where we're going," Ian announced. "Spoiler alert: the parable involves a public shower room."

They all looked at him, just as confused as before.

"Here are the scriptures that I wrote for you to read by next week," Ian said, handing out notecards to the four of them. "Oh, and a couple of final comments. Moof," he added, pointing to Moof, who was trying to read the notecard right-side up. "It will be your turn to bring the snacks."

"Okay, Ian, anything vegan?" he asked. "I'm trying to watch my weight."

Ian glared at him.

"Junk food it is," Moof answered for himself.

"And John is designing the uniforms for us," he said, smiling at John.

"It'll be silk that just falls off the skin and makes you feel free," John said happily.

Ian stared blankly at him, but then clapped his hands and said, "Okay, that's a wrap."

With that, everyone began to walk out. Once most had left, it was just Ian and John. Ian turned to him. "We're not ready for our uprising yet. We're too young," Ian said.

John nodded. "Rebellions take years to build up, Ian. We're just getting started." Ian agreed with this notion, said adieu to his friend, and headed back home.

That night, Ian was having very strange dreams—and not the fun kind. There were weird orbs and hooded men with gray hair marching in lines down a deserted hallway. A gravelly voice suddenly called his name, and he woke with a start. He looked around his room—empty except for the stacks of paper he had used up when trying to come up with parables for the group. He sighed and got up to get a glass of water.

Dressed in his PJs, he retrieved a glass from his desk and flicked it. It shimmered and filled with grape juice. After taking a swig he set it down. He went to turn back to bed before noticing something odd outside his window and went to have a closer look.

Outside his house stood a huge, ugly mountain oddly plopped in the middle of the desert. "When did that get there?" he said to himself.

He had the inexplicable urge to climb it, though he knew it was probably a bad idea.

"Nothing good comes from climbing up weird mountains," a homeless man on the street once told him while he was trying to get food at a food stand. He was right: when are spontaneous mountains a good thing? He decided to ignore it, at least until morning, and slipped back into his bed. Lying on his back, he tried to get back to sleep by counting the founding fathers.

"James Wilson, John Dickinson, Robert Morris ..." he mumbled out loud, and he drifted back to sleep. This lasted for one minute, though, and his eyes bolted open when he heard the gravelly voice from his dream again. This time, though, it sounded like it was right next to him. He sat up quickly and looked around. Still nothing, but he wasn't buying it this time. Getting up again, he looked back out to the mountain still towering over the palace. Deciding he was going to give whoever was doing this a piece of his mind, he put on his royal jacket, grabbed a solar lamp that worked almost a quarter of the time, and headed out.

When he reached the bottom of the mountain, it started to rain hard. Ian looked at his wet palm and saw that the rain had blackened. Drawing a deep breath, he began to climb, holding up the flickering lamp. The mountain itself was a crude brown and looked like it was rotting. There was some semblance of a path, though it wasn't an easy trek.

As he climbed higher and higher, the air seemed to thicken, and it was beginning to be more difficult to breathe. He was also having trouble climbing around the weird rock formations that were scattered around the rising ledges.

Things only got stranger the higher he got. He saw a mountain goat a couple of ledges away. After waving to it, however, the goat made a strange noise and then jumped off the ledge and out of sight below. Ian uncomfortably continued on.

He tried going around the two trees locked in a slap-fight and finally managed to get to the top just before daybreak. The mountain had flattened to a large plateau that looked off into the seemingly endless desert.

"Uh, stupid evil mountains," he said, dusting himself off.

"It's quite beautiful, isn't it?" said the low, gravelly voice from his dream, suddenly beside him. Ian looked next to him and jumped back when he saw an old man sitting in a wheelchair. He wore large, thick glasses, sported balding, short gray hair, and had a crooked nose. Dressed in a suit and tie and puffing a cigar, he wasn't looking at Ian but out toward the horizon, where the desert met the edge of the city. The sun was just beginning to peek out.

Ian tried to keep his composure, admittedly hard to do. "Yeah, just breathtaking," he replied carefully.

"Have a lollipop, Ian," the stranger said as he held up a comically large green snack. Ian took it from him.

"Thanks," he said, licking happily.

The stranger smiled greedily. "Isn't this nice, Ian? I give you a lollipop, and you give me your soul."

"Give you my soul?" Ian said between licks.

"Yeah, but who needs those anyway?" the stranger replied. "Here, have a parking permit," he said, handing Ian a torn piece of paper. Ian looked at it.

"This expired thirty years ago," said Ian, looking at it warily.

"Oh, those are only suggestions. And you didn't complain when I gave you that lollipop I dropped in goat manure on the way up here," said the stranger indignantly. Ian threw the lollipop on the ground in disgust and glared at the stranger, who didn't react. "The fact that it was free was enough to keep you happy."

"Who are you?" Ian pressed.

"Who am I? That's the question that drives the lives of everyone," the stranger replied airily.

Ian countered heatedly, "I'm in no mood for riddles right now. It's way past my nap time. Why did you draw me up here?"

"I did no such thing. You wanted to be here, Ian. Why do you think that is?" the stranger said, now grinning again.

"I don't know, I'm stupid?" Ian said, even more annoyed now.

"Because everyone, at the end of the day, picks the easy way out. People will always pick the free option, no matter the cost to others," the stranger answered to himself. He turned to Ian, his wrinkly face more obnoxious now. "I'm here to offer you a deal. A new deal."

"What?" Ian asked, not interested but admittedly slightly intrigued.

"You will have all the free stuff you want. Think about it. Unlimited breadsticks, free toenail surgery, a free pass to see me perform a Helen Keller musical," the stranger said, sounding like a salesman.

"Cool," Ian said, pretending to be impressed.

"Yes, cool," said the stranger, who struggled with this last word. "I will need a little something in return, though."

"So it's not free."

The stranger ignored him. "All you have to do is to give me your soul. Pledge your undying support for the rest of time, no matter how much I take advantage of your loyal support," he declared, grinning.

Ian crossed his arms. "All people like you want is to raise taxes and control everyone's lives," he said, the disgust ringing off his tongue.

"Well, Ian, have you ever thought why we raise taxes and control people's lives?" the stranger asked him.

"Why?"

"Because it's fun," the stranger answered cheerfully. "Now, here, take this," he said, dropping on the ground a giant stack of papers that reached all the way up to Ian's belly button.

"What is this?"

"It's your socialist contract where we will be pulling the strings," the stranger said. "Read it carefully. It likes to jump around a lot, and section 7 may cancel out section 6, but it does the job."

Ian angrily took the giant stack of papers and threw them off the ledge, where he heard the sound of a goat screech. He then turned toward the stranger. "Listen, you old, wrinkly wheelbarrow, I don't know who you think you're talking to, but you are speaking to the son of Backwards Dog," he declared. "And I will not be so easily baited into bad trade deals with pre-set terms."

The stranger shook his head. "You don't want us as your enemies, Ian. I'm warning you," he snarled, his voice carrying a weight of impending danger.

"Who are you?" Ian asked again, this time clenching his teeth.

"Oh, let's just say I'm a friend of your father's."

"Why would Ron send you to harass me?"

The stranger gave an unnerving smile. "Wrong father. You think you and Backwards Dog can change what we have created? No, you will fail, and you will pay the price."

"What you built, huh?" Ian said. "Well, color me not impressed."

"This is bigger than you, and the son of some rebel god will not defeat us," the stranger spat at him.

"Ah, so you're some commie gods that love to revel in the suffering of the many, I get it," Ian said, understanding now.

"It's not your concern. I would watch my back if I were you, boy. It's getting hairier by the day."

"Later, I have some governments to topple," Ian said, having had enough of this conversation, and began to stroll away back down the mountain.

The stranger in the wheelchair started to slowly wheel after him. "Wait, come back here, young man. I'm warning you," he barked behind him. "You get back here, mister." The stranger's wheelchair got caught on a misshapen rock, and he spun off the ledge, crashing into the crevices below. "You'll pay for this, Ian!" the stranger cried before falling out of sight.

Ian dusted his hands and hurried back down the mountain. When he reached the bottom, the sun was fully out, and birds chirped happily around him. Feeling quite pleased with himself, Ian went back inside and returned to bed, sleeping peacefully, which he believed was a gift from Backwards Dog for his unwavering loyalty. However, dark forces do not give up their desire for power so easily, and they were certainly plotting their next move against the holy son. For now, though, Ian slept.

Chapter 15:

The Story of Ian and the Big Dude

I an was now thirteen. He had just begun puberty, but his voice would not quite deepen for another five years. He did, however, develop the ability to conceal body odor, a great skill for a teenager. He was also a growing boy, though he ended up taking his mother's height instead of his father's, much to his disappointment.

Over the past few years, Ian mainly focused on studying political and economic theory with his followers, as he wanted to better know what his goal was. He also encouraged his followers to read texts that opposed what they were aiming for, thinking it was important to understand what your enemy believed. The meetings improved, and Ian was finding his new groove.

Ron continued to implement his radical powers as far as they could be stretched. Ian's research had revealed that it was actually more financially viable not to work than to have a steady job due to the extreme welfare that King Ron's Department of Nannies was handing out. The windmill project Ron had started years ago was finally up and running, though it came with the sacrifice of the rare Rondithmuth Swallow.

One day, when Ian was trying to read an "educational" book about anatomy, Backwards Dog interrupted him. "Ian, my son," he said in his common low rumble of a voice.

"I, eh, it's a homework assignment," Ian said.

"Ian, you know that I'm all-knowing, right? I know what you're doing, and I know you burned down your school."

"Sorry, Dad," Ian apologized, not having any response to this. He had come to realize that you shouldn't argue with the deity who is also your daddy.

"Yeah, yeah, yeah, I'm not here for that, and I have a meeting about pardoning Loki. I need to get to it, so let's get this over with."

"Oh yeah, who was that old man who was trying to tempt me?" Ian asked. "He said he knew you, and it didn't exactly sound friendly."

"Oh, Ian, the complicated weavings of the metaphysical world knows no bounds," Backwards Dog said casually as if he were a lecturer in a philosophy class.

"What?"

"I could not have made that clearer," Backwards Dog replied. "The bottom line is you need to watch your back, as parties don't want you achieving what you do. Now, they can only do so much due to laws and contracts that are in place, but it doesn't mean they can't try to influence things. Just be careful."

"All right," Ian said, just happy the conversation was not about his book.

"Also, I'm glad to see you've gained some followers. Good, now we need to wait and see what happens."

"Just wait and see?" Ian asked in slight annoyance. "How long am I supposed to read 'Human Action' before I lose my mind?"

"Patience, my young prodigy."

"I don't want to be patient. I'm tired of this waiting around," Ian complained. He waited for a comeback but didn't receive one. It appeared Backwards Dog was gone. "How rude."

So, Ian waited and waited and waited. He wanted something to happen, anything. That old man wasn't sounding so bad now. But that old cliché, about being careful what one wishes for, is a cliché for a reason. Ian would learn this lesson the hard way.

On this particular day, about a week later, it was Ian's turn to take the canned coconuts over to his sister's well. He strolled across the town, walking in a cool, jazzed-up way. He passed by, as usual, the many beggars and homeless people looking for food. When he got to the well, he shooed off the little kids who liked to paint the sides and throw large objects down the hole.

Ian called out to them and yelled, "Hey, read the sign. No feeding and no trash down the well." They all scurried away like rats, and Ian went up to the well and opened the can.

"Here you go, Kimmith," Ian said, and he tossed the can down the hole.

"Ow!" Kimmith's voice echoed up after a thud.

"I keep telling you to get in a turtle position when I toss it," Ian yelled down.

"I can't move in here," she called back. Ian really didn't have a good defense against this and decided to leave the conversation. As he walked away, a bird hit one of the windmills and fell down the well. Kimmith screamed, and Ian turned around to see what the commotion was.

After there was silence, though, he turned around again, but when he did, he smacked into a large hunk of person behind him. From the sheer force, Ian flew back into the side of the well, nearly falling in.

"What's going on up there?" Kimmith yelled from the well. "Is there a llama up there or something?"

When Ian shook his head to get rid of the hammers and sickles that were running around him, he stared up at what he had hit, or more accurately, crashed into.

Towering above him was an enormous kid, probably eleven or twelve. He had to have been almost eight feet tall and around four hundred pounds. He had more hair under his armpit than Ian had on his head. If Ian hadn't known any better, he would have thought he was looking at a giant gorilla or something, as his entire body was covered in thick brown hair that was raining with sweat. The giant kid wore nothing but a loincloth around his lower half, probably due to there not being a store that sold clothing in his size. The boy peered down at what had brushed against him. He growled in a low tone that reminded Ian of a tuba.

"What is that thing that is getting in my way?" the boy growled, vibrating the sand below him. Ian, eyes wide like an owl's, couldn't speak clearly.

"Just well, the coconuts throw," he said.

The boy stared at him, perplexed, drool dripping down his open mouth.

"I'm Ian. What do they call you?" he asked in a high-pitched voice.

The boy made a low noise that sounded like a whale burping. "Nobody has ever talked to me. They just see me and say, 'Look out,' then run away," he said in a sad, low growl.

"So, I guess I'll just call you Look Out, then," Ian replied, trying his best to sound friendly.

The boy rumbled and put his enormous hand to his chin. "Look Out is nice name," he said, sporting an unnatural smile. "Now, I must kill the king," and he began to take long strides away. Ian quickly got up and scurried after him.

He called after him. "Wait, what are you doing?" But there was no answer.

Meanwhile, Ron was in his throne room holding court. Gretchen was seated next to him, bored as usual, stomping on the ants that were invading the palace. "I'm sorry, but I fear the song you sang for us was too offensive to at least five marginalized groups. I must sentence you to life in prison," Ron said to a man holding a lute in front of him. Before anything could happen, though, the front doors crashed open and flew to the side, crumbling into the wall. Through the dusty hole where Ron's front door once stood came Look Out, who stormed toward Ron and Gretchen. Shocked, Ron staggered up as his guards rallied around him. Gretchen looked up a few seconds after the chaos and stared at the giant boy curiously.

"What is the meaning of this? How dare you interrupt important kingly matters!" Ron bellowed, though fear was rampant in his eyes.

Look Out picked up a large piece of rubble on the ground and held it up high.

"No more king," he cried out. Ron kneeled down in a panic.

Just then, though, Ian climbed through the hole. "Hold it right there, stinky pants!" he spat at Look Out.

Look Out looked over his shoulder. "You again?" he said.

"Leave them alone," Ian snarled.

Look Out stared at him, seeming to comprehend the words Ian said to him. He then shook his head and raised the piece of rubble again.

"No more king!" Look Out bellowed again.

Ian ran even closer to the giant than he wanted.

"Stop this! I challenge you to a duel, Look Out," Ian yelled at the giant. Look Out slowly turned around and glared at Ian, intrigued. "But you must spare them."

"Nobody who challenge Look Out live to talk about Look Out," Look Out said confidently.

"There's a first time for everything," Ian replied.

"Ian, what are you doing?" Gretchen yelled at him.

"I may disagree with my father on many things, but even he doesn't deserve to be smushed by an overgrown manchild," he said, smirking at Look Out.

Look Out smiled back, showing yellow teeth that were obviously difficult to brush. "Meet me in center of town, near well, in twenty-four sixty minutes. I suggest you make most of them. They be your last," Look Out said, and he strolled out of the palace and back out of the hole he had created, laughing all the way.

After this, Ron sent the court away and ordered a janitor to clean up the mess. He went up to Ian, who was now looking quite pale. "Thank you, Ian, but you don't have to do this."

"No, I do. We can't have a reputation for letting giants kill our leaders," Ian said.

Ron smiled, nodded, and walked away, leaving him with his thoughts.

Ian called an emergency meeting with his followers and told them what was about to happen.

"Why didn't you just let him do it?" Moof asked, confused.

Ian sighed. "As I've said, I'm not going to just kill my stepfather and take over the city, then we're no better than the people currently in charge. We will set an example, not follow one." He turned to John. "John, I need you to get me as many weapons as you can get." John nodded and ran out of the room. Ian turned to Mark. "Mark, I need you to figure out what exactly Look Out is and who sent him."

"Okay, Ian," Mark said, and he ran off after John.

"Moof, you, uh …" Ian said, turning to Moof, who looked at Ian with anticipation. "Go find some snacks. I've got to bulk up."

Ian went home to train for his fight. In his room, he punched bags of sand that he tied to the ceiling, bench-lifted some pipes that he found in the basement, and stacked boxes of Styrofoam one after the other. When he was done, the phone in his room rang, and he picked it up.

"Yello?" answered Ian.

"Hey. Ian, it's Mark. I did some of that research you wanted me to do."

"And?"

"I believe the Coffee Party sent him. They've been quiet the last few years but not entirely gone."

"They must've used the time to find Big Bertha," Ian said, cursing the Coffee Party for always being problem children. He still hadn't really forgiven them for trying to kill him, nor did he really intend to because, well, they had tried to kill him. "Well, thanks, Mark. It's good to know." He hung up. Ian still hadn't seen or heard from John, but he was sure he would find him in the morning before the duel.

The next morning, he got up and dressed in his royal fighting attire, which included a cape. He waited a few minutes before leaving just in case John came by, but after too much time had passed, he had to leave. Walking down the familiar path he had taken just yesterday when he wasn't about to fight a side of beef, he got to the well and saw a crowd anticipating the fight that would finally see the end of the king's weird son. Ian sighed and stood inside the circle of people. After waiting a couple of minutes, the ground began to shake, and many of the onlookers scattered away as Look Out rumbled into view and stood across from Ian.

"David," Look Out said to him.

"It's Ian," Ian said indignantly.

Look Out smiled, not seeming to really care. "Let's get this over with. Look Out has things to do."

"John, where are you?" Ian whispered. As though John was eavesdropping on him, he heard John from across the way.

"I'm here, Ian," John called, and Ian saw him push his way through the crowd.

"Where's my weapon, John?" Ian asked when John got to him.

John hesitated. "Um, uh, here," he said, and he handed Ian a limp stick.

Ian took it and stared at it. "John, this better just be some sick joke."

John, though, shook his head. "I'm sorry Ian, it's almost impossible to find actual weapons in this city. I got stopped on the way over here for having this," he said, pointing to the stick in Ian's hand.

"Well, I guess it'll have to do, then," Ian sighed. John nodded and drifted back to the crowd. Ian looked up at Look Out, who was smearing thick mud on himself. Ian followed suit by diving and rolling in the dirt and sand. He stood up and stared down his opponent.

"Do your worst, little man."

Narrowing his eyes, Ian yelled and held up his stick, throwing it as hard as he could at Look Out. The stick bounced off the giant brute's chest and shattered, shards hitting a bystander nearby. Look Out smiled gleefully.

"Batter up," Look Out said, and he grabbed a hunk of plywood lying on the ground and began to spin around like a hammer thrower at the Olympics. When he had gained enough momentum, he thrust the plywood at Ian, who only had a second to dive to the ground to dodge it. Look Out laughed at Ian, who dusted himself off and stood back up.

"Careful, big boy. You look a little dizzy," Ian said to Look Out, raising his arm toward him. "Maybe you need to sit down." He pushed his arms out, and a force blasted toward Look Out, who was driven back as if he was walking through a hurricane. However, the beef of a boy was able to keep his balance, and he gave a condescending grin to Ian, who realized he might be in trouble.

"Ian, I'll help you," John called from the crowd.

"John, this is a duel, meaning only two," Ian said. "Learn your Japanese."

Unfortunately for Ian, his rant to John took his eyes off Look Out, who had thrown another piece of plywood at him, this time knocking him square in the chest and sending him flying backward. Ian was able to jump before hitting the ground and began to levitate into the air. The crowd gasped, and even Look Out seemed befuddled.

"You could say I'm flying by the seat of my pants," Ian quipped, though the crowd booed his joke. Before Ian could make another bad joke, he was hit in the shoulder by a parade of cabbages that were coming in like missiles from Look Out. Ian spun out and crashed to the ground.

"You're mine now," Look Out said, and he began charging toward Ian like a rhino. The force from his steps knocked Ian to the ground again after he had stood up from his crash. He looked up and saw Look Out barreling toward him. He was stuck and didn't know what to do. He closed his eyes tight, bracing for the impact. After a moment, though, Ian felt nothing but heard a loud whooshing sound and then the gasps and screams around him. He squinted his eyes open. Look Out was nowhere to be seen. He opened his eyes all the way.

"Where did he go? Can he turn invisible now?" Ian panicked.

John went up to him warily. "Uh, Ian, when he got close to you, he suddenly, like, went away," he said ominously.

"Went away?" Ian said, puzzled.

"Like, forever. He shot in the air and out of sight," John said.

Ian pondered this new information. "Are you sure? I've always thought that you needed glasses," he said speculatively.

"Look around you, Ian," John said, and Ian saw many of the citizens looking at him with fear. He left the circle, and the crowd bolted from where he was walking.

John caught up to him. "Are you okay, Ian?"

"What do you think? I think I just killed someone and shot them into space," Ian said.

"Well, I mean, he was trying to kill you."

"Yeah, I guess you're right. It was self-defense," Ian said, smirking a little.

"You should watch yourself, though. I think you're more powerful than you think you are," John said, slightly worried.

"Yeah," Ian agreed, and they parted ways, though he was already in his own world, thinking.

Ron was happy to see Ian alive. That evening, he, Ian, and an uninterested Gretchen celebrated. Ian got to choose the vegetables used for the salad. No beans were seen that night. When he went to bed, he couldn't stop thinking about what he had done to that boy, who, for all he knew, was still flying out in space somewhere. This was a lot of power to have, and that both excited and frightened him.

Chapter 16:

The Story of Ian and John's Double Date

I an was now the age of sixteen. He had learned about the birds and the bees at fifteen after watching two sloths at the zoo one Tuesday afternoon. Ian had come to terms with his powers. This took a couple of years, though, and he had to get used to the stares he got when walking down the road or in a public bathroom.

It was concerning, though, that the brand of Ian's movement had been hurt by the incident with Look Out. People didn't want to associate themselves with someone who, with a single thought, could blast somebody into outer space. Ian wondered if he could do that at will or if Backwards Dog had given him a temporary boost to help him out. Regardless, he had gained no followers outside of his four original members, and honestly, he was comfortable with that.

One day, Ian came down from his room, as many of his other stories begin. He sat down and grabbed some salad. Gretchen was seated across from him while Ron was seated at the end of the table, sipping some blood-red wine and writing a law banning cows from farting. When he was done, he noticed Ian at the table and smiled.

"Oh good, Ian, I'm glad you're here. I have something to tell you," Ron said. Ian stopped eating mid-chew and looked warily at his stepfather.

"What is it?" Ian asked. Gretchen had put down her *Paraformal* fashion magazine—featuring clothes for seers, gypsies, and astrologers—and was now paying attention.

Ron put down his wine glass. "Well, you have just turned sixteen, and when one becomes of age, it is time that he is married off to another family in order to strengthen our political position," he said.

Gretchen looked back and forth from Ron to Ian, who still hadn't chewed.

After no response, Ron continued, "So, within the next month, I will be arranging, with another royal kingdom, a marriage with a suitable daughter."

Ian finally swallowed his food. "Uh, Father, I hate to break it to you, but this is not medieval times, as much as you seem to wish it were," he said, mouth holding back other words wanting to be spoken.

"What is my name?" Ron asked him.

"Ronald," Ian replied.

"King Ron," Ron answered himself. "So, while it may not be medieval times, there are still kings around, and this king says you shall marry whoever I want you to."

"I'm a little too busy to get married," Ian replied.

"Busy with what? Hiding in your room? I know what you're doing in there," Ron said harshly.

Ian thought about the notes on how to overthrow the government he had been writing the previous night.

"You don't know what I'm doing. What am I doing?" Ian snarked back.

"I can't talk about it in front of your mother," Ron stated. Ian sighed in relief. Gretchen snorted, though it backfired, and tea came out of her nose.

"Oh, I see, all right then," Ian said. "But I refuse to be married to some short-haired gender studies major."

"This argument is over now. Have a good day," Ron said, then left for work and went out the door.

"You too," Ian yelled back. He looked at his mother, but Gretchen had hidden behind her magazine.

Ian finished his breakfast and went over to John's place. He told him what had happened.

"Well, Ian, it's true that you don't really get out much outside of political meetings and complaining to me," John said, handing Ian some coffee. He sat down next to him and removed his tea-making apron.

"You know, John, sometimes I do want a yes-man," Ian said.

"Okay, I know you think everything your stepdad says is stupid. And while that's mostly true, he may not be wrong about this," John said, trying to talk him down. Ian glared at him darkly, and John pretended he needed to use the bathroom.

The next day, Ian was in his room playing with his army men, who lacked guns. He was floating them in the air with his mind and smacking them into each other when John walked in. "Oh yeah, guy kneeling in protest, how would you like to face the mighty power of a guy waving at his friend? Hah, hah, hah," he said, and the plastic smacked into each other.

"Ian? Are you busy?" John asked, and the entire army floating in the air fell at once, clattering to the ground.

"What can I do for you, John?" Ian asked irritably.

"Well, remember yesterday when we were talking about you getting out more?"

"No." He knocked over a tower of blocks with his hand and stood over the rubble. "Yes, yes '... hah, hah, hah. Take that, you Marxist totalitarians. Your seizure of private property and single-brand products will never see the light of day."

John tried to continue. "So, I've been seeing someone, and they have a friend who I think you might like."

Ian gave him a condescending look. "Why is everybody suddenly pimping me out?" he asked no one in particular.

At that moment, Ron came into the room. "Ian, I have good news. I've found you a match. You're going to marry the princess of Lesotho," he said.

"What? I don't even know where that is," Ian said.

"It's in Africa—know your geography, Ian," Ron said. "Oh, and get ready to learn some Southern Sotho," he added. And with that, Ron left. John turned back to Ian, who was irate.

"It's not pimping. It's a double date," John tried to explain.

Ian angrily sighed. "Ugh, fine. If I do this, will you help my father get off my case?"

"I will, Ian."

"Fine, when is it?" Ian asked, still a little annoyed.

"Tomorrow night."

"Oh, thanks for the heads-up," Ian said before relenting. "All right, but meet me here."

The next afternoon, Ian changed into his black dress shirt, black dress coat, black dress pants, black socks, black shoes, and black tie. A little before seven in the evening, the Soviet doorbell rang, and Ian answered it. John was on the other side, dressed in a colorful puffy suit coat and tight dress pants.

John looked at Ian's attire. "Ian, you do know the date is supposed to be able to see you, right?" he said sarcastically.

"A plane could see you, John," Ian said back to him.

"Let's just go. We're going to be late. They're meeting us there."

They left for the restaurant they were booked for. On the way there, John lost Ian in the dark a couple of times, but they finally made it only a few minutes late.

"I can't believe we're late," John grumbled.

"Well, it's not my fault your shoes are so tight you're waddling along like a penguin," Ian said.

John pointed to two people sitting in a booth in the corner. "That's them," he said, and they walked over to them. They looked up and smiled at the two of them.

John introduced them and said, "Ian, this is Jordan, my date. And this fine girl here is—"

"Debbie. Debbie Stabmenow," the girl finished, viciously shaking Ian's arm up and down.

"Nice to meet you," Ian replied awkwardly. Ian sat next to Debbie, while John sat next to Jordan. If awkwardness could be described in food, the atmosphere was leek soup.

"What would you guys like to drink?" Jordan asked as a French-looking waiter came up to them. "I'll have a mojito," she said to the waiter.

"And I'll have a Long Island Iced Tea minus the tea," Debbie said happily.

After John had ordered what Jordan was having and Ian accidentally ordered a Cement Mixer, they started talking. More accurately, though, John was talking with everyone else listening. He was just getting done telling a long-winded story.

"And so then I found out, I didn't have any ice," John said, smiling. Jordan chuckled. Ian rolled his eyes, but Debbie started laughing hysterically. In her excitement, she grabbed a fork from off the table and stabbed Ian right in the wrist. She continued to belly laugh while Ian yelled out in pain, grabbed the end of the fork, and tugged repeatedly, to no avail.

Just then, the waiter came back. "Are we ready to order?" he asked.

Debbie raised her hand, still trying to contain her laughter. "I'll have a leg of lamb, rare," she said.

"Madam, are you sure? I strongly advise you not to," the waiter tried to plead with her.

She frowned and angrily ripped the fork out of Ian's wrist and pointed it at the waiter. "Now you listen to me, you glorified plate jockey. I'm having rare leg of lamb, and my honey buns over here will have some rare veal," she spat.

The waiter looked at Ian in disgust. "You sicken me, sir," the waiter said to him, then walked off.

"Hey, I didn't get to order," John complained. Ian put his head on the table, and Debbie started scratching him behind his ear.

At this point, he stood up and said, "Come on, John, let's go to the little boys' room."

John looked up at Ian, attempting to protest, but eventually stood up and followed him. "But I'm hungry, Ian," he pleaded.

"Just get in there," Ian said, and they went into the bathroom. He entered one of the stalls while John chose the one next to him.

"Ian, why are we hiding in the bathroom?" John asked through the stall.

"Look, John, I agreed to this night under the assumption that your date's friend wasn't a psychopath."

"What, Ian? You had lamb last night, and the city uses them for sacrifices all the time. They say that sacrificing a lamb a day keeps fiscal responsibility away."

"You're not making your case, John," Ian replied. He flushed and left the stall, with John following suit. They started washing their hands.

"Oh, she's just a little quirky. She's not that bad," John replied.

Just then, Debbie burst through the door, went up to Ian, and yanked a strand of hair out of his head. "Yes. That's just enough," she said, looking at it gleefully. And with no other words, she left the bathroom and the door shut.

Ian gave John a sarcastic look that seemed to burn into his forehead.

"Okay, fine, she's weird, but we can't just ditch them. I like Jordan," John said.

"Sometimes, John, sacrifices have to be made."

"What are you sacrificing?"

"My sanity," Ian replied bluntly.

"Okay, but what are we going to do?"

"Just follow my lead," Ian said, and went out the door. John followed behind, a worried look on his face. They went back to their table. Ian's food was ready on the table, bleeding. Debbie looked up at him and smiled, blood dripping down her lips. Jordan just sat at the table uncomfortably.

"Dinner's ready, Ian," Debbie said happily.

"Oh, I'm not really hungry, and it's such a beautiful night. I thought we'd all go somewhere special," Ian said.

"Where are we going?" Jordan asked, uneasy.

"It's a surprise," Ian replied.

"Oh boy, a surprise," said John excitedly.

Ian kicked John's foot. "Will you shut up?" he whispered, and John slunk behind him.

Debbie jumped up. "Oh, I love surprises," she said excitedly.

"Good, well, go grab your things and get ready," Ian exclaimed. "We'll be waiting outside."

"Okay," Debbie said. Ian and John headed out of the restaurant. The night was now a little chillier than earlier, and the fluorescent lamps flickered erratically.

"What now, Ian?" John asked him.

"We're going to fake our deaths."

John looked at him like he must have misheard him. "Fake our deaths? Ian, that's insane," he cried.

"Well, first, we're taking our dates for a romantic sand ride," Ian continued.

"With what wagon?" John asked.

"This one," Ian said, smiling, and with a whip of his hand, a fairly large red wagon appeared before them.

"How's it supposed to move?" John asked.

Ian's smile faded. He may have forgotten about that part. He looked at John carefully, went to the handle on the wagon, and then back to John, and smirked. John saw this.

"No, no, no, Ian. Come on," John pleaded. Just then, though, Jordan and Debbie came out of the restaurant, and it was too late.

"Wow," said Debbie in amazement, and she jumped into the wagon. Jordan followed suit. Ian looked to John.

"Followers gotta follow." He hopped in, and John slowly went to the front of the wagon, lifted the handle with all his might, and began to drag them away from the restaurant. Debbie clapped happily as John made grunting noises, and Ian had a pleased look on his face.

"Where am I going, Ian?" John asked, not hiding his contempt.

"To the top of that mountain, John," Ian replied and pointed to the mountain that he had walked up years ago. It looked about as rotten as ever, and no one seemed to notice or care that a mountain had just appeared out of nowhere, but Ian had come to just accept the stupidity of the city he lived in and move on. John looked back and gave Ian a death stare but then dragged them on. After a long pull, he finally managed to drag them to the top. The ride had been rough, especially since the mountain was still cursed and evil, with them having to dodge a deranged beaver battling a giant aardvark. When they reached the flat of the mountain, John collapsed and fell to the ground in a heap.

"So dramatic," Ian said, shaking his head.

"Oh my, this is magnificent," Debbie cried.

"Look at this, guys." Ian pointed to some dirt on the ground. "There once was a crazy guy in a wheelchair who stood on this very dirt."

Jordan and Debbie got out of the wagon for a closer look. Well, more accurately, Debbie ran over while Jordan reluctantly followed. Ian then heard Ron's voice from the bottom of the mountain, and suddenly, he had a headache.

"Ian? Is that you?" Ron inquired.

"Yes," Ian replied sharply.

"Is that company I see?" Ron asked, and Ian noticed that he was looking through binoculars. He could also make out Gretchen yelling at one of the servants behind him.

"Yes," Ian answered again.

"Would they like some salad?"

"I doubt it."

"Okay, have fun," Ron said, and he went back into the palace.

Ian picked up John from the ground and threw him into the wagon before following him in. Ian then heard Ron's voice again.

"What are you guys doing?" Ron asked from outside again.

"Just faking our deaths," John yelled down, and Ian's headache suddenly got worse.

"What?" cried Jordan, and she and Debbie spun around.

"Quick, Ian, they're on to us," John shouted to him.

Ian panicked, lifted the wagon's handle, and began to jerk forward to move it closer to the edge of the cliff. However, each time he jerked, he only managed to move a few inches.

"Faster, John," Ian shouted to him, and they jerked harder and faster without much more success.

"That's enough!" Debbie yelled, and they all looked over to her. Debbie plunked down on the ground. "I don't need you to fake your deaths to make your point about how you feel about me. I just wish people would be honest with me first before running away. You don't know what that's like," she sobbed.

Ian thought back to the dinner party when he was three, the battle with Look Out a few years ago, and how the people around him reacted to him when he did something they thought was strange. There was an odd feeling in his chest, and his brain was acting kind of funny. At first, he thought he might be having a heart attack, but then he realized this must be what empathy felt like. It was weird and he didn't care for it.

Ian sighed and sat up in the wagon. "Debbie, we're sorry. We never meant to hurt you. We were just more scared of you than anything. We should've just said that, though, instead of running away," he said, and John nodded.

"Thank you," Debbie said, wiping her eyes.

"All right, John, I hope you learned a valuable lesson today," Ian said and began to climb out of the wagon.

However, before Ian could step down, John noticed the wagon was beginning to slide backward toward the cliff's edge.

"Uh, Ian," John said.

"What?" Ian asked, done with everything at this point. The wagon fell off the ledge and began flying down the mountain.

John covered his eyes. "Ian, do something!"

"Uh, uh, hold on," Ian desperately tried to steer the handle, but to no avail.

"Use your powers," John pleaded. Ian tried, but nothing happened.

"Stupid evil mountain," he yelled. They held on tightly before slipping off the bottom of the mountain and soaring into the air, rushing toward the palace. They screamed together as they crashed into Ian's room. They landed on the bed, which now looked as if someone had taken a wrecking ball to it. They climbed out of the wagon and collapsed on Ian's destroyed bed.

Ian turned to John. "John, no more double dates," he said. John silently nodded.

Just then, Ron came into the room to see what the commotion was. "Ian, what the voter ID have you done? You're lucky that, per the broken window theory, your little accident will create jobs," Ron said sternly. He went to leave and then turned around. "Oh, by the way, I've called off that marriage with the Lesotho kingdom. I've discovered that their primary export is textiles, which are environmentally unfriendly, so that's not going to happen."

"Okay," Ian managed to say, not exactly caring at this point. It turned out that crashing into walls was pretty bad for headaches. Ron left, leaving Ian and John exhausted from their long night. They never heard from Jordan or Debbie again because they thought Ian and John were too weird for their tastes. After the disastrous date, Ian swore off women altogether, though that only lasted two years.

Chapter 17:

The Story of Ian's Second Temptation

Two years later, Ian was eighteen years old and had just been accepted to Rondithmuth University for the next fall. The university initially didn't want Ian due to his certain beliefs and rumors that he may be a witch doctor. But after Ron made a strongly worded threat to the university—he said he "would rather be seen dead than see one of my descendants not go into higher education"—Ian was let in, though he was put on academic probation to begin his college career.

With the fall term coming, Ian decided that he was going to take a break from rebelling for the summer. The rest of his followers made it into the university as well, so there would be plenty of time to plan revolutions later. However, this particular summer week happened to be tax week in Rondithmuth, Ron's favorite week of the year. With Ian turning eighteen, he needed to fill out his taxes.

The tax parade was going on downtown, featuring music, marching revenue agents, and a mascot, Audity the Happy Tax Audit, who went around asking children if their parents had paid their taxes yet. At the end of the parade, on a majestic coach that was drawn by donkeys, sat King Ron and Queen Gretchen. Ron waved to the crowd and made the money sign with his hand while Gretchen slunk in her seat, trying to avoid the fruit being thrown at them. Ian took this day to hide in his room and get to work.

He was at his desk, with an enormous tax code sitting in one corner, along with a thick packet for him to file. Ian was scribbling numbers and looking through the pages of the code in deep concentration.

"Let's see here. Take your gross income from two years ago and divide it by the age of your mother-in-law from twenty years ago. If no mother-in-law exists, skip this section," Ian said out loud to himself.

He flipped to the next page. "Unless your own father has bought a rake in the past 2 to 7 years, then subtract the price of that value of the purchase from the amount of income you think you'll receive 60 years from now, 5 years ago." Continuing, he scribbled some more. "Got it," he exclaimed. Just then, John came into the room.

"Next, if you've stolen money from any entity, please write down that number here and multiply it by the number of days last year that you went to the bathroom more than four times. If you donated funds to King Ron, neglect this page entirely," Ian read and scribbled again, then turned the page. "And now, for final payment, calculate your gross income and multiply that by the number we're thinking between 1 and 1,000. See Form 108YME for reference."

"Hey, Ian," John said.

Ian looked up in acknowledgment and then back down at his sheet, realizing that he had completely lost track of where he was. After a moment where he swore he had died from a broken heart, he angrily threw the entire unstapled tax code in the air, sending pages flying everywhere around the room. He glowered at John, who uncomfortably grabbed his own butt.

"What's so important, John, that you've now wasted ten hours of my day?" Ian snarled.

"Oh, I, uh. Oh, I forgot."

Ian's eyes flickered, and he stood up. "That's great, John. Just great. Stupid social engineering piece of junk." He kicked the pages that were lying on the ground, crushing them.

"Calm down, Ian."

Ian whipped around to John. "No, I will not calm down, Johnnn!" he shouted. "I hate being an adult. This must be why suicide rates in this city skyrocket during tax season." He walked toward the door.

"Ian, where are you going?"

"Out, and I won't be back for a long time," Ian said, leaving the room. A minute later, he came back and grabbed his coat. "It's chilly," he explained, and stormed back out, leaving John behind.

Outside the mansion, Ian began marching down the street, where the parade was still going on. Audity, the tax mascot, bounced up to him.

"Hi there, friend. Are any of your parents a tax cheat?" it asked, and Ian promptly lifted his hand and blasted the mascot back into the crowd. The crowd around him cheered and began throwing their fruit at Audity, who was rolling around in a heap on the ground.

It was around eight in the evening, and the sun was going down, causing a sharp breeze to pierce the air. Ian continued on his way, angrily cursing taxes. He cut across town and ended up on the side where Ron had forgotten to install streetlamps. Ian walked in the darkness until he saw a building lit up among the dark structures around it. He figured that it was a pub of some sort, as he knew people felt a need to drink a lot in this city. He waltzed in, ignoring a sign above the door reading, "*You Walked in Here Because You Didn't Read the Sign.*"

When he entered, the room was dimly lit and reeked of dirt and cigars. The bar near the center of the place was dusty and filled with even dustier customers. Ian slouched deep into a cushioned chair off in the corner. As he observed his surroundings, he noticed a young woman across the way, watching him intensely. Ian stared back for a moment but recoiled after he started feeling uncomfortable. She had glanced away but, out of the corner of his eye, he thought he could still see her observing him.

Ian didn't order a drink, didn't watch whatever sporting event was on the fuzzy television, and didn't pay any more attention to the woman.

He just wanted to sit and stew in his anger at what life was handing him. A life of high—literally godly—expectations.

Concentrating so much on his anger, he failed to notice in time when a large man sat down on top of him. Feeling the pressure, he looked up at what little he could see of the man on top of him and poked him in the side to get his attention. "Excuse me, I'm sorry to bother you, but you're currently crushing me," he said, trying to keep his cool.

The man, who looked like he had obviously had too many drinks that night, looked down at himself. "What the? Oh, my Backwards Dog. The chair is talking to me!"

The drunk stood up, drink in hand, wagged his finger at Ian, and said, "I thought I told you chairs to stop bothering me."

Ian tried to sit up but couldn't. "Listen, you redneck nincompoop," he said. "I've had a long day, and I'm warning you now, I'm not in the mood for your stupidity."

The man did a shot and slammed his glass on the floor, causing the people surrounding them to jump and see what was going on. "You don't scare me, you stupid chair," he said and began to approach him.

Ian narrowed his eyes, remembering the approach Look Out had taken two years earlier toward him, although this one was a little more wobbly. At once, the man suddenly began to get bigger and bigger, and—like a balloon—he was inflating. Ian sprang up. The woman across the room sat up and was watching him again.

"Whoa, whoa, whoa. I'm sorry, Mr. Chair, I won't bother you again," the man pleaded. Ian smacked the man's belly and the drunk began to roll across the room. He continued to bowl his way around, and then squeezed out the door and out of sight.

Ian plunked back down and looked up at the ceiling, cursing the tiles for not being two-sided shapes. When he looked down from it, though, he saw the woman from across the room standing in front of him.

She had brown skin and dark, flowing hair. Her large, brown eyes worked well with her over-glossed red lips. She was shapely, with wide hips but a fit figure. The woman beamed down at him. Ian immediately sat up in the chair he had been slouching in and dusted off the crumbs from the Parmesan cheese tower he had made next to his salad that morning.

"Wow, that was quite an impressive scene there. I like a man who takes charge," she said. She sat on the arm of his chair, put her arms around him, and whispered into his ear. "So, what's a nice young man like yourself doing in a place like this?" she asked, her nasal voice cutting through Ian's ear.

He smirked and deepened his voice. "Oh, just sitting around counting the ceiling tiles."

She grinned, bobbed her head to the side, and said, "Mmm, I like a man who counts ceiling tiles."

"You have good taste," Ian replied, and he slicked his hair back coolly, though it whipped back in its messy place. While having lush hair since birth had its benefits, it had refused to work with him as he had gotten older—now he typically looked like he had rolled out of bed and gotten his head stuck on a carpet.

"So, what do they call you?" she asked, batting her doe eyes at him.

"I'm Ian, son of the king," Ian bragged.

She smiled at this and placed her hand on her cheek. "I'm Aoc," she said slowly.

"Aoc, huh. What a pretty name," Ian said dreamily.

"I know," she replied.

"Some people might think it sounds like something you're hacking up, but not me," he stated. "Or a crappy acronym."

She again gave him a seductive smile. She stroked her hair behind her head and leaned forward.

"So, Ian, what do you like to do for fun when you're, what's the word? Alone?" she whispered.

"I play with my blocks and plot to topple totalitarian regimes." Ian had just realized that the room seemed to have gotten smaller, like it was now just a small box with just the two of them.

"Ooh, what else do you do?"

"I'm the head of a secret group that fights for conservative principles," he spilled out.

"Oh, you must be that Holy Ian they have been talking about."

Ian wasn't sure how she knew about that. As far as he was aware, only his group called him the Holy Ian. It happened after a long night of partying, and Moof started to chant it when Ian was playing "Ants in the Pants." It was probably John who blabbed.

"Yeah, that's me," he finally said.

"Wow, you're bigger and sweatier than I expected," she said, smiling. She put her finger in her mouth and rubbed his hipbone.

"So, Holy Ian, what can you do with your, what's the word? Powers?" she asked seductively, her words wrapping around him like a wet, warm blanket.

Ian grinned from ear to ear like an idiot. "I can show you."

"Mmm, show me," she begged.

Ian conjured a crinkled-up ball of paper in his hand and held it up to her so it glistened in the damp light.

Aoc smiled and put her hand on the paper. "Ooh, that's impressive," she said in a whisper. "But could you show me something more, big?"

Ian conjured a bigger crinkled-up ball of paper in his hand. Aoc smirked, stuck her finger slowly in her ear, and turned it back and forth. She then toyed with Ian's earlobe.

They talked for about an hour. Well, mainly Ian talked, with Aoc hanging onto every word. "Mmm, tell me more about flexible spending and game theory," she begged Ian, who obliged.

After Ian was done ranting about the prisoner's dilemma, Aoc pursed her lips at him and got closer.

"So, Ian, tell me … What. Makes. You. Tick?" she asked, gently poking his knee at every word.

Ian, confused, said, "I'm sorry?"

For the first time, Aoc's smile faded for just an instant before returning in full. "I mean, what makes Ian so special?" she asked.

Ian didn't respond, and she sighed and then went right back to smiling.

"What I mean to ask is, what would have to happen for Ian to lose his powers?"

"Hmm, I guess I never thought about it," Ian replied, hand to his chin.

Aoc scowled. "Well, try!" she shouted viciously, her voice oddly lower. After this, though, she gave a wide grin and put her hand across her cheek.

Ian had jumped at Aoc's outburst but tried to think quickly for an answer. "Well, I guess if one wanted me not to be able to use my powers, they would probably have to kill me," he said rather uncomfortably.

"Mmm, sounds dangerous," she replied, seemingly satisfied now.

"Yes, that is true. You're so smart and funny and wise, Aoc," Ian said dreamily.

"Who, me? I'm just a silly bartender," she giggled. Suddenly, she grabbed Ian's elbow tightly. "How about you and me get out of here? We can go somewhere where no one can see what I, I mean, we are doing."

Ian swallowed something in his throat that didn't feel right. "Um, sure, we can go to my place," he suggested.

She licked her lips, smearing her lipstick. "Sounds perfect." She pulled him up from the chair with surprising strength and led him out of the pub. They walked down the dim street that was even more deserted than earlier. Aoc said nothing as she led him along. Ian turned around and noticed he couldn't see the pub anymore, even though they had just left.

"Um, where did the pub go?" he asked her.

"Some things only appear when needed, Holy Ian."

Ian didn't know what exactly this meant, but when Aoc squeezed his arm tightly, he forgot what he was thinking about.

"Have you ever heard of a succubus?" Aoc asked him after a long silence.

"Um, are they those weird soft things that hang on the faucet of the shower?" he asked.

Aoc rolled her shoulders in a way Ian thought was a little too flexible, as her neck went almost ninety degrees to the side. "No, they are demons that take the shape of beautiful women to trick men into their doom."

"Oh. Why do you ask? They don't actually exist, right?" Ian asked, more to himself than her.

She didn't answer him, and they continued on their way. They finally made it back to the palace and went in. It was around midnight. Ron was snoring in his room while Gretchen was sitting on the couch in the living room watching *Mythical Captors*.

"We're here in the Scottish Highlands looking for the notorious beast of the bean nighe. We're going to find it, capture it, then sell it on the black market," the man on the TV said.

"Ugh, I hate beans," Ian said in disgust.

"Come, Ian, no time for silly tales," Aoc said, and she led him up to his room. She then looked at him. "I'm going to get ready in the place where people defecate. Wait in your room on your bed," she said.

"Okay," Ian said in a cracked voice. She turned, and he saw from the side what he swore was the face of an old, wrinkly man, or woman. It was hard to tell in that flash of an instant. Jumping back, he yelled.

Aoc turned around and beamed at him, her face as pretty and not old as ever. "Something wrong, my Holy Ian?" she asked.

"No, nothing," Ian said. He listened closely for his mother coming, but he only heard the television.

"Careful, the Bean Nighe is a disgusting old hag who will curse you with misfortune if you have direct contact with it. Kind of like your mother, Bill," the TV man said.

He went into his room and saw the mess he had left earlier. Tax papers were scattered everywhere. Ian quickly tried to scoop everything up and shoved it into his closet.

He looked at his bedsheets, which had a large picture of Calvin Coolidge on them. Raising his hand in the air, the sheets immediately turned into motorcycle sheets. He ran to change the Ronald Reagan poster plastered above his bed, but tripped on some blocks and fell onto the mattress.

At that moment, Aoc entered the room. Ian quickly went for a pose, but ended up just arching his back like he was trying to do a handstand.

Aoc was dressed in a sweater and snow pants. "What do you think?" she asked slowly and softly.

"Wow," Ian replied, then fell over from his pose.

She smiled and pursed her still ruby-red lips. "Let's get started. Go to the back of the bed," she said.

Ian went backward so fast he slammed into the headboard. "Okay," he said, smirking.

Aoc then pulled out some rope and lighter fluid.

"Oh, you're that type of girl," Ian said, eyebrows raised.

"Let's get you all tied up so you can't move," she said almost inaudibly.

"Okay," said Ian, smirking again, though this time more uncomfortably.

She went up and tied his arms and legs down to the bed.

"Wow, these are pretty tight."

"That's the idea."

"Okay," Ian said, though he wasn't exactly sure why he did. His mouth was kind of just saying things now.

Aoc then started pouring the lighter fluid all over him.

Ian raised his hand. "Uh, not to kink-shame or anything, but this seems kind of dangerous," he said.

"Well, how else am I going to set you on fire?" she stated simply.

Ian nodded his head. "That makes more sense, then, because— wait, what?" he said, finally catching on that things may not be what they seemed.

Aoc let out a vicious laugh. "Oh, Holy Ian, thank you for making this so easy. Is this really the best Backwards Dog can do?"

Her face then morphed into an old woman's. Her once smooth visage was now wrinkly and withered. She wore a crooked nose and narrow red eyes.

"Who are you?" he cried.

She raised her crusty eyebrows. "That, my frisky holy friend, is none of your concern. The important thing is"—she lit a match and held it up—"you won't be around to tell this story."

She began to move the match slowly toward Ian. He wiggled and tried everything he could to break free, but his powers weren't working. Something was stopping them.

At that moment, John came into his room. "Ian, I made a cream pie for you, to make up for earlier." He took in the scene and gasped. "Oh, I'm sorry, Ian, I didn't know you had company."

Ian tried to lift his head up. "John, some woman or thing, I'm not really sure, tied me up and is going to set me on fire," he yelled.

John looked at Aoc, who was just about to drag the match across his wet skin. Then he ran toward her. "You leave my Ian alone," he shouted and smacked the pie into her face. She screamed, backing up, hand over her face as she tried to wipe the pie off her. In the process, she backed into Ian's closet, and the tax pages he had stuffed into it earlier flew out and knocked her over.

"Nice one, John," Ian cheered from his bed, but Aoc, like a whale breaching, came out from under the tax pages, angrily glaring at the simpleton that had foiled her plan. She let out a blood-curdling screech and charged at John, who had now, for the second time that day, grabbed his butt in discomfort.

"Quick, John, the lighter fluid," Ian shouted.

John grabbed the can quickly and threw it at Aoc. The can ignited, and with the match still in her hand, she burst into flames.

She shrieked, "You'll pay for this, Holy Ian, eventually."

"Who do you work for?" Ian demanded.

"The ones who wait, the ones who wait," she was only able to scream, still burning in flames. She then disappeared into a column of black, fiery smoke, leaving only a black stain on the floor where she had burned.

Both Ian and John took a deep breath. "How did you get here?" Ian asked.

"Moof saw you walking in a daze with some strange woman. He was worried you were in some sort of trouble, so he called me because I was closer to your house. So here I am," John answered, holding his hands up like he had just won a prize on a game show.

"Ah," Ian said, embarrassed. "Untie me, please."

John loosened the rope and freed him. When Ian stood up, though, his legs were completely asleep, so he fell over onto the floor. John looked down at him. "Ian, do you want help up?" John asked.

Ian shook his head. "No, I think I'm just going to lie here the rest of the night," he said in a muted voice through the floor.

"Okay, good night, Ian," John said, and he went to the door.

"Good night, John," Ian said, muffled by the floor.

After John left, Ian lay there for a little while, thinking about his life choices. "The ones who wait" kept going through his mind. He would need to ask his dad about that at the next random encounter. It certainly didn't sound good. As he thought more, though, he fell asleep, dreaming incredibly weird dreams that he didn't want to discuss.

Chapter 18:

The Story of Ian
in the Goose's Den

Ian's close call with being burned alive by a crazy demon woman was kept mostly under wraps, especially from the king, who did ask at breakfast the next morning what those sounds were in Ian's room.

"I woke up to some yelling and weird sounds last night, Ian. Care to elaborate?" Ron said after shoving a plum into his mouth.

"Oh, I think you were just hearing noises from Mother's program. She was playing it pretty loud," Ian said, promptly chewing on some lettuce.

Gretchen glared at him from the opposite side of the table. He was used to this, though, and had learned to just look away and ignore her.

Ian also persuaded both John and Moof to keep silent on the matter, as it was not a good look for a holy savior to be bamboozled by a succubus.

"It went downhill for Odysseus ever since he got tricked by those sirens," he told them in confidence.

Ian himself was shaken by his encounter and didn't fully recover for some time. Every time a woman passed by him in the street, he would either walk to the other side of the road or start babbling about Nozick's entitlement theory, which no one seemed to understand or see the connection, *for there was none.*

Backwards Dog visited him the night after his close shave with death, interrupting him as he ripped up every book page that had a picture of a woman. "Ian, my son," the voice of his father droned around his room.

Ian had still not exactly gotten used to this and jumped, ripping the book in his hand in half. "What?" Ian asked. "Can't you give a signal to let me know you're coming?"

"I did. You obviously didn't hear the owl outside the window."

"How was I supposed to possibly put two and two together?"

"You shouldn't be the one demanding answers. Mr. Almost Gets Set on Fire by a Succubus," Backwards Dog said judgmentally.

"You could have intervened."

"When you get a date with Persephone, you don't blow it. She never comes out for anybody," Backwards Dog defended. "And regardless, you're supposed to not be tempted. Eyes on the ball, son."

He lowered his head. "Sorry. She spoke about the ones who wait. What was she talking about?"

Backwards Dog hesitated for a moment before answering. "They are the progressive gods who have been slowly and patiently turning the world into the dystopia you see today. It took them centuries to achieve their goal, and they aren't exactly keen on losing so many years of progress."

"So they're still after me?"

"I have been able to hold them off with some sanctions," Backwards Dog said. "So, for now, they shouldn't bother you, and you can continue on your mission. But I would still be careful."

"Ah, sorry about getting almost killed by a demon woman."

"Temptation from supernatural beings can be tricky. You are not the first, and you won't be the last to fall for their tricks," Backwards Dog said almost warmly. "Just be more careful in the future."

"All right, thanks." He waited, but as per usual, there was abruptly no response, and he went back to his pictures in his books, happy that he could maybe have some peace for a little while.

Two months later, though, Ian was officially off to college. He arranged to stay in an apartment near the college with Moof as his roommate. John wanted to be roommates with him, but Nancy had insisted that he stay home to preserve her youth. It would be nice to get away from Ron and his mother for a little while.

Ian decided that he needed to understand his enemy's way of thinking in order to defeat it, so he declared a major in Rondithmuth Is Great Politics with a minor in Indoctrination Studies. He also got a warm and fuzzy sensation when he thought about making gender studies majors cry.

On the first day of classes, Ian set out from the apartment and went down to the Rondithmuth University campus. He passed by the large glass bubbles around the edge of the sidewalks that were deemed to be "Emotional Recalibration Chambers."

He went into Kant Hall, where he would be taking his first college class, "The Evils of Conservatives 101."

He arrived at his classroom, which smelled oddly of soy candles and something Ian swore he had smelled in Ron's wine cellar. It smelled more like burnt oregano than grapes and cranberries, though. He took his seat, leaving a two-seat buffer between himself and any girl, and got out his textbook, *Progressive Perspectives: An Unbiased Analysis of Traditional Ideologies.*

The professor was a young man wearing a blue flowery shirt, blue bell-bottoms, and no shoes. He wore his long black hair in a braid that went down his back. After putting his backpack behind his desk, he took out a piece of paper, cleared his throat, and addressed the class of around twenty.

"Good morning, and welcome to your first class, where we will open your mind so you have an intellectual awakening, allowing you to explore the one true path for societal harmony. I will be your guide, Professor Running Bear O'Sullivan," he said in an airy voice. He looked at his sheet. "Now, I will need to read the names, and you will tell me if you are present. Do I have a Prince Ian?"

Ian raised his hand. The professor narrowed his eyes, looked at the sheet again, and smirked maliciously. "Ah, Mr. Prince Ian himself.

I'm a big fan of your father's. I've given funds to him and have gone to many parties that he's thrown," he said.

"Yeah, you look and smell like the type who would," Ian replied, eyes fixed on the professor. The grin faded, then reappeared on the professor's face.

"Yes, well, it's a pleasure to have the son of a great leader in our midst," he said graciously and clapped continuously, which the rest of the class mimicked.

He then went through the rest of the attendance, took out the expensive textbook he'd written and made everyone buy copies of, and began flipping the pages.

"Chapter One will start with defining what a conservative is, and why they are so dangerous. In order to find one and hold them accountable, you must be able to identify one," the professor said, his voice trailing off near the end. "Can anybody tell me how you can tell someone is a conservative?"

A girl answered from behind Ian, causing him to jump. "I heard they use outdated technology like landlines?" she asked.

"Good job. Conservatives are well known to never be progressive enough, and this includes technology," the professor replied. "Anything else?"

A boy a few seats over from Ian answered. "I heard they are all afflicted with some form of anatomical abnormality," he said.

The professor nodded. "That's a good guess. Though not entirely proven yet, there is strong evidence, uncovered by us intellectuals, that conservatives are more likely to have unorthodox features that will be explored in chapter three of our lessons," the professor said.

"I have one," Ian said loudly.

The professor stopped, looked at Ian suspiciously, and then smiled. "Go on, Prince Ian," he said.

"Aren't conservatives supposed to be able to process the consequences of actions instead of acting on emotional impulses?" Ian snarked.

The professor's eyebrows lowered, and he bit his bottom lip. "Actually, according to my research, which was verified by friends in my circle, conservatives all have brain function indicating that they were dropped on the head when they were young," he sniped back.

"I don't think I really want to hear what people from your circle—" Ian started before being interrupted by the sound of fighting outside. Everyone got out of their seats and left the room.

When Ian squeezed through the crowd, he saw three young men beating up another young man in the middle of the hallway.

"So, you think you can offer us a policy that gives us more freedom of economic choice and get away with it?" a skinny Hispanic man yelled at the poor man.

"More individual freedom," the young man tried to say through the punches, sounding like a bad radio signal. Ian then recognized that the man being beaten up was Moof.

The professor from Ian's class ran up and separated the men from their target. "What the Thatcher is going on here?" he exclaimed.

One of the men, who had combed-over black hair, a square head, a polo, and cargo shorts, spoke up. "He told us that we should be accepting of all dangerous political ideologies," he complained. The professor glared at Moof and smiled.

"Ah, I see. Well, carry on then," he said, and he went back into his classroom.

Ian approached the men and smiled at them. "Good morning, gentlemen. Lovely day to be mindless drones, is it not?"

A tall, skinny man with parted brown hair and a white button-down shirt turned around and looked down at Ian. "You stay out of this, Prince Weirdo," he sneered.

"You know, I don't think I've ever met a group of more pathetic-looking goons than you three clowns without the cool shoes," Ian quipped.

The Hispanic one, who had short black hair, bushy eyebrows, and a large forehead, stepped toward Ian, offering a better look at the expensive-looking suit laced tightly around him. "Do you know who we are? We are the sons of the most dominant oligarchs in this city. I am Julian." He pointed to the short man and said, "This is Pete," then pointed to the tall man and said, "And this is Rob."

The tall man frowned. "I told you my name is Beto. I'm getting in touch with my Hispanic roots."

"Your family's from Dublin, Rob," Pete pointed out.

"So, you're denying my identity, are you?" Rob said, crossing his arms.

"Fine, sorry, Beto," Julian sighed.

Ian laughed and got the men's attention again. "As cute as your bickering is, I believe we still have the matter of what you're doing to my friend here," he said.

They grinned like they'd all taken a laxative by mistake.

"We are a zero-tolerance campus for ideologies that spread hate. That's why we work to suppress them and belittle them as much as possible," Rob said, chuckling.

"Oh, big men, right? Picking on the minority who just happens not to fit into your insane little square," Ian said.

"And what exactly are you going to do about it?" Julian mocked.

Ian's eyes narrowed. "This," he said, and he threw his arms up. Immediately, the three goons rose into the air and were hung from the ceiling fan above them. They began to spin around and around until they flew off and crashed into the recycling can across the hallway.

Immediately after this, though, a loudspeaker erupted above him. "Would the Prince Ian please report to the Dean of Intolerance's office immediately," it said.

Ian sighed and went on his way.

When he got to the office, a large man with thick, round glasses sat at the desk. Pictures of him sitting in lawn chairs during protests and rallies dotted the desk and walls. He glanced up at Ian and glared at him. "Mr. Ian, I'm Terry Maddler. Please sit," he said in a whiny voice.

Ian sat on the floor as the dean was using both chairs to sit in.

"Now, Ian, we here at the university were reluctant to have you, due to your, let's just say, evil ways of thinking," he said.

Ian nodded mockingly.

"But King Ron was quite aggressive in ensuring that you were accepted and let in. And in a show of good faith toward the King, we did. However, we accepted you under the condition that you'd keep your dangerous views to yourself. Do I make myself clear?"

"Oh, I don't think you could be clearer," Ian responded dryly.

"So, I'll overlook this incident this time for your father's sake. But I will be watching you closely, so you better not screw up," Maddler said, out of breath from talking for so long.

"I understand completely," Ian said, standing up and leaving. Lost in thought, he didn't notice that he was about to smack into people. When he collided, Julian, Pete, and Rob whipped around and beamed mischievously.

Ian beamed back in kind. "Gentlemen, how have you been? Last time I saw you guys, you were flying like the vultures you are."

Julian frowned. "We don't like being thrown in the air and put on fans, Ian," he said.

"I would think not, but I'm not one to judge out loud," Ian responded.

"You'd better watch yourself, Ian. Nobody who messes with us does it again," Rob warned.

Ian wasn't intimidated, though. "Listen, Bobby ..."

"It's Beto," Rob snarled.

"Listen, Bobby, if I were afraid of a vindictive dunderhead like you, I wouldn't be able to live at my own palace," Ian said.

"Watch your back, Ian," Julian chimed in.

"Yeah," Pete added, and with that, they strolled away.

That evening, Ian was making his bed. Moof came out of the bathroom and lay on his own bed. "Hey, Ian, thanks for sticking up for me," Moof said.

Ian pulled his sheet over the mattress and then looked at Moof. "No problem, what's a holy savior for if not to defend his loyal followers," he said, and the sheet snapped loose.

"Yeah, but people never really stuck up for me before. I was always just called the weird boy with the weird name that no one could pronounce."

Ian smiled. "Two things: one, you don't have the most complicated name in the city, that belongs to the man whose name I can't pronounce. And two, people who call you weird have obviously not met me."

Moof nodded and went under the covers. Ian went back to making his bed. Twenty minutes later, he got under his covers as well.

That night, around one o'clock in the morning, while he and Moof were sound asleep, Ian awoke to the sound of a vase smashing outside the door.

"Dammit, clean that up," a voice said.

"Moof? Is that you?" Ian asked with a yawn.

"No, I mean, yes," the voice responded. "Go to sleep, Ian, and don't worry about suspicious noises."

"Okay, good night," Ian said, and he drifted off again, ignoring the sound of what he thought was a drill pounding into his door. After a moment, he awoke to voices again.

"Dude, I think the door was unlocked, actually," one of them said.

"What? Why didn't you say anything?" another voice cried.

"You looked pretty intense, and I didn't want to bother you," the first voice responded. The voices then stopped, and Ian began to drift again. Suddenly, though, he was jolted awake by a bag being thrown over his head.

"Hey, what in the safe space?" Ian cried from the bag. "I'd better be being taken to a surprise party or something." He felt his arms and legs being tied together and was picked up. He was then dropped.

"What was that?" one of the voices asked in a loud whisper.

"My fingers slipped," the other voice replied.

"Just pick him up," the first one said, and Ian again felt himself being lifted into the air and carried off. He then felt himself being thrown somewhere. It seemed like a carriage, and sure enough, Ian felt a tug and then the ground moving.

After about a ten-minute wait, he felt the ground halt and was grabbed again. After being carried for a few more minutes, he was thrown down again, this time onto the ground that smelled like the time he had stolen eggs from a chicken farmer, eggs he later used to coat his father's office window.

He was propped up, and the bag was ripped off him. It was pitch black, and he couldn't see in front of his face. After a moment, though, a bright light broke out and revealed that he was in a weird room—almost cave-like. The floor was soft and wet, and the walls were layered with what appeared to be numerous bird droppings. A loudspeaker then came on, startling him.

"Good morning, Ian. I bet you didn't think this would happen, did you?" the voice said gleefully.

"With the year I'm having, I'm not shocked," Ian replied.

The voice gave a sarcastic laugh. "Humor won't be saving you, Ian. We're going to play a little game. How does that sound?"

"I'm guessing you don't have Candy Land in mind."

"No, more fun. It's more of a 'Saw' kind of game."

"Ah, sounds lovely, I can't wait. Do I get to play the man behind the chair?"

"Here's how the game works," the voice said, ignoring him. "Somewhere in this room is your loyal sweet friend. Your challenge: Find him before it does."

"Hah, this is going to be so cool," another voice said through the speaker. Ian recognized it and smiled.

"Pete, is that you?" Ian asked. "I should've known this was the work of the three wicked stepbrothers."

"Rob, I mean Beto, release Max," Ian heard the voice that he now recognized as Julian's say.

"Max?" Ian pondered aloud to himself. Out of the shadows, Ian saw a goose waddling toward him, and he laughed. "That's it? Oh, you guys are just sad."

The goose then honked at Ian and started running toward him. "Uh-oh," Ian said. He tried standing up but quickly fell over because he was still tied up. He took a quick glance and saw the goose right in his face, giving him a clear look at the black-and-white patterns.

"Nice, Max. Now, let's just take a chill pill here. I'm going to slowly stand up and back away. That's all I want to do," he said, grimacing, and he very carefully loosened the rope around his legs.

The goose honked loudly and bit Ian on the nose. Ian fell backward and scampered up as quickly as possible. He started running as fast as he could, as the goose sprinted after him, honking madly.

Ian raised his hand in the air. A flight of stairs appeared before him, and he ran up them. However, he fell off the edge, flat on his face, because he had forgotten to finish building the stairway. The goose flew down from the stairs and landed on Ian's back.

"Get off of me," Ian cried, but the goose simply honked and pecked at his hair. Ian stood up and sprinted, but it remained stapled to his back, continuing to peck the back of his head.

As he aimlessly meandered around the room, he suddenly tripped over something. He looked up and saw Moof tied up to a chair with slices of bread stuffed in his mouth.

"Moof?"

Moof gave a muffled answer. "Mmmmm," he got out.

"Exactly what I was thinking," Ian replied.

"Mmmmm."

"What?"

"Hmmmm!" Ian turned around and saw Max staring him down, showing off its razor-sharp ridges around its tongue.

Ian stared back intensely. "All right, I can't think of anything badass to say that relates to geese, but I'm going to tear you a new father," he said.

The goose replied with a furious honk and charged at him. Ian raised his hand, waiting for his moment. The goose glided into the air and then dived toward him like a missile. Ian waited, and waited, until at the last moment he pushed his hand forward.

In that instance, the goose froze in midair, and then floated to the ground, slowly deflating and shrinking until it gently touched the floor. It stood still, silent and harmless—a lifeless plushie of a goose. Ian sighed and turned to untie Moof. He grabbed the stuffed goose and handed it to Moof.

"Here you go, for your troubles," Ian said.

Moof snatched it from his hands. "Funny," he said, not laughing.

"I thought so," Ian replied.

"Can we get out of here?"

"Hold on. I have something to take care of first." Ian went to the back of the den where the goose had wreaked havoc. He raised his hand to the wall, and it exploded, leaving a hole into another room on the other side.

In the room, Rob, Julian, and Pete were sitting on the floor in a circle, laughing and rolling a ball back and forth. Julian saw Ian and staggered up in surprise, followed by the other two. They all looked stunned and were sweating heavily.

"So, Ian, I see you have fallen into our trap," Julian said unconvincingly.

"Wow, and you three came together and thought of it all on your own. I'm impressed," Ian shot back.

Pete angrily tried to throw the ball at Ian, but it fell in front of his own feet.

Ian shook his head in disappointment. "You three are going to rue the day you ever messed with me," he said.

Seconds later, the three of them were running out of the den, with green gas spurting out of their backsides.

Ian and Moof laughed and headed out like they had just left a comedy club. However, before they knew it, they ran right into Ian's professor, Running Bear O'Sullivan.

He glared at Ian and then noticed the goose sitting under Moof's arm. "What have you done to the university mascot, Max the Marvelous?" he said.

"What?" Ian said blankly. He eyed the plush goose that now looked like something one would win at a bad carnival game.

"You killed our mascot, the only thing that is allowed to cheer our sports teams as they win participation trophies. You'll pay for this, Ian," he snarled.

"It was an accident," Ian protested, and Moof shook his head feverishly.

"We'll just see how the Dean of Intolerance feels about this," the professor said, not hiding his smug satisfaction.

"I think he'll see it my way," Ian said, though he didn't feel very confident on the inside. "I'm in the right."

"Oh, that's the problem. You're on the right," the professor said.

"I was kidnapped. I was defending myself," Ian said. "The dean will definitely not look too kindly on that. Mark my words."

And that was how Ian got expelled from Rondithmuth University.

Chapter 19:

The Story of Ian and the Coffee Party

Ron was very upset about Ian getting expelled from the university. "I bent over backwards to get you in there, and, as usual, you undermine me at every turn," he said at the dinner table after Ian came home that afternoon to tell them the news.

"It's not my fault that they are completely unreasonable and suppress everything that even remotely contradicts their shallow way of thinking," Ian shot back, raising his voice.

"That shallow line of thinking is my way of thinking. And in case you have forgotten, I am the king," Ron said, raising his own voice.

"Well, maybe we've figured out the problem," Ian said, eyes narrowed.

"What did you say?" Ron asked, narrowing his own eyes.

Gretchen, who was just trying to eat her baked beans in peace, turned pink. Ian slammed the table, jamming his pinky, and left the mansion.

He went down the road, still furious at his stepfather. After making it to the well and sitting against the stone, he pondered his situation. Was this the moment he had been waiting for? He always knew the moment would eventually come and he had waited so long for it, but he never thought about when it would happen.

But as Ian was in his thoughts, he suddenly saw something coming at him in the distance. He squinted his eyes for a better look, and then they popped open when he realized what was happening. He raised his hand in the air and stopped an arrow dead in its tracks as it hovered in the air, frozen where it stood inches from his face. He scampered up and yanked the arrow from midair. The shaft was marked "CP." The Coffee Party—again trying to take him out. He broke the arrow angrily and stormed off, tired of the constant distractions. He needed to act. After walking for a while, he knocked on the door of a lonely little shack in the poor part of town. When the door opened, he saw Mark in the doorway.

"Hello, Ian, do you want to come in? We have some coffee," Mark said in a now-deep voice Ian was put off by.

"No, but what I need you to help me with involves coffee. I need you to come with me to take down the Coffee Party and convert them to our side," Ian said, but Mark looked at him, puzzled.

"Why me? Why not John or the boy whose name you can't pronounce?" he asked.

"Because you're good at sneaking around and finding out things. Plus you've got the whole loner thing and the pathetic life. You'd be perfect for a conservative group. I want you to pose as one of them. And to let me in their main building where I'll scare the crap out of them."

"Well, thanks for the um, compliments, I think. And far be it from me to defy you. When are we doing it?"

"Tonight, we head out now. Get your things," Ian replied, and Mark closed the door. A few minutes later, he came out in a dark hood that concealed much of his face. Ian put on his own dark hood, though this one went over his entire face.

"Ian, can you even see?"

"Listen, you fuzzy blob that sounds like Mark, just worry about getting me in," Ian said, and Mark shrugged and led him down the road, guiding him by the shoulder.

They set out to the outskirts of the city and into the outer region near the river. "Are you sure this is where their headquarters is?" Ian asked as they approached a lonely-looking old coal mine that sat near the edge of the village. Mark nodded.

"Yes, Ian, my sources tell me that this is where they do their operations," Mark whispered.

"Good, you go in there, and then when you are ready to let me in, blow this." Ian handed him a rusty cornet.

"Is this clean?" Mark asked, looking at it.

"As clean as you need it to be. Now go." Mark headed for the mine while Ian hid behind some mine carts nearby. He saw a couple of men approach his follower, check him, and then let him pass.

He waited and waited. After two hours, Ian started to drift as the sun set, giving the area a creepy aura. The only light came from the dim glow of the mine shaft. He was awakened by a buzzing sound coming from the shaft. Realizing this was the signal, he crept his way to the entrance. There were no guards in sight, only the hooded figure of Mark, whom Ian could barely make out.

"Is it done?" Ian asked quietly.

"Yes, not so pathetic now, am I?" Mark said proudly.

"I meant that as a compliment."

"Sure, Ian, whatever you say. What's next?" Mark asked, visibly annoyed that his night was being stolen.

"You're going to tell me where the leaders are and then go back to them to avoid raising suspicion."

Mark nodded and led him into the shaft. Mark took a torch and led Ian through the pitch-black corridor, which had wooden doors dotted along the walls that apparently housed the members. They passed through and went down deeper into the shaft, eventually landing on flat ground that ran over an old railway track that had been unused for centuries.

They made it to a door where a light was shining under the crack. Mark opened it, and Ian followed close behind. "Go now, I'll stay back here until I see an opening," Ian said, and Mark went back to a group of men who were seated in the corner of the large room. A conference table dominated the room, and many men and women were clustered around it, standing up, deep in conversation. Ian drifted closer and listened carefully.

"You're telling me that son of his somehow escaped our grasp again?" a man with a thick gray mustache and a military-like coat asked another man who was obviously a soldier.

"This is proof enough, Simon, can't you see?" a young woman, probably slightly older than Ian with short dark hair, said from across the table.

"Quiet. We have to get rid of King Ron's line of succession if we are to destroy him. We have to act now. Food is scarce, and we can't keep going forever," the man called Simon responded.

"We must wait for the Maud'Ian, who will come and free us," the woman pleaded.

"We can't wait for some prophecy that no one even remembers where it even came from. In order to overthrow tyranny and install our democratic government, we have to act now and not wait for some savior," Simon replied.

Ian pondered what they were saying. The Coffee Party was trying to do what he was doing. They just didn't know about him. He needed a way to convince them that he could be an ally, not an enemy. As he was thinking through this crappy plot twist, though, Ian failed to notice that his hood had caught fire after he had leaned on a torch on the wall. He let out a yell, startling the entire room. He ran over to a table where people were drinking coffee, grabbed a mug, and dumped it on himself, scalding himself further.

The soldiers surrounded him.

"Hands up, and get down," one yelled. Ian smiled and raised his hand. Their bows and arrows crumbled to pieces. They looked at him in terror and ran out of the room. Ian felt his burned face and gently rubbed the burned skin, which healed it.

The people in the room looked at him in shock. Simon stepped forward. "What are you?" he asked nervously.

"I am Ian, son of the King."

"What do you have, a death wish coming here?" Simon barked.

"You speak to me like that again, and it'll be you with that wish."

"I will not be intimidated by a treasonous maggot. We should've killed you when we had the chance as a little brat," Simon yelled, but Ian held up his hand, and Simon's mouth immediately closed. He tried to open it, but it was stuck. Panic filled his eyes, and he collapsed to the ground, hands together, pleading. Ian shook his head.

"Now, in case you haven't noticed, I'm not exactly like other men. I am the King's son by name, yes. But my true father is up there," Ian said, pointing to the ceiling.

"You're the illegitimate son of Rusty the butcher?" a man from the back asked.

"No, I am the son of Backwards Dog, born with a destiny to restore freedom to this land," Ian proclaimed. Mark sat up from his chair.

"It is true. I follow him myself. He is true to his word," Mark said, and Ian smiled at him.

"How do we know you're who you say you are?" the woman that was arguing with Simon earlier said. "How do we know this isn't some trick?"

"If I wanted you dead, I would have already done it," Ian said. "But I'm acting rationally. Which doesn't exactly sound like a liberal, does it?" The room seemed to nod their heads in agreement.

"So you're not a liberal? Big deal. That doesn't mean we should follow you," an older woman near him said in a hiss that reminded him of his mother. He shook his head.

"I need you. And you need me. I don't see why we shouldn't come together to fight our common enemy," Ian said.

"You're—You're the Maud'Ian. The one who is gracious," the woman from earlier stated and got down on her knees. Ian hesitated, not knowing what she was really talking about. He remembered vaguely hearing something similar somewhere when he was very young, but he might have been dreaming it. The dream involved a giant worm, so, of course, this was a little bit silly.

"I only know that I am Ian and that I am holy," Ian said.

"It means the same thing, Ian," Mark replied. "They were telling me about it earlier. You are who they are looking for."

Ian nodded. "Well then, it is time that you join me and my followers. Step forward and join us, and we shall restore freedom for all," Ian called. The crowd rejoiced and cheered, and everyone went to their knees, except Simon, who had somehow gotten his big mouth back.

"I'll be married to a goat before I bend the knee to the son of a tyrant," he said, grabbing a spear from the table near him and raising it in the air. However, before he could throw it, the woman from earlier smacked him with a banjo that was also lying on the table, and he fell over, knocked out.

"And who are you, miss?" Ian asked the woman.

"You can call me Margaret. Margaret Burns," she said, loosening her tied-up hair so it tumbled over her face.

"Margaret Burns, I hereby declare you one of my main followers and the leader of the Coffee Party division of my group. Backwards Dog bless you," Ian said, smiling.

The whole room called out, "Backwards Dog bless you," and she blushed red.

"It will be an honor to serve you, my Maud'Ian," she said.

"Good, now mobilize the men and women. You are to set off for the city in a week. Your jobs will be to surround the city and take out any vantage point as I lead the assault with my army into the city," Ian said. Mark approached him.

"Uh, Ian, what army are you talking about?" Mark asked. "You don't have an army."

"You'll see, my friend," Ian answered cryptically. "You'll see."

The Coffee Party pledged its allegiance to Ian; it was the first large conversion to Ian's movement. Simon was barred from participating after he attempted to strike Margaret, though she promptly punched him in the nose before he could get a shot in. They said their goodbyes and left the mine shaft. It was not how he had expected this night to go.

He had expected to be coming back annoyed that he had just beaten up a bunch of jerks, but as it turned out, those jerks thought a lot like him. The irony.

Ian and Mark headed back into the city and met with John, Moof, and the boy whose name Ian couldn't pronounce, and informed them of the plan. The stage had been set.

Ian returned home to the palace. Before he could get to his room, though, Ron came in from the living room.

"Where have you been?" Ron asked, concerned.

"I was out with friends. I needed to get away and let loose for a little bit," Ian replied.

"I heard you were attacked at the well," Ron said. "By that evil Coffee Party group." Ian's eyes darted away from Ron's gaze.

"Yeah, it wasn't that big of a deal." Ron frowned.

"Not a big deal? You are my son. They won't get away with this. I signed an order this evening, barring any talk of rebellion or unhealthy viewpoints in this city and its regions," Ron said, and Ian's heart did a kickflip.

"And," he continued, "I am hiring you to personally oversee the roundup of all groups that seek to harm us and our city. Maybe it's time you pulled some weight around here. And my leg has been cramping lately."

Ian almost threw up in his mouth but managed to get out, "I'll do my best." Ron smiled and left the room, leaving Ian somehow more depressed than when he had left earlier. Ian, the great rebel hunter, certainly didn't have as good a ring to it as Maud'Ian. It did not matter, though. He had to do what he had to, and there was no going back.

Chapter 20:

The Story of Ian's Guerrilla War

The man whose name Ian couldn't pronounce entered the large, abandoned factory on the outskirts of the city. He turned around to make sure he hadn't been followed. It had been one week since the joining of Ian's followers and the Coffee Party. The Coffee Party had proven a useful ally in disrupting the trade chokepoints for Rondithmuth's commerce with distant cities in other parts of the continent. Just today, the shipments of new red tape were stopped and turned around by Margaret and her men.

Ian had summoned him to the factory immediately, though Ian had decided to use bats to transport communication back and forth. This was fine, though letters usually arrived at night and seldom reached him until the next day. He spotted Ian on the factory floor, arguing with several large figures he couldn't quite make out.

He called down. "Ian?"

"Hey, get down here," he said. "Ow, don't bite my ass!"

The man whose name Ian couldn't pronounce went down the metal stairway. When he got to the bottom and started walking toward Ian, he noticed that the figures around Ian weren't people—they were gorillas—many gorillas, probably two hundred. They glared at him suspiciously, and some beat their chests at him and grunted. He kept his distance.

When he got to Ian, he found him arguing with John.

"Ian, for the fiftieth time, I said a guerrilla war, not a gorilla war," John pleaded. Mark shook his head beside him.

"What kind of dumb name is *guerrilla* anyway? People actually know what a gorilla is," Ian protested weakly.

"Guerrilla is derived from the Spanish word guerra, which means war, and guerrilla means little war. It comes from nineteenth century Spain during the Peninsular War against Napoleon, which was often fought in small-scale, irregular ways of combat," Moof, who was lying on a lawn chair, said.

Ian turned to Moof. "Oh, now you speak up," he said.

"Ian, how did you even get them here?" the man whose name Ian couldn't pronounce asked.

"I asked Backwards Dog to provide, and the next morning, when I opened the door, I found them wandering around my front lawn, eating the bananas from the compost bin," Ian answered.

"And what exactly are we going to do with them?" John asked.

"First, they will peel our bananas for our lunch. Then we will lead them into battle," Ian said proudly and patted one on the back. It lurched, knocking Mark to the ground.

"You can't lead an ape into battle, Ian; they have to be trained," John pleaded.

"If Noah could potty-train all those animals on the Ark, I think I can train a few of our distant ancestors," Ian replied defiantly.

"Leave me out of it," Mark said, throwing his hands up.

"That's fine. I have another job for you guys to do anyway," Ian said, and they stepped closer, and Mark rubbed his shoulder.

"I need you all to go down early before the battle and barricade the doors of the oligarchs. I need them to be willing to negotiate when we seize power," Ian said.

They all nodded, and Moof wrote down what Ian said on his arm.

"We will start the attack in two weeks. Scout your positions. Know their weaknesses," Ian said, and the four nodded. "Now, who wants to help me train our army?"

They all groaned and left Ian with his gorillas. He shook his head in disappointment and turned to a gorilla next to him that was scratching its butt. "They may be my followers, but they will never be as loyal as you fellas," he said.

The gorilla got up and walked away to sniff a female. Ian rolled his hair back, straightened his glasses, and got to work.

The next two weeks were the hardest Ian had worked in his life, as it turned out it was difficult to convert a bunch of gorillas into an army. There was a steep learning curve from the beginning.

"All right, let's line up here," Ian said on the first day of training to the scattered group of apes. "Hey, where are you going?" he yelled as most of them wandered off to the other side of the room.

"Look at me when I'm talking to you," Ian said the next day to the gorilla he had named Sergeant. "Don't throw that banana at me."

With much work and a harvest's worth of bananas, he had them standing in formation after one week. He addressed his army. "Next, I want you to charge forward and knock out the cardboard cutouts of Ron," he said, pointing to the poorly drawn-on boxes across the room. "Get ready ... charge."

They ran forward, grunting and howling. "No, no, no. In a straight line," he pleaded. "Where are you going? Stop running around in circles, Sergeant."

Ian started pulling on his lush hair, which was beginning to fall out. "Did I tell you to sit down?" he asked one near him who had laid down for a nap. "Hey, stop throwing bananas at each other."

It took him another three days to get them to charge correctly. He decided that it was good enough and laid out his plan. He decided that he would have them charge into the city, then just have them run around and do whatever.

"Is that understood, Sergeant? Hey, how many times have I told you to stop picking fleas off the privates?"

The next day, both John and Mark came in to show Ian some things they had gotten for the battle. John had gotten his hands on some armor for him to wear. When he put it on, however, it weighed him down so much that he tipped over and fell to the dirt, unable to stand back up until John helped him.

"John, why is this thing a metric ton?" he demanded.

"It's armor, Ian. It's heavy," John replied. "If it's a problem, I can shorten it to just reach your armpits." Ian thought about it for a second but decided to just see how it would play out.

Mark presented Ian with a sword that he had gotten from a seller from outside of the city, as the selling of swords and weapons in private hands was now banned. "Here you go, Ian," Mark said. "Though, if you're the czar of political imprisonment, why don't you have a sword already?"

"I dropped it down the well where I was practicing. Kimmith caught it as it fell, but she couldn't get it back out," Ian replied and grabbed the sword from Mark.

It was so hefty, though, that it immediately fell to the ground in his hand. He tried to pick it up but couldn't. "Where are you people getting this metal?" Ian asked.

"That sword once belonged to Charlemagne himself," Mark said.

Ian examined it. "Really?"

"That's what the guy with the one eye said that sold it to me."

"Well, I still can't pick this stupid thing up."

Mark shrugged. "I guess you'll just have to practice."

On the day of the planned invasion, Ian got a bat from Margaret saying the roads out of the city had been blocked and that everything was in order. Ian called over the man whose name he couldn't pronounce.

"What is the report from the city? Where are the soldiers?" Ian asked.

"They're just kind of milling about, Ian. They don't expect a thing."

"Good, then we can begin. Go down and get ready," Ian said, and he turned to the formation of his gorillas while the man whose name he couldn't pronounce ran off.

Ian donned his armor and slunk forward gingerly. "My loyal gorilla friends," he said to the apes. "The last few weeks have been some of the most rewarding of my life. But instead of reflecting on how sad that is, I'm going to ask you to ride with me to triumph and prosperity, and I promise you all the bananas you can dream of." The gorillas all grunted and hollered. "Mark, sound the alarm," he cried. Mark reluctantly put his lips to Ian's cornet and played it through the loudspeaker placed on the factory roof.

Ian yelled to his gorillas, "To glory," and they all meandered toward the city, with Ian lagging close behind.

Meanwhile, Ron was eating his brunch salad when he suddenly heard the obnoxious sound of a horn blasting through his window. Surprised, he dumped his relish everywhere. "What in the due process was that?" he exclaimed.

A guard from outside came running in. "Your Grace, we have a problem," he said.

Ron wiped his robe. "Yes, we do. This isn't machine washable."

"Uh, no, sir. We've seen a number of unrecognized individuals starting to come into the city," he said hesitantly.

"Is it those Coffee Party people that keep blocking my salad shipments?"

"No, we're not sure, but there's something else."

Ron frowned. "What?"

The guard hesitated. "We're kind of locked inside."

Ron looked as if someone had just misgendered his goldfish. "Then get it open," he snarled. The guard began to beat on the door. At that moment, another soldier yelled from the window.

"Your Grace, we have identified the army. It appears to be a troop of gorillas approaching the city," he yelled to him. Ron stared blankly out the window.

"I'm going to pretend like you didn't say that, and you're going to tell me something else," Ron said with a furious undertone.

"But sir, it's true. Some of our men were already mauled by one of the beasts." Ron yelled out in frustration and went back to the door, where the guard was still desperately trying to open it. Eventually, the guard from outside managed to help them break the barricade of wood that had been lined against the door. Ron bolted out and found two of his men holding a man who looked familiar.

"Your Grace, we found this young man barricading Oligarchs Nancy and Chuck's home. We also caught three others and have them locked up," one of them stated. Ron looked closely and finally recognized him clearly.

"Oh, John, my boy, why have you done this? You disgrace your adopted family," Ron said, shaking his head.

"But I honor my real parents," John replied stoically.

"Then your parents were fools," Ron replied. "Take him away." The guards led John away. Ron turned to another one of his men. "Where is Ian? I need him here, he's supposed to be putting this stuff down."

"We haven't seen him, Your Grace," he replied.

"Well, take a letter for me, and send it to the city outskirts. We'll send our little revolutionary an ultimatum," Ron said.

"Yes, Your Grace."

Meanwhile, Ian was dragging his sword behind him and duck-walking down the road into the city. He ran forward in small sprints, then halted, out of breath. When he got into the city, he unleashed the gorillas to do their work, and they obliged.

Many went to the fruit stands first, tipping them over. The people around them cried out in terror and ran away. Other gorillas were just running around, knocking things over. It was chaos. Ian had gotten what he wanted.

After an hour, he haphazardly gathered all his gorilla troops together. "My great ape friends," he said. "Today is a day that will be celebrated for generations. Your commitment to scaring and running around has been admirable, and we have frightened the enemy into submission. We have them right where we want them."

He looked at them like a proud father. "And in celebration, all of you will get one extra banana as a reward. Hand me my banana box, John," he said. He waited. "John?"

He looked around but saw none of his followers anywhere. "Mark? Moof? Man whose name I can't pronounce?" he called out into the crowd of gorillas.

Just then, Ian saw something attached to the back of one of the bananas a gorilla was eating. He went up to take it. The gorilla growled at him, and Ian plucked off what was attached and quickly handed the fruit back, then ran away.

He looked at what it was. It was a rolled-up piece of parchment, the kind he'd use to swap Ron's grocery list with his own before handing it to the butler. He unrolled it and found it to be a letter. It read:

Dear Jerk,

We have your followers. Your coup attempt on our city has failed, and your followers will be tried for treason. Unless you want them to suffer more, you will turn yourself over to my son, Ian, who is in charge of taking care of pathetic runts like yourself.

Surrender and submit to my rule and I may just spare you and your people. You have 24 hours.

Kind Regards,

King Ron

Ian looked up from the letter, anger and fear swelling inside him. Ignoring the gorillas battling for mates, he headed out of the city, dragging his sword behind him. If this was a fight that Ron wanted, then he would have it.

Chapter 21:

The Story of Ian's Great Escape

Ian found Margaret near the intersection of "Collectivist Square," by one of the city's entrances. The Coffee Party was turning around the carts and carriages of cauliflower and cabbage that Ron had ordered for his upcoming "Lenin Day" celebration.

"Unless that cabbage is for the poor people of Bolshevik Bay, turn that cart of yours around," she barked at a man who quickly rode away in fright. Ian ran up to her.

"Margaret, something terrible has happened," he cried.

"Oh, hello, my holiness, here, have an oca," she said, handing him a weird-looking yellow thing. Ian took it and put it in his pocket for later.

"Thank you, but I must talk to you. My stepfather has taken all of my followers," he said.

"He has?" she said in surprise.

"Yes, and that means that it is only a matter of time before they come for you and the rest of the Coffee Party. You have to get out of here."

Margaret shook her head. "No," she said. "We will not simply leave and abandon you like this. You are our Maud'Ian." Ian smiled at this and placed his hand on her shoulder.

"Thank you, but I want you to take your people out of this city before they capture you. Head out and look for somewhere to settle. It is no longer safe here," he said. She removed Ian's hand from her shoulder and smiled grimly.

"All right, I will send them out to scout for locations. However, I will stay behind and help you get your followers back."

"Thank you, Margaret. This means the world to me," Ian said, a holy tear streaking down his cheek.

"I'm ever at your service, Maud'Ian," she said, more cheerfully now.

She sent her men and women out of the city. They left, not knowing where or how long they would be on the run. Ian and Margaret watched as they disappeared into small black dots against the endless sand. Margaret looked worried, but she turned her attention back to Ian.

"So, what's the plan, Maud'Ian?" she asked.

Ian's face made an uncomfortable-looking thinking movement. "Um, I don't know, I was kind of hoping for some help from Backwards Dog," he replied sheepishly. She looked at the sky for a moment.

"Well, it appears he's on break for the moment, so I think we're on our own," she said. "Luckily, I think I have a plan." He looked at her, eyebrows raised.

Meanwhile, Ron was on his throne looking furiously at the four men kneeling in front of him. He had called an emergency court hearing the very evening that he had captured the men. The many oligarchs and guards waited anxiously around him. Gretchen was nowhere to be found, but Ron did not have time to worry about this.

He banged his gavel on his throne repeatedly, even though the room was as quiet as a jet engine when it's turned off. "Order! Order in this court," he yelled. His voice echoed off the expensive-looking walls. He leaned in toward the four men, who were looking stoic except the lumpy-looking one, whose thawb bore a distinct wet spot.

"So, you four. John, Moofapafadapolis, Mark, and uh …" he said, rummaging through the scroll in his hand before tossing it behind him. "Well, I guess it doesn't really matter, does it?" He smiled and leaned back in his chair. "You are all charged with conspiracy to kill the king, blowing irritating horns when I'm trying to relax, and not kneeling when the bagpipe anthem of Rondithmuth was played over the radio. How do you all plead?"

"Not guilty," John said firmly.

"You have all been found guilty," Ron said, ignoring him and sneering gleefully. "So, now we get to determine how badly you wish to be punished. Tell me who your leader is?"

They knelt silently. Ron shook his head. "My apologies, I must have accidentally whispered. I said, who is your leader?!" There was still no answer. He sighed dramatically. "People with their loyalty and principles. Makes me sick."

"We'll never tell you that Ian is our leader," the boy whose name Ian couldn't pronounce blurted. Ron smiled and jumped out of his chair.

"Ho ho. You just made a big mistake, uh, you," he barked, stabbing his finger at the boy who was now as pale as a ghost, like, the white kind, not the tinted blue kind. Ron turned to one of his men. "Guard, find the local knot maker, Ian, and bring him here at once."

At this moment, Gretchen had crept in and taken a seat next to Ron, who was not paying attention. "I should have known that slippery little knot maker was the leader of this pathetic rebellion. Well, let's see him wiggle out of this one," Ron gloated. "Take them back to their cells." The guards dragged the four men out of the room. Ron sat back down happily and noticed Gretchen sitting there, hiding a grin.

"It's over, dear. We have finally found the culprit," he said. Gretchen rolled her eyes.

"Yes, Ron, you're a regular Sherlock Holmes," she replied in her ever-pleasant tone.

That night, Ian, dressed in an all-black wetsuit, and Margaret, holding a paper cup with string in her hand, huddled in a dark alleyway near the city's outskirts.

"So, you remember the plan, right?" she asked Ian, who was trying to make his wetsuit fit better.

"Yes, for the hundredth time, I dig a tunnel with your guidance toward the jail where they're holding my followers. I dig up from their cell, and we escape into the night. Pretty simple."

She shook her head. "No, not simple. Any wrong turn is the difference between you digging into the cell and into a river."

Suddenly, Ian felt something sharp poking into his back. He looked over his shoulder and saw a man in a zebra-striped shirt with a mask over his eyes pressing a stick against his back.

"Give me all your money," the zebra man said. Ian sighed exasperatedly and raised his hand behind him. The man flew in the air and was jammed into the building beside them, seemingly stuck halfway in.

"Don't interrupt. I'm busy," Ian said, turning his attention back to Margaret. "It'll be fine. I have Backwards Dog on my side." And with that, he got out a little green plastic shovel and began to dig the sand below him.

"Good luck, Maud'Ian," Margaret said, and she handed him a cup with a string attached. "I'll talk you through where to go."

"Good, thanks," Ian said, and with that his head disappeared into the sand.

There was a problem, though, as Ian began to dig as quickly as a plastic shovel could. It turned out that sand is hard to dig a tunnel through. Every time Ian made progress, the sand would collapse behind him. He tried to prop up the sand with inflatable pool toys but with limited success.

"Okay, Ian, you're approaching the jail if you've been heading in the right direction," he heard Margaret say through the cup.

"Got it," he replied, continuing to dig. After twenty minutes or so, the sand above him collapsed and revealed hard concrete. He put his mouth to the cup. "I believe that I've entered the jail."

"Good, now you need to drill up to get through the concrete," Margaret replied. "Try not to make much noise."

"Well, duh," Ian said, and he turned on the drill in his hand.

Somehow louder than a fireworks display, Ian wildly tried to drill up, eventually breaking a hole through the top. He quickly turned the drill off and poked his head up through the hole.

He looked around and realized that he had missed the cell and had ended up in the guards' staff room. Two guards lay sprawled out on the couch, fast asleep, drool dripping onto the other. Ian carefully climbed out of the hole and stood up. He crept by the sleeping men, trying desperately to keep his footsteps to a light tap.

When he reached the door leading out of the staff room, he peeked around the corner. He saw a guard approaching, holding a flickering fluorescent lantern as he wandered down the dark corridor. Ian quickly changed into a monk outfit that was lying on the coat rack and entered the hallway. Wearing a dark hood over his not-bald head, he casually strolled toward the guard. As Ian got closer, the guard noticed him and eyed him with suspicion.

"What brings you in here this evening, uh, monk?" the guard asked Ian, who jumped.

"Uh, the daily monk tax to the security department was due today. I was making the payment," Ian replied, his voice unusually higher than normal.

"Ah yes, that was due today, wasn't it?" the guard said. "Well, on your way," and he walked by him. Ian gave a sigh of relief and continued on his way.

"Ian, are you okay?" Margaret asked suddenly through the cup.

"Uh, yeah, a slight change in plan." He found his way to the cells and crept in. In one cell, he found one of the men who had been arrested for sarcastically thanking the tax collector for taking his money, lying down, hungover from a previous night of drinking his sorrows away. Next to him, though, Ian found his four followers sleeping in their cramped cell, each sharing a small bed that looked like it was rotting.

"Hey, guys, wake up," he said in a low voice. John woke up, saw Ian's silhouette in the darkness, and smiled.

"Ian, it's you," he said loudly, waking up the others.

Ian hushed him. "Will you be quiet? I'm in the middle of a covert operation here."

"I knew you'd rescue us," said the man whose name Ian couldn't pronounce.

"Oh, you know I wasn't going to abandon you. Now, step back. I'm going to blow this door down," Ian said, and his followers stepped back against the wall. He took a deep breath. He got ready to huff and puff, but before he blew the cell door down, he heard the sound of a guard tripping in the other room.

"What the? Hey Joe, get Jimmy. I tripped over some string over here," the guard said. Ian felt his paper cup get yanked out of his hand, and the guard stormed into the room. "Hey, you monk, you can't be in here," he yelled and went to grab him. Ian raised his hand though and magically pushed the guard backward into the wall, knocking him unconscious.

"Get us out, Ian," Mark cried.

"Yeah," said the hungover guy in the cell next door. At that moment, though, ten more guards came in, blocking the door.

"You there, arms up and on your knees," one of them shouted.

"Hang on, is that who I think it is?" pondered the guard next to the one ordering.

"Yeah, that looks like Prince Ian," another said.

Ian hesitated. "Uh, later, guys, I can't stay for a drink," he said. He then threw the oca from his pocket at the guard nearest him, knocking him unconscious, then blasted a hole in the ground with his hand and jumped down out of sight. The guards ran up to the hole.

"Bill, go get in there and follow him," the one guard ordered.

"I can't fit in there," a larger guard replied.

"Of course you can't," said another.

"Are you fat-shaming me, Barry?" Bill cried.

"No, no, please don't report me," the man, apparently named Barry, replied hastily.

"Enough of this," the guard, who was obviously the leader, yelled. "Find him." They scattered.

Outside of the jail, Ian poked his head out of a hole that was somehow in the middle of a little girl's room. He crawled out and tiptoed through the room. The girl stirred awake, saw him, and screamed.

"No, no," Ian cried. "Don't be scared, I'm just your holy savior." The girl's father burst in.

"Who are you? What did you do to my little girl?" the father growled. Ian didn't really have a good excuse, so he ran by the father, pushing him over, and rushed out the door into the night.

The next day, Ron was again holding an emergency court session. He was looking furiously again at Ian's four followers.

"So, it appears that the knot maker named Ian was actually not the leader of the rebellion," Ron said with an ominous calm. "You think you can pull the wool over my eyes. I look through wool for breakfast."

He stood up from his throne, eyes flickering. Gretchen, who had been forced to attend this session, looked worriedly from her chair next to Ron's. "So, I will ask you one more time, who is your leader?" Ron asked in a dark tone.

At that moment, though, the guard from the jail burst through. "Forgive me, Your Grace," he said.

"We'll see about that," Ron replied.

"Your Grace, I bring news of an attempted breakout of the four followers."

Ron raised his eyebrows. "Really? Do tell," he said, eyes flickering.

"We have linked the attempted breakout to Prince Ian," the guard declared. Gretchen almost fell out of her chair. Ron simply chuckled though.

"Hah hah hah, that's a good one," Ron laughed. "You almost had me there for a second."

"But, but," the guard stuttered.

"But you see, that is impossibly laughable, as Ian has been here this whole time," Ron said, pointing to the empty chair next to his throne. He then narrowed his eyes, trying to figure out why there was no Ian in the chair he was pointing to.

"But Your Grace, with all due respect, Ian could've been out last night and still be here in court," the guard tried to explain, though to Ron's deaf ears. He stood there, still in silence, not moving a muscle. No one in the court was moving either, frozen with anticipation.

Suddenly, Ron grabbed the salad bowl on the arm of his chair and threw it across the room, smashing it to pieces. He breathed heavily, his eyes darting around the room, desperately looking for his son somewhere in the crowd of oligarchs. The guard had ducked away to the back of the room.

"Find Ian," he said to Gretchen through his gritted teeth. Gretchen tried to give him a similar glare, though it was not working as usual.

"I, I don't know where he is," she replied gingerly.

"Find my son!" Ron bellowed, and she scurried out of the room. "How dare he! He has betrayed his country, his family … and me."

His head whipped toward the guard hiding in the back. "Find him! Bring him here! Until then, he is no son of mine!" he shouted, and the guard flew out the door. He turned to the guards standing near Ian's followers.

"Throw them back in their cells. They'll pay for this. Give them the ultimate punishment for deplorables like them," he screamed, and the guards dragged them away. He turned toward his shocked court.

"I will not be torn down. Not today, not tomorrow, not ever," he yelled at them, who all quickly nodded like bobbleheads. He finally turned to his guards standing near him.

"Guards, get me the tongs. Get me the tosser. Get me the spinner, the whisker, and mixer. This is the worst day of my life!" And with that poetic salad-based fit, Ron stormed out of the room, leaving behind a very uncomfortable party of people.

Chapter 22:

The Story of the Plagues of Rondithmuth

That night, Ron was in the kitchen, standing in front of the counter and a cutting board. He was angrily hacking at any vegetables he could find. Greens, purples, and oranges flew around the room haphazardly. Gretchen, who was awakened by her husband's angry grunts, entered gingerly.

"Ron, what exactly did the radishes do to you?" she asked sarcastically. Ron didn't look up from his cutting board.

"Your son," he replied simply. "Your son has decided to disgrace me."

"Ron, I'm not sure why you're surprised. You've known him for eighteen years," she said, taking a seat at the table.

Ron sighed and threw the knife down. "I know, but I can't just let this slide. He has to be punished."

"Then punish him, but I don't think it would be helpful to kill him and make him a martyr. You will only make things worse."

Ron turned and eyed her curiously. "Since when do you care about Ian's welfare?"

Gretchen glanced at the ceiling and bit her lip. "He's my son," she finally replied.

Ron nodded and took a deep breath. "Fine, I'll hear him out if he wishes to speak cordially. But I wouldn't hold my breath," he said.

Gretchen gave a soft smile, which was incredibly difficult for her to do. "Thank you, Ron."

Ron nodded silently and left the room, leaving Gretchen alone at her table. She looked up again at the ceiling, then at the box of oats on the shelf. "You better hold up your end of the bargain," she said, and she stood up as well and went back to sleep.

That morning, Ian was walking through the main road near the center of Rondithmuth. Officially on the run now, he covered his face with a cloth, which kept fogging up his glasses in the heat of the desert. Because of this, he kept knocking into things and people. Several women screamed when he accidentally grabbed them in a place Ian would later refuse to elaborate on.

He had gone to assess the security of the city at that moment, against the advice of Margaret, who said it was too dangerous. He saw that the number of guards seemed to have increased, and also observed wanted posters with his face on them, as he was now declared public enemy number one.

Suddenly, though, he heard some sort of crying and screaming coming from the center of the town near the well. Holding his cloth tight to his face, he sped toward the source of the noise. When he got there, he saw a man with his head in a pillory. Two guards stood behind the man, methodically tickling his neck with a feather. "Please, please, no more, I can't take it," Ian heard the man cry. He crept closer, then realized who it was. It was the man whose name he couldn't pronounce, looking worse for wear. Ian got within earshot, avoiding the guards' gazes.

"Psst, hey," Ian whispered. The man whose name he couldn't pronounce looked up.

"Dad?" he asked.

"What? No, it's Ian."

"Ian!" he yelled.

Ian hushed him. "Quiet. Now, what's going on here?"

"I'm serving my first day of humiliation."

"Humiliation?"

"Yes, we're supposed to be humiliated to learn our lesson," he said, and Ian frowned.

"This is an outrage. I've had enough of this," Ian said, and he stormed off.

"Ian, wait, where are you going?" the man whose name he couldn't pronounce called after him. "I have an itch. Can you scratch it?"

Ian ran through the crowd of people who were laughing at his friend, being sure to kick mud on them whenever he got the chance, and arrived at the palace, his home, though that seemed like a long time ago, even if it had only been a couple of days.

He burst through the front door. Ron was in the kitchen, sitting at the table, unsurprisingly eating a salad. He looked up at Ian, who was visibly shaking at the door.

Ron gave an unconvincing smile. "Ian. Have a seat. It's time for our brunch salad," he said casually, as if nothing of consequence had occurred recently. Ian cautiously approached the table, scraped the chair across the floor, and sat opposite the king.

Ron slid the salad ingredients and a bowl toward Ian's side of the table. Ian ignored the bowl and didn't take his eyes off his stepfather.

"I demand to speak with you," Ian said coldly.

Ron looked at Ian with amusement. "Speak with salad in your mouth. Don't be rude," Ron said, gesturing toward the bowl. Ian sighed, and begrudgingly took the bowl. Ron smiled in approval. "Now. What were you demanding that I, the King, do?"

"Why did you arrest my followers? I demand that you release them at once," Ian said, not returning the smile.

Ron popped a pepper in his mouth. "Your little playmates insulted their kingdom and King. They must die or be looked at scornfully," Ron replied simply. "I chose the last option out of mercy. Was I mistaken in doing that?"

Ian angrily grabbed a cucumber and shoved it in his mouth. "They were simply expressing themselves. They have a right to an opinion."

Ron sliced an artichoke heart and placed it in his mouth. "Yes. The correct opinion, that is determined by his elders. Which means me."

"I won't ask—"

"Ian." Ron pointed to Ian's plate. Ian grabbed an eggplant and crammed the whole thing in his mouth, choking a little.

"I won't ask again. Let them go now," Ian repeated.

Ron rolled a carrot down his throat and finally gave in to a frown. "You've always been such a little problem child. Ever since you were tossed to me," he spat, and stood up. "You're no son of mine."

Ian shoved a hard-boiled egg through his gritted teeth. "And you're no father of mine," he replied in kind, but got tired and sat down again in his chair.

"You want to see real fairness? I'm going to lock up all your followers indefinitely and you can watch as they rot in prison," Ron said.

Ian shot up out of his chair again, seething. "You will pay for this," he said, storming out of the palace.

He went all the way outside the city walls and sat in the middle of a small pond, floating on top of the water's surface, pondering his thoughts. He looked at his reflection, sighed, and splashed the water. His moment of character progression was interrupted by a booming voice above him.

"Ian, my son," the voice called.

Ian was so surprised, he lost his concentration and fell into the water. He waded his way back to the shore, soaking wet.

"Sorry, Ian, I forgot that you haven't looked at me for six hours like I've been watching you," Backwards Dog said to him as Ian shook himself like a fuzzy animal.

"So, you saw that thing that I was doing when I got up?" Ian asked, face turning red.

"Yes, Ian."

"I can explain."

"Ian, I'm not here about that. I'm here about the situation you're currently in."

"What am I supposed to do? I don't have my people to help me."
Ian, befuddled, sat on the ground. "I'm alone."

"You are not alone, Ian. You have followers and people who believe in you," Backwards Dog said. "But this isn't the place to do this. You must settle somewhere where you can start fresh and spread from there."

"Like a virus?"

"I would say like a blooming flower in your speeches," Backwards Dog said, and Ian nodded in agreement.

"So, how am I going to get my followers back?"

"Leave that to me, son," Backwards Dog said simply.

Ian smiled brightly, feeling hope for the first time in a couple of days.

That night, the city was dark and quiet, with the only light coming from the dimly lit fluorescent bulbs flickering as usual in the poorly built streetlamps cluttered on the sides of the roads. Nobody was around except for a few homeless people hovering around the lights like moths. Whacking at the flies that were trying to eat the morsels of scraps they had managed to find, as well as the mosquitoes that were trying to eat them, they suddenly looked up in surprise after a large bang went off in the distance, shaking the ground below them.

Over the horizon, a massive storm was heading for the city. Lightning lit up the sky, and thunder rang in the ears. The homeless ran for cover. A group of people on top of the windmills, turning them to provide the city with power, jumped off after lightning struck the turbines, setting them ablaze.

Sleeping soundly in his bed, Ron was awakened by the crackling thunder and screaming.

"What, the private school?" he cried, jerking up from his luxury pillow. Gretchen remained asleep next to him, somehow snoring just as loud as the storm.

Ron jumped out of his bed and ran to the window, where he saw the windmills burning. He rushed toward the phone, but the electricity went out before he could dial the number. He set the phone down and said to himself, "Years of other people's money, wasted. Now I have to go get more."

Ron sighed and went back to bed. The next morning, he was making salad by candlelight when Ian came down from his room wearing purple, striped pajamas.

"Morning, Father, long night?" Ian asked brightly.

Ron stopped what he was doing. He wasn't about to show weakness to Ian. "Slept like a baby," he replied, and spread some olive oil over his bowl.

"I'm guessing you didn't see what happened, then?" Ian asked, a little surprised.

"I heard. It's a shame. Rebuilding will take months, and prisoners are indeed scarce right now," Ron snickered.

Ian winced in anger at the last part but kept his composure. "Maybe it's a sign," he said instead.

Ron grabbed some tongs and tossed his bowl. "I agree. It's a sign that we aren't doing enough to fight global cooling," he said, and Ian rolled his eyes. "Scientists I paid say that when the world gets cooler, there is an increase in disasters and more violent storms."

"Makes sense," Ian played along.

"So, tomorrow, I will declare a ban on using electricity after six in the evening," Ron stated proudly.

"So, you don't think this is a sign about your actions against my people?" Ian probed. Ron put down his tongs and smiled at his son.

"Ian, I'm not even going to dignify that with a response," he said. "So, if you'd like to have some salad, you're welcome to it. If not, I ask you, respectfully, to please get out of my sight."

Ian didn't need an excuse and left the room, annoyed at Ron's stubbornness. But Backwards Dog had told him to have faith and patience. He could swallow his pride for one day, maybe.

That night, a couple of blocks down the way, the Hugo Black Rondithmuth Courthouse stood quietly over the people outside it. It was empty and dark, no doubt due to the electricity curfew that had been established for a day now.

A lone office worker sat hunched over a desk, typing into a typewriter by candlelight. He didn't really understand what he was typing, but he knew government employees were never fired for failing at their jobs. So, he wasn't sweating it—he had already sweated enough, thank you very much.

He was wearing a dress shirt and dress pants, though he had unbuttoned his shirt to let any cold evening air into the oven of a building. He grabbed a sheet and stamped it, got up, and walked toward a chute with "To Somewhere" written above it. He was about to walk away when he heard a sound coming from the chute. It sounded like rumbling. His first thought was just to walk away and ignore whatever long problem was waiting behind him. But against his better judgment, he crept up to the hole in the chute and peeked in.

He immediately regretted his decision as pages upon pages of government documents flew out, blasting him backward. He lifted his head off the floor and saw that every corner of the room was now filled with whiteness and black ink.

The man stumbled up frantically and went for the door, slipping on the papers covering the ground as if he were walking on an ice rink. He fumbled his way to the door, wrenched it open, and sped off.

Meanwhile, King Ron and Queen Gretchen were eating a salad at dinner time. Ian was nowhere to be found, which was just fine with Ron.

"Does it taste better?" Ron asked Gretchen, who was looking at her spoon as if it were covered in tar.

"If by 'taste better' you mean it tastes less like crap, then no, it doesn't," she replied, sneering.

A frantic knock on the door startled them.

"What the Laffer Curve?" Ron exclaimed.

He got up to answer the door. Gretchen took advantage of the distraction and threw the salad out of the open window. Ron opened the door and found the man from the courthouse panting, out of breath, in his doorway.

"Sir," the man huffed.

Ron waved his hand in dismissal. "Please, son, call me King."

"King Ron. Trouble. Office. Paper. Cuts," the man panted.

Ron scowled at his low-level worker. "Young man, you're talking nonsense," he said. "Take me to wherever the problem is."

The man nodded and led Ron down the few blocks to the courthouse.

Outside the building, people gathered around, looking at the scene coming out of the building. Papers spilled out of the windows. People were being buried under the piles that poured onto the streets.

"Move aside! Make room for the King," a guard shouted to the crowd after spotting the gold crown sparkling under the moonlight.

Ron, who had gathered multiple other guards with him, approached the courthouse, looking up in disbelief at the state of his precious building.

The guard went up to Ron, dumbstruck. "My King, it appears that every government mandate and document has multiplied and is now flying around the whole building," he yelled above the crowd's ruckus. "The building has been evacuated as we speak."

"Never mind the evacuation. How could this have happened?" Ron yelled back.

"No one is sure, my King."

Out of what seemed like the ether, Ian emerged from the crowd and approached them, casually holding a turkey leg.

"Oh, Father, what has happened?" Ian asked flatly, and he took a nice chunk out of the side of the leg.

Ron took a deep breath. Not even this made him willing to give his son the satisfaction.

"It appears that our drawer infrastructure is crumbling, Ian. I will have to create a stamp tax to pay for renovations and bigger drawers," Ron said. The guard next to him raised his eyebrows in surprise. Ron leaned into Ian and whispered, "I'm sure you're not responsible for this, right?"

Ian smirked at him and replied, "I'm only a man, Father."

Ron scowled at him. "Don't patronize me, Ian. You once flooded the city with beans because you didn't want to eat your dinner," Ron barked, making Ian chuckle at that memory.

He gathered himself, though, and simply said, "I assure you, I have nothing to do with this. Maybe this is a sign to release my people before anything else happens."

"Oh, you would like that, wouldn't you, Ian?" Ron accused.

"Well, yeah."

"Well, just like the oil production you want, it's a pipe dream," Ron spat, and smiled at how witty he was.

"We shall see," Ian replied calmly.

"We shall," Ron echoed. He turned his back to Ian and left for the courthouse, hoping to retain all the documents he could.

Ian took another bite of his turkey leg and disappeared back into the crowd. Faith and patience. That's what he had to do.

The following night, two guards were lying down at the top of the guard tower near the large gate that opened into the city. They were dressed in light armor—it was hot, after all—and their silver helmets shone bright under the clear moonlight. The life of a tower guard wasn't an interesting one. Most of their time was spent squinting through clouds of bugs, trying to make out wagons approaching the gate. The rest was sitting around, hoping nothing would show up. Most of the time, nothing did, and it was long days of boring conversations that were always repeated eventually.

"What are you doing after work?" the one guard asked his partner after failing to come up with anything else to talk about.

"I'm going to some dinner at one of the oligarchs' mansions," his partner answered. "My wife wanted to go meet them. She loves the parties."

"Do you like them?" the guard asked, not concealing his judgment.

His partner shrugged. "Not really. Snobby as all get-out. It's like walking into a condescending roast where you're being insulted, but you should be thankful for it," he explained. "And Backwards Dog forbid you touch a shrimp without kneeling and begging. One tends to lose their appetite after that. Still, it's better than this, though."

"Yeah, can't argue with that," the guard replied, and put his arms on the back of his head like a pillow.

"True that," his partner agreed, and stood up to stretch. His eyes suddenly widened as he looked out at the horizon, and he kicked the guard, who was still lying on his back.

"Hey, get up," he said, kicking him in the shin.

The guard sat up. "What? Don't kick me."

"Get up," his partner repeated, and the guard sighed and stood up, muttering to himself. He looked where his partner was staring and dropped the spear that he was gripping; it landed on his partner's foot.

Out on the horizon, as far as the eye could see, were what had to be millions of migrants camped outside the walls. They crowded around each other, and their voices blended together into an endless hum that filled the air like a plane flying overhead. The two guards looked at each other in shock.

"I think I'm going to have to rain check the party."

Ron was awoken by another bang on the door. After angrily walking down the staircase in his robes, he found two watch guards standing awkwardly in his throne room.

After they told him what had happened, Ron angrily paced in front of the two guards, who looked like they would rather be anywhere else, maybe even the party. Gretchen was seated next to Ian, who was sitting in a metal rocking chair in the corner, smirking while eating a donut. She was so angry at the guards for disturbing the season finale of "Weird Crap Faked on Camera" that she had thrown a couple of Ron's little wooden Bolshevik miniatures at them, splintering them to pieces.

After Ron desperately attempted to put them back together, he turned to the two uncomfortable guards. "So, you're saying they just showed up? How did you miss them coming?" he asked angrily.

"My King, I swear that they just seemed to appear out of nowhere," the one guard pleaded.

Ian chuckled in the corner and then choked on his donut. King Ron whipped around and stared at him intensely.

"Is something funny about this?" he asked Ian, who hacked up the last of his donut, then stared coolly back at Ron.

"Well, ignorance is amusing, so yes," Ian replied.

"What do you want us to do, my King?" the other guard interjected.

Ron turned back to the guards, then smiled smugly.

"Well, as much as Ian finds this funny, we can't just leave them out there to die. We will begin to ration the food supply here even more than we already do. Everyone will be able to eat."

"Just not a lot. Everyone must suffer, right? I assume you're exempt from this, of course, right, Father?" Ian prodded.

"A king needs his vitamins to be able to rule effectively," Ron explained.

"Don't forget about the dressing," Ian added, and at that remark, Ron stormed out, slamming the door behind him. Gretchen sighed at Ian and stood up.

"Stop riling him up. I can't keep him from killing you forever," she said.

"Sorry, Mother, it's just so fun," Ian replied. Gretchen rolled her eyes but also gave a small smirk and followed Ron out the door. The two guards stood around awkwardly.

"You are dismissed, guards. Go and be unproductive somewhere else," Ian said.

"Yes, sir," they responded together and clinked their way out of the mansion.

The next morning, outside the courthouse, which still had papers being swept out of it, many people were surrounding small carriages with food piled in the back. Ron entered with some of his guards and approached a grocer, dressed in an apron, who was nervously standing by the carriages, trying to hold the crowd back.

"Is everyone being fed the portions I ordered?" Ron demanded.

"Well, we have run into a little bit of a problem," the grocer said slowly. Ron looked at the grocer with amazement, as if someone could not be so useless anywhere else in the entire world.

"What do you mean by problem?" Ron hissed.

"There isn't enough food to go around, even in the small portions you've set. There are simply too many for us to handle," the grocer exclaimed.

"These are new taxpayers," Ron said, scowling. "We'll make it work."

"But we can't—"

"Then I will find someone who will," Ron said. "Take him away. Why I even let businessmen operate in this city is beyond me."

The guards surrounding Ron grabbed the grocer and took him out of sight. King Ron walked up to the carriages.

"All right, everyone. Ready your plates," he called. "Guards, grab the butter knives and start slicing."

Ian watched on from the distance, wondering how much longer he would have to wait. His followers were not cut out for prison life, especially the man whose name he couldn't pronounce. He knew that he was supposed to be patient, but Ron was being so stubborn, he didn't know who would break first. He looked up to the sky.

"Father, it is time to take it up a notch, please," he pleaded. He waited for an answer but, of course, got none, as expected. You operated on Backwards Dog's time, not the other way around.

That night, Ron walked down the stairs into the kitchen, dressed in his red-starred nightgown. Yawning, he went to the fridge and took out a bowl of salad that had been put there the previous night.

Ron walked to the dining room table and took a seat. He took off the plastic wrap that covered the bowl and looked down into it, ready for his late-night snack. His mouth dropped open when he saw what was inside.

Ian was lying on his bed reading *Free to Choose* by Milton Friedman when he heard Ron's terrified scream from downstairs. Ian looked up at the ceiling of his room.

"Oh, so you've answered?" Ian said, smiling.

Back in the kitchen, Ron was rummaging through the entire fridge, picking things up and looking at them, only to toss them angrily aside. Ian came down the stairs, adjusting his glasses and dressed in a fluffy bathrobe with money patterned on it.

"Father, May Day Spring Cleaning isn't for another six months," Ian said.

Ron looked up and gave Ian a death stare. "Oh, you think this is funny, do you?" Ron snapped. "You've gone too far this time, Ian."

"I haven't a clue what you're talking about."

Ron gave a mad laugh. "Really? So, you can't explain this."

Ron shoved the bowl into Ian's hands. Ian looked into it carefully. The once-fresh salad now sat decayed, its once-crisp greens a murky black mush infested with black maggots that danced over its surface. This time, Ian couldn't contain his chuckle.

"Everything is rotten. Every vegetable in the house. Even the frozen peas for your mother's footbath," Ron yelled.

"Please don't bring that up," Ian replied, but Ron was ignoring his son's nasty sarcasm. He finally sighed and glared at him, looking defeated.

"Well, Ian, I don't know how you did it, but that's it. If you want to experience making your own stupid decisions, have at it."

Ian stopped chuckling and looked at his father, surprised. "And my followers?" he probed.

Ron pondered this for a moment, then replied, "You can have all the traitorous runts you want. Let it be known, though: If you leave, you may never return, and I will be keeping an eye on you."

"You will remain blind, though, I'm sure," Ian replied.

Ron was done with the game, though. "You have until dawn to-morrow," was all he said.

"Understood."

With that, Ian left the kitchen and returned upstairs, leaving Ron amid a pile of black greens. He had gotten what he had wanted, but it did not seem as glorious as he had pictured it. It didn't matter, though. The work had just begun.

Chapter 23:

The Story of Ian's Bearden

Ian entered his room and looked around, taking a last look at his childhood and thinking about what lay ahead. He thought about that succubus incident and the double date he had with John when he was younger. He then thought about what a weird childhood it had been.

He grabbed a backpack and packed his things. He then performed a miracle that enlarged the inside of his backpack so he could pack his books, sheets, pillows, paintings, and other items that he needed.

The door creaked open behind him. Gretchen entered the room, and Ian looked up. She stared at Ian's backpack and the lack of a Harriet Martineau poster on the wall.

"So, it's true," Gretchen said.

"It is," Ian replied, not really knowing what else to say.

"When I gave birth to you, I thought you were a curse that was sent to punish me," Gretchen said.

An awkward silence followed.

Ian raised his eyebrows. "And?"

"What?" she asked blankly, and Ian shook his head. Gretchen sighed. "I did what I was supposed to do. You're here now, so you do what you want. You're not my burden anymore." In a normal world, this response would have shocked Ian, but after so many years, it really didn't bother him anymore.

"Thanks, Mom. You've always been the supportive one," Ian quipped. Gretchen left the room without a response, leaving Ian alone again. He finished packing, took one last look at his childhood home, and then left.

Back in the kitchen, Ron had finally finished clearing out the refrigerator. Gretchen came in. Ron looked up at her, looking exhausted.

"So, you just let him go?" Gretchen asked him accusingly.

Ron slapped a rotten peach on the table, and it made an unappetizing noise. "The entire crop is destroyed. Who knows what he would have done next?" Ron said. He thought for a moment. "Oh my Marx. The wine!" He ran out of the room to the wine cellar, out of sight. Gretchen shook her head, grabbed some oats from the shelf and sat down, thankful that she had that wonderful taste.

Meanwhile, Ian's followers were just waking up from another night in jail. Mark threw off Moof, whose foot was in his face. "Get off of me," Mark cried, and Moof fell to the floor, waking up John and the man whose name Ian couldn't pronounce.

"Why do you do that every night?" asked the man whose name Ian couldn't pronounce.

"It's not my fault I move in my sleep," Moof said, getting off the floor.

"Stop the arguing," John said, rubbing his eyes. "What would our Holy Ian say?"

"He'd say you all smell terrible," Ian said from outside the bars.

John would've jumped out of his shoes if he were wearing any.

"Ian!" John shouted.

"You're here," Mark added.

Ian took a bow. "Yeah, we're leaving the city," he proclaimed. "It's time we fulfilled our promise."

"We're finally becoming a barbershop quintet?" Moof asked.

Ian looked at his follower with disappointment. "Of course we are. But first, we must find a place to settle and establish our own city."

"And where is that?" asked the man whose name Ian couldn't pronounce.

"We have to meet Margaret at the gates of the city," Ian said.

"We'll follow you anywhere, Ian," John said as Ian unlocked the door with the guard's key, and his followers stepped out to freedom.

"Well, you *are* my followers."

"True."

They left the jail and went to the gate, where Margaret was waiting. Next to her stood something that Ian had never seen up close before. It was a camel with a single hump. It looked anxious as it kicked up some sand.

Margaret smiled at Ian. "Hello, Ian, I'd like you to meet Bob," she said.

Ian went up to the camel. "Very nice, but why is he here?" Ian asked.

"Well, he's your ride, of course, Maud'Ian. Every holy figure needs a divine mode of transportation," she said, and Bob licked Ian on the ear. "We found him after he escaped from a circus nearby."

"The circus, huh? I thought King Ron banned those for having clowns," Mark said. "They're 'discriminatory against the uglies,' I believe the order read."

"That's the thing, the circus was abandoned, and all the performers went into hiding. Not long ago they were taking refuge from the Rondithmuth soldiers, and we stumbled upon it," she said. "And that's where we found him. Alone and needing help."

"Well, he'll be a noble steed, I'm sure," Ian said. "We should head out, though. Everyone got what they need?"

After John left to get some toothpaste and say goodbye to Chuck and Nancy, they headed out of the gate and didn't look back. Ian got on top of Bob, who didn't appreciate this and threw him off. "Bad Bob," Margaret said, as Ian got up, dusted himself off, and tried again. After twenty more attempts, he finally was able to stay on Bob, and they were off.

The next few days were long and tiring. The endless desert was no joke. Ian constantly had to conjure some wine into water just to keep the group hydrated. After four days of nonstop riding, though, they finally made it to a forest, which seemed to have not been contaminated for an eternity. Ian and his followers, aside from Margaret, had never seen a forest before. They were unaware that green nature even existed outside of vegetables and cacti. They had heard rumors, but it was more glorious than they could've imagined.

They entered the still woods, walking along a run-down path that must have been a hiking trail in the distant past but was now overtaken by nature. The only sound was the snapping of twigs under their feet.

"Ian, how many times have I told you? Don't read and ride—you're scraping against a tree," John said to Ian, who was scraping against a tree that had drifted near the path while reading *The Virtue of Selfishness*.

"You know, John, most divine followers are supposed to just be in awe and follow. It's in your job description. I'm no fool," Ian retorted.

"Ian," Mark said.

"What?" Ian replied, annoyed and wanting to get back to his book.

"You have sap in your hair."

Ian ignored this, only washing his head when no one was looking, and they continued on their way. The forest seemed to go on forever, much like the cursed desert they had just escaped, only more cramped and buggy. They also appeared to be lost, as his group constantly reminded him.

"Hey, we need to find shelter," the man whose name Ian couldn't pronounce said. Ian was trying to get Bob out of a thicket.

"He's right, Ian. We need to rest," John said.

"And what exactly do you want me to do, John? Just come across a giant cave to stay in?" Ian said before smacking into a sign that had an arrow with the word "Cave" painted on it.

"Was that your holy intervention, Ian?" Moof asked.

"Uh, yes," Ian said, trying to lead Bob back toward where the sign was pointing. "Now, let's head that way. It sounds safe." As they passed by, Moof knocked over the sign and missed the part of the message that said, "Do Not Enter, You Idiot."

They went down the beaten path and eventually approached a large hole that opened into darkness on the side of a hill. It was pitch black and seemed to be endless. Ian picked up the sandwich John had in his hand and tossed it into the cave. It flew out of sight.

"Hmm, seems deep," Ian observed. "Moof, you check it out." Moof looked at Ian, petrified.

"What? Why me? Surely there is someone better," Moof said.

"Yes, and that's why I'm trying to keep them around. Now, show me how committed you are to the movement, and go into that hole and see what's in there," Ian said.

Shaking and grumbling, Moof reluctantly headed into the cave and immediately disappeared into the darkness. They waited an hour, or maybe fifteen minutes. Nobody was really keeping track. Mark and the man whose name Ian couldn't pronounce were playing Go Fish while Margaret was trying to catch rabbits in the field. John was attempting to give Ian a back rub, which Ian resisted until he felt John's magic touch.

"Got any threes?" asked the man whose name Ian couldn't pronounce.

"Um, go fish," Mark said hesitantly, quickly changing out one of the cards.

"Ow, why did you do your finger like that?" Ian said, and he threw off John's arm.

"Sorry, Ian, you seemed tense," John said.

"Because you're digging your finger into my back."

"Guys, should we look for Moof? It's been, um, some amount of time," Margaret pointed out.

Ian, who was looking for a topic change, agreed with her.

"We can't see anything, though," Mark said. Ian saw a lit torch planted near the mouth of the cave and scoffed.

"Now that's just lazy," he said, taking the torch, and they headed inside. Occasionally, he would touch the flame of the torch when it was starting to go out.

"Ian, what are you doing?" John asked, concerned.

"I'm making holy miracles, John. Get with the program. I'm not an idiot," Ian said before burning his hand.

As entropy suggests, though, everything must be more chaotic. So, Ian's flame suddenly went out, and they all crashed into each other. Ian got up, found the glasses that had fallen off of him, and then smacked into something. He heard a loud scream in front of him, causing him to fall over again.

The torch suddenly lit back up, revealing Moof's face. "Oh, it's just you guys. Good, I'm glad to see you," he said, helping Ian back up.

"I wish I could say the same. What did you find?" Ian asked.

Moof shook his head. "Nothing. I couldn't see anything. I think I've been walking in a small circle for who knows how long," he explained.

"Moof, are you sure you're not a cartoon?" Mark asked.

"Well, I guess we'll just see where it ends," Ian said, and he led his group onward.

When they finally reached the end of the cave, it opened into a cozy little corner. Ian held the torch up and saw that right in front of him was a large, curled-up ball of fur.

Moof looked ecstatic. "Wow, it's a giant blanket for us to sleep on."

"And you wonder why Ian sent you in first," Mark said. "It's not a blanket. It's a bear that's sleeping."

Ian held up his hand. "Now, let's not jump to conclusions," he said, picking up a stick from the ground and holding it up.

"Ian, please think and don't poke the bear," John begged.

Ian rolled his eyes. "Ugh, I'm tired of thinking. It's time for action." He began to poke the ball of fur repeatedly. The group behind him held their breath.

"Ian, please," John said through his teeth.

"Shh, John, you don't want to wake up your imaginary bear," Ian mocked. The blob of fur started to stir, though.

"Uh, Ian," Mark said.

"Will you people stop worrying, already? I'm the Holy Ian," Ian said. The blob lifted up, and Ian dropped the stick onto the ground with a thud. The bear lifted its head and stared at Ian, who looked as though someone had walked in on him while in the shower. Towering over him, the bear gave a low growl, and Ian began to slowly step back.

"All right, I think it's time to go now," Ian said to his group. He looked behind him and saw that his followers were no longer behind him. "Ugh, some followers."

He bolted, his torch flailing around wildly. He managed to escape the cave after he saw the daylight and ran out of the hole. He turned around and lifted his hand. The top of the hill collapsed and dirt fell to the ground, blocking the hole into the cave. When it was done, he let out a deep breath.

"Someone should really put a sign up or something," he said. He realized then he was not talking to anyone. He called out for his followers, eventually finding them hiding in trees, rabbit holes, or just standing around on the path. He gathered them together.

"All right, that could've gone better," Ian said.

"You think?" Mark said, and Ian glared at him.

"All right, let's not assign blame here. It's not entirely Moof's fault," Ian said.

"Hey!" Moof yelled.

"I said let's not assign it. So, I think it's time that we come up with a new plan," Ian said. They all nodded and stood in an awkward silence. "So, what do you guys got?" They all looked at him blankly.

"Well, being that you're the holy savior, we'd thought *you'd* have an idea," Mark said.

Ian gave an overdramatic sigh. "Fine, get in here," he said.

They all leaned in. Ian did like the feeling of being listened to. "We need to find a place to settle quickly. We have limited food and supplies," he said.

"But Ian, you said that you have a magic backpack," John said.

"Shut up," Ian snapped, red in the face. "So, we'll split up into teams. We could cover more ground anyway. John and I will go northwest. Mark and Moof will go south."

Mark looked at Moof and sighed.

Ian continued, "And the rest will head southwest. We'll meet in the middle and see what we've found."

"That sounds good, Ian. The rest of the Coffee Party is already out scouting, but we haven't heard anything in a while," Margaret said.

"Well, I guess we'll have to be on the lookout then," Mark said.

Ian nodded in agreement. "Well, it's settled, then. Good luck, everyone. Let's meet up again here in one month."

They all nodded, got together with their partners, and headed off in other directions, unaware of the plans the world had for all of them.

Chapter 24:

The Story of Moof & Mark's Greek Tragedy

Moof and Mark walked through the hills and around the rolling meadows. It had been a long and often contentious journey. It turned out that Mark didn't really care for Moof after having been around him in the middle of nowhere for weeks, and Moof's feelings were mutual.

"Did you eat the bologna last night while I was sleeping?" Mark asked as he rummaged through the bag hanging over his shoulder.

"What? I was hungry," Moof replied.

"Yeah, for my food. Keep your grubby hands off," Mark said, angrily closing his bag.

"I thought it was mine. It was dark," Moof explained. "I'm sorry, Mark."

"Sorry, sorry, sorry. How many times do I have to hear that before it comes true?" Mark asked furiously.

Moof put his hand on his chin and began counting to himself.

"Ugh, why did our savior have to leave me with a fool?" Mark exclaimed, and he angrily shoved the bag back behind him.

"He said that he thought it would be interesting," Moof answered.

"Shut it," Mark cried, and he pushed Moof, causing him to stumble backward.

Moof, who was quite a bit larger than Mark, looked at him, stunned. "Why did you do that?" he asked, rubbing his chest.

"Because I can't take you anymore. I haven't had a peaceful day in weeks because someone has to have a stupid answer for everything," Mark replied coldly.

Moof stumbled up and loomed over Mark. "That's not true. Ian sent me into the cave," he said, and he shoved Mark, who almost lost his balance on the hill.

"Stop shoving me," Mark said, responding in kind. Moof grabbed him, and they wrestled to the ground.

Oblivious to where they were going, they rolled down the hill, falling on top of each other. They eventually slammed onto the bottom of the hill, with Moof crushing Mark. He angrily rolled Moof off him and glared at him irritably.

"You could've killed me, you oaf," Mark cried.

"You started it," Moof replied.

"No, you did."

"No, *you* did."

They began wrestling again. However, they were interrupted by the sound of hooves galloping around them. Looking up, they saw six sets of hooves circling them like a pack of hyenas. They immediately held each other in a panic, with Moof holding Mark's face to his enormous chest. On the back of one horse was a tall man with flowing blonde hair that seemed much too clean for the wild. He was dressed in plated blue armor and smiled down at them.

"Whoa, my friends," he said in a gallant voice. "Do not fight amongst yourselves. You may have your differences, but I assure you, a house divided will surely fall much faster than from outsiders."

Moof looked at the man in confusion, as if he was still processing the third word, but Mark answered him quickly. "Who are you? And why do you look like you've stumbled into the wrong fantasy?" he asked, judgmentally.

The man gave a hearty laugh. "Oh, I think I'm going to like you," he said. "Allow me to introduce myself. I am Solon Monfort, chief officer of the city of Demockcrata."

"Demo what?" Moof asked cluelessly.

"Demockcrata, the city of choice," he replied boldly. "Where all of the people's thoughts are of equal value under the eyes of the maker." Both Moof and Mark smiled.

"Freedom from kings and dictators?" Mark asked, astonished.

"Not a king or dictator in sight, good sir," Monfort replied, pretending to scout the surrounding area just in case.

Smiling, they both stood up. "Can we see it?" Moof asked excitedly, and Monfort continued to smile like he had just seen a baby gorilla cuddle with a puppy. It was quite possible that the man's mouth was actually stuck, but one couldn't be sure.

"Hmm … that is up to the men and women around us," he said, and he looked at the other five, three men and two women, all of whom were wearing the same armor as Monfort. "What do we say to the question of taking our new friends to our fair city? All those in favor raise their hands." All six, including Monfort, raised their hands high in the air. Monfort looked around approvingly. "It is set, then. Come, my friends. You will come with us."

They started to walk next to each other. "Thank you, sir," Mark said, and Moof nodded as well.

"Do not mention it. It is the will of the people. Now, shall we let our friends on our horses, or shall they walk alongside us?" he asked around. "All in favor of horses raise their hands." All six raised their hands. "Good, pick a rider and hop on behind them." Mark hopped on behind Solon, and Moof picked a young woman who didn't look very pleased with his decision.

They were off and headed back toward the base of the hill. As they rode along, a long, flowing river split the green field in half between the tree lines. "Mr. Monfort, do you have anything to eat? I wasn't able to because someone ate my bologna while I was sleeping," he said, glaring at Moof from behind him.

"Well, I do not have any food," Monfort said in front of him. "But Jerry back there has a bologna sandwich."

Jerry, an older man with a short white goatee, looked at Monfort, startled. "All right, who says we give Jerry's sandwich to our new friend Mark? Those in favor, raise their hands," Monfort proclaimed. Everyone but Jerry held their hands high.

"All right, it's settled, then. Jerry, give Mark your sandwich," Monfort said to a sullen Jerry.

Jerry didn't reply, and Monfort shook his head. "Jerry, come on, you know the rules. Your ideas are not above everyone else's," he warned. Jerry threw his sandwich across the way to Mark, who looked at it happily. Jerry sulked in the back for the rest of the trip while Mark enjoyed his meal and Moof enjoyed his company.

"Have you ever been to a cave?" Moof asked the woman escorting him.

"No," she stated.

"Do you want to go to a cave with me?" he asked, hopeful.

"No."

After what seemed like hours, Mark noticed that the meadows were becoming less of the dark, lush green grass with wild blue flowers and more brown and mushy grass with wilted dandelions. The path they were following seemed to somehow get worse the closer they were to the dot in the distance, which Mark assumed had to be the great city that he was constantly hearing about from Monfort.

"You'll be amazed at the wonderful camaraderie of the city. Everyone has an equal part of the government. Every decision the government makes must go through the people first," Monfort had stated. "And please don't grab around the hips. It tickles."

They finally reached a half-finished wall, which was flanked by a rusty-looking gate that made an awful sound when Monfort demanded it be raised. The guards then voted on whether it should be raised. After the unanimous vote, they entered the city.

It seemed all right at first glance. Houses and cottages made of wood and cobblestone lined up and down the gravel road. People wore silk tunics and kirtles, in stark contrast to Mark and Moof's light thawbs and sandals.

At the town's heart stood its centerpiece. Looking over a large, two-story community center was a large statue with a sign nearby: "Here lies the founder of this Democratic Utopia, Fabian Populi." In front of the brick building sat a large bell, which Monfort said was used to summon the people to vote. The bell looked very worn. The city was nothing like Mark and Moof had ever seen before. The days of sandstone buildings were well behind our two companions.

They dismounted, much to the delight of the girl escorting Moof, and were let into the grand community center. Rows and rows of chairs lined every corner of the room. There did not seem to be much room to move.

"Have a seat here," Monfort said, gesturing to a pair of grimy wooden chairs, obviously meant for guests. Monfort left them and went out of the building. They heard the bell clang over and over again.

"Hey, uh, Mark?" Moof asked.

"What?" replied Mark, who was happy to finally have a moment of peace.

"Aren't we supposed to be finding somewhere not civilized so we can settle with Ian?" Moof asked him.

Mark shrugged. "Why would we need to build something from scratch when we might have a perfectly good city right in front of us?" he answered.

"But isn't Ian supposed to lead us to a better world?"

"Ian is supposed to lead his people to a better, free life. He led us out of Rondithmuth. He has accomplished his goal," Mark said. The door opened, and a mob of people began to pour into the room and sit in their seats. "We'll tell Ian later," he said quietly.

Monfort came in and sat near them, close to what appeared to be the central seat. Many people were still wearing what looked like their work clothes.

"Jerry, round up the others who aren't here. This meeting cannot start until everyone has arrived," Monfort ordered Jerry, who was trying to eat the sandwich that he had missed out on earlier.

After half an hour, Jerry returned with two grumpy-looking men dressed in mining gear. "Monfort, we were holding up the mine that we were drilling. We could've missed one vote," one of them said.

"Nothing is more important than expressing your opinions," Monfort said before the sound of a crash rumbled the ground, shaking the chairs. "Now sit down."

After they reluctantly sat down in their seats, Monfort stood up. "Welcome, noble citizens. I'll keep it simple since we were delayed. We have two new friends staying with us. We need to vote on whether they should stay or not. I'll just say that they are good men who respect democracy and its importance for a functioning society. So, those in favor of allowing them to stay, raise your hands."

It was not unanimous. About two-thirds of the room raised their hands. Monfort did a quick count with his finger. "Good, it is agreed that they are allowed to stay. Now, where shall they stay?" he asked the room.

A tiny little old woman struggled out of her chair. "I think they should stay in the nice little bungalow across from my house," she said. "It's a lovely place for couples."

Mark went to protest, but Monfort spoke before he had the chance. "All those in favor of this proposal, raise your hands," he said. Most of the room raised their hands. "Good. Now, the final matter for our new citizens. Who here believes they should be allowed to vote?"

It was close this time. Mark and Moof couldn't tell who had won, though Moof didn't really look like he was entirely paying attention.

"Why should they be able to participate in our sacred duties after they just got here?" asked an irritable man who looked like the kind of person who would deny a baby milk just because.

"Because they are part of the community, and it is their responsibility," a woman from the corner of the room cried out. The crowd mumbled in agreement.

"Well, it seems that it is a yes," Monfort said, attempting to calm the room. "So, Moof and Mark, it will be your responsibility to vote here whenever a meeting is called. You must attend and drop everything you're doing. If you do not attend, the first offense is a month in solitary. The second is banishment forever. We will only provide you with a farewell pie to live off of on your way out. Do you understand?"

They both nodded their heads. "Good," Monfort said. "Meeting adjourned, then. Back to whatever you need to do." The room dispersed, with the miners shoving through and quickly running out down the road.

Mark and Moof headed down with the old woman who had suggested the home across from her place. "It's a lovely little cottage. The last people that were there simply adored it," she said as they marched past the nearly identical-looking homes along the road, each painted a bland color and patched with over-trimmed grass on the small front lawn.

"What happened to the last owners?" Moof asked.

"Oh, they both got very ill," she replied.

"Oh, and they passed then, huh," Mark said.

"Oh no, they missed our vote on the type of potato that would be served at the Democracy Day Celebration. They did not look like they had the appetite to eat the pie on their way out. What with how sick they were," she said, reminiscing. Moof looked at Mark, worried. "Oh, here we are."

They had arrived at one of the identical houses, though this one had a number plate, 76, on the mailbox near the front door. They thanked the woman—by then, they had forgotten her name, so it does not appear in this story—and went inside.

The inside was just as neutral as the outside—nothing terrible, but nothing perfect. All the necessities were there, but they were standard and seemingly of the same crop as all the other furniture they had seen in the city so far. They sat down at the four-sided wooden dining table and each took a breath.

"So, what do you think?" Moof asked Mark, whose tranquility seemed to have been interrupted yet again.

"What about what?" Mark questioned. "It's all we ever wanted, isn't it? No kings, our voice can finally be heard."

"What about Ian?"

"What about him?"

Moof looked at him, startled. "We can't just abandon him. We are his followers," he said.

Mark rubbed the top of his forehead and sighed. "Look, I'd love to go and get Ian. But you heard them. We can't miss a vote. And I'm not about to lose what I've been looking for my whole life over someone who thinks he's better than us," he said.

"But he *is* better than us," Moof pointed out, and Mark stood up.

"If you want to go and risk your life, go ahead. But leave me out of it," he said, and Moof sank into his chair.

"Fine, whatever you say, Mark," Moof replied sheepishly.

For the next two weeks, the moods of our two followers could not have been more different. Monfort had not been exaggerating when he said the city took voting seriously. Mark and Moof were in the middle of their new jobs as sanitation workers when a meeting was called to determine if Sally Winters should get a promotion for her electrician job. Unfortunately for Mark and Moof, this was called right after Moof had broken a pipe in the arsenal basement, and water began to pour everywhere. They had to leave it, though, to vote, and when they came back, the entire basement was flooded up to the ceiling.

Mark brushed it off as a necessary sacrifice, while Moof just wanted dry pants. Mark was all too happy to determine, with the city, the name of the one-way street between Freedom Drive and Bolivar Boulevard. Moof, on the other hand, didn't understand why he was voting whether the police uniforms should be dark blue or sky blue.

They barely spoke to each other outside of work. Mark was far too busy researching any issue that could possibly arise to pay attention to Moof, who was caring less and less as the days went by. On one fateful Thursday afternoon, though, this would change.

Mark was at the water department office readying some votes on permits for the next meeting. "I need you to fax these to the voting office," he told the secretary. She inhaled sharply, and Mark got the message. "Oh, my bad. Those who favor faxing the vote requests to the voting office raise their hands." He and his secretary, the only other person in the room, raised their hands. She smiled, took the papers, and slipped them into the machine.

However, the machine started to smoke after the papers weren't received.

"What is happening?" he asked.

"I asked for a vote on getting a new fax machine to replace this old one, but it was denied at the vote," she replied, backing away. Flames burst out of the machine, melting it and everything around it. The flames started to spread, crawling up the walls like a spider. Mark grabbed his secretary, and they headed toward the door, but the flames blocked their way, trapping them. They went down to their knees and huddled closely, trying not to inhale the smoke that was quickly filling the room.

Meanwhile, Moof was coming back from his lunch. He was just polishing off his bagel when he looked up and saw smoke coming out of his office. Without hesitating, he ran into the building and up the stairs to the third floor, where the office was.

When he arrived, he saw the door blocked by debris and smoke. Covering his mouth and taking a deep breath, he barreled through the door, knocking the debris aside. He saw Mark and his secretary passed out in the corner. He ran over to them, threw the secretary over his back, picked up Mark, and dragged him out of the room.

"Don't worry, Mark, I've got you," he said to a drowsy-looking Mark. He crashed through the fire and debris and back out of the room, which was beginning to leak fire into the hallway.

Moof muscled his way down the stairs, carefully trying not to smack Mark into the stair railing, to no avail. Finally, he hustled out of the front door of the building and placed Mark and the secretary on the ground.

"Mark, are you all right?" he asked his friend.

The secretary came to and sat up, but Mark didn't. "Mark, come on. You've come all this way. It can't end like this," Moof begged, rubbing Mark's sooty face. He raised his hand in the air, preparing to smack him awake, when suddenly Mark coughed and came to. He looked up at his bulky friend and sat up.

"What the stimulus package was that?" Mark asked out loud.

Moof smiled and sighed in relief. "Don't do that again," he said.

"Don't worry, I'll try not to," Mark said, standing up and looking at the scene before him.

"We have to do something," Moof said.

"Agreed, let's get some hoses and call the firehouse, and …"

Before he could finish, Monfort came flying from around the corner. He ran past them, screaming, "Emergency vote now. Emergency vote now."

"But Monfort, we need to act now," Mark said, trying to stop him.

Monfort threw Mark's arm off of him. "There is no time for arguments. Can't you see the fire? We need to vote now," Monfort replied before disappearing out of sight.

Without the opportunity to protest, they headed down to the voting hall.

Inside was pandemonium. People were yelling, panicking, and screaming verbal insults at each other. Monfort banged the gavel in his hand so hard that it split in half.

One person cried out, "We need to use the carpet at the carpet store to put it out."

"No, you idiot, use the drinking water reserve to help throw buckets of water at it," another replied.

"We have hoses, people. Just let us do our jobs," a firefighter pleaded over everyone.

"All right, enough!" yelled Monfort, and the crowd finally went tame. "First, we need a roll call. To make sure everyone is here."

After ten minutes of counting and miscounting, then counting again, the roll call was finally finished, leaving Mark incensed and Moof worried.

"Next, we need to vote on whether or not the fire is an issue," Monfort continued slowly. Every arm shot into the air like a bullet. "All right, now we need to discuss possible solutions to this problem."

"Carpets. Carpets," the woman from earlier shouted.

"Okay, those in favor of carpets raise their hands." Monfort tried to keep calm, but the dam broke again, and people began shouting.

Mark looked outside, where the flames were now engulfing three buildings: the water building, the air filtration building next door, and the geology department. He then looked back at the crowd. Someone had decided to punch the person who had suggested someone stick their carpets somewhere not very ladylike. Mark finally snapped.

"Enough, shut up!" he screamed, quieting the crowd again.

"Thank you, Mark," Monfort said. "Now, let's continue the vote."

"No, you shut up too," Mark continued, prompting gasps from the crowd. Moof looked like he would have stuck his head in some sand if any were available. Mark didn't care, though. "You people are insane. There is a crisis, and you're all wasting your time voting on pointless crap when there are people in this very room who know—and are probably willing to do—exactly what must be done."

"Do not speak to us like you know better. You haven't even been here a month," said the woman who lived across the street from them.

"She's right, and don't think we're not going to hold Moof there accountable for taking action without consulting the community first," Monfort said, glaring at Moof, who went pink.

"What was he supposed to do? Let me die?" Mark said furiously.

"Sacrifices must be made for the sake of democracy," Monfort replied.

"This is not freedom. It is the oppression of the majority," Mark said.

"Then that majority should hold a vote," Monfort said. "All those in favor of banishing Mark and Moof, raise their hands."

"Don't bother. There is no need. We're leaving. We won't be around to watch this place fall into chaos," Mark said, and he grabbed Moof and headed toward the door. "Oh wait, we're already there." He went out, slammed the door, and headed toward the gate, dragging Moof along with him.

"You'll come back," Monfort cried from a window behind them. "You people always do. Do you think freedom is safe out there? This is your sanctuary. You'll never be free again."

With this, Mark turned around. "I follow the Holy Ian, the son of Backwards Dog, and I will not go into that world so quietly," he said, and he kept walking.

"Nice one," Moof said.

"Thanks."

"But Mark?"

"What?"

"I'm hungry. Can we wait for the pie?"

"I don't think we're going to get to that," Mark replied as they passed by the now-burning street.

"Oh, well. Can I have your sandwich, then?"

Mark sighed and took a sandwich from his bag. "At least you asked this time," he said, handing it to him.

They left the city behind, heading out of the unattended gate.

"What was that place, Mark?" Moof asked after they stopped half-way up the hill that, just two weeks prior, they had fallen down together.

"It was a warning, Moof," Mark replied, taking a bite of a tomato—once a mushroom—that Ian had given him.

"A warning of what?" Moof asked.

"A warning that democracy is not perfect and can't be absolute," Mark replied. "Kings and dictators are terrible, but a majority rule is just as bad."

"Ah, that makes sense," Moof said, and with that, they ate in silence. "But Mark?"

"What?"

"What's a democracy?"

After they finished, they continued up the hill, eventually reaching the edge of the woods. They headed through the branches and leaves, where their hope still resided, awaiting them.

Chapter 25:

The Story of the Paradise of Gult Gulch

While Mark and Moof had traveled through the south to find their utopia, Margaret and the man whose name Ian couldn't pronounce were heading northwest, searching for anything that might be serviceable for settlement. After 400 miles, though, nothing but rocky desert seemed to plague the land they had wandered into. They had entered the Worselands, as Margaret had called it. In place of Rondithmuth's sandy wasteland, they found hard, coarse rock where the only life seemed to be the withering twigs that occasionally stuck up out of the ground. Ground that was hard on the feet and ugly on the eyes.

"We have to turn back," said the man whose name Ian couldn't pronounce, after a particularly exhausting hike through the hellscape. "There's nothing in sight."

"We can't turn back. We can't let the Maud'Ian down," Margaret said, and she continued on, ignoring the bunions on her feet.

"We need food and water," he said, trying to keep up, but she didn't answer. She didn't want to waste her energy on an argument. The man whose name Ian couldn't pronounce was all right company, but he was quite the complainer. Even a professional cynic would say that he was sometimes a little much. The man whose name Ian couldn't pronounce didn't hate Margaret. In fact, he liked her company. But she did tend to be stubborn for his taste, often taking his thoughts with a grain of salt.

They continued on their way. After another three days, Margaret was about ready to let the man whose name Ian couldn't pronounce have his way. "Fine, let's just go. We can't go on anymore. There's nothing over—" she said before stopping in her tracks.

They had stumbled on the end of a large cliff that dropped straight down. Looking across, they saw a large gulch carved into the land.

More astounding, though, was what they saw down below. "Are those buildings?" asked the man whose name Ian couldn't pronounce. Sure enough, Margaret saw, down below, a cluster of tiny houses, almost toy-sized from this height. A long road ran down the center of the gulch until it ran into a large steel structure that rose high into the air. Margaret realized that it was a dam, with water thrashing against the other side.

"We have to get down there," she said.

"I'm not jumping," said the man whose name Ian couldn't pronounce, looking down at the bottom of the cliff.

"No, we go around," she said, pointing to a path that headed down around the gap.

"Oh." That was the other thing. Margaret tended to make him look stupid, which was terrible for the mood, especially if one was trying to impress.

They went around and came upon an opening revealing a city reminiscent of an old Western town. Small shops and booths were scattered around small ranch homes. A wooden sign nearby bore the faint image of a transparent hand, its outline just visible in the sun, and read, "Now Entering Gult Gulch."

"What is this place?" asked the man whose name Ian couldn't pronounce. They went down the dirt road into the town, but they were stopped by a gate guarded by two men holding rifles and standing still like two pissed-off statues.

"Do you have a pass for entering Blaken Road?" one of the guards asked them.

"Um, no," said the man whose name Ian couldn't pronounce, confused.

"Then that will be six Blakes, please," the other guard said.

"What?" Margaret asked blankly.

"I don't have time for this. No Blakes or passes, no entry," the guard said. Margaret frowned. "Look, buddy, I don't know who you are, but—" she began, but out of the structure attached to the gate came a tall, tan man in a tight-fitting suit. His toupee fluttered in the wind, and his smile screamed someone who might take candy from a baby.

"What's going on here?" the man said, looking between the guards and Margaret.

"Sir, this woman doesn't have any Blakes or passes. You said no Blakes or passes, no entrance," one of the guards said quickly to the man in the suit, who was obviously an important figure. The man put his hand up, and the guard went silent.

"Calm down," he said, and he went up to Margaret and gave her a large, toothy smile. "And who might you be?"

Margaret blushed. "I'm Margaret, and this is, um, well, you wouldn't be able to pronounce it," she said, pointing to the man whose name Ian couldn't pronounce, though the man appeared to assume that the man whose name Ian couldn't pronounce was just a ghost.

"I'm Victor Blaken. I'm the owner of this road between Carnegie and Quebec and the founder of Free-Flowing Industries, which is in charge of that magnificent dam up there," he said, pointing to the dam that seemed to loom over the town like a god.

"Nice to meet you," Margaret said, her voice slightly higher. The man whose name Ian couldn't pronounce lingered behind her, arms crossed.

"Why don't you allow me to show you around the freest town in the Western Hemisphere?" Blaken asked, putting his arms around her and leading her while the man whose name Ian couldn't pronounce jogged to keep up. "And you must be starving if you've been out in that dreadful world out there."

"Yes, I am," Margaret said, almost frothing at the mouth over the mere mention of the word "food."

Smiling, Blaken handed her a cup of black coffee. "It's good for you. Makes you strong, productive, and self-righteous," Blaken said, and Margaret took a sip. Blaken led them by the barrier and down the dirt road, holding up a different pass at each checkpoint, which seemed to be on every corner.

"Who's in charge here?" asked the man whose name Ian couldn't pronounce, looking for some sort of courthouse or something.

Blaken looked behind and saw what he had assumed was a gnome Margaret had taken with her. He laughed. "Freedom, my sneaky little friend. Freedom," Blaken said. "There is no government to get in the way of our individual liberty."

Margaret looked like she had died and gone to heaven. Blaken noticed this and continued. "Yes, if a service is needed, the private sector will provide it and be better than any government could hope to be," he said.

Margaret buckled almost to her knees, and the man whose name Ian couldn't pronounce caught her, though Blaken helped her up. "I know. It's everything a person who values themselves could dream of," he said. "Here, have another coffee." He handed her another cup, seemingly out of nowhere.

"What about police?" asked the man whose name Ian couldn't pronounce. He couldn't shake the thought of getting mugged.

"Private police force. Here's their business card," Blaken said, handing Margaret a card with a fee scale depending on the level of crime they would be responding to. Margaret looked dreamily at the card, enchanted by the idea of an efficient police force, failing to see the fine print that offered a premium membership perk for wrongful arrests and a two-for-one arrest deal for the next two weeks.

"What about schools?" pressed the man whose name Ian couldn't pronounce.

"Private all the way. If you can afford it, you get the best," Blaken said.

"It's everything I've ever dreamed of," Margaret said, taking in the sights in wonder.

"What happens when you can't afford these essential services?" the man whose name Ian couldn't pronounce asked skeptically.

Blaken looked like he was getting very tired of the gnome's questioning. "Darwin talked about nature taking its course. Survival of the fittest," he said. "If you yourself are capable of prospering, this city will allow you that opportunity."

"Well, it looks fabulous," Margaret said. "Where can we stay?"

"Well, we have some hotel rooms set up for now. I have a beautiful one right next to my place, as a matter of fact," he said. "And I'd be more than willing to lend you some money until I can help you find a job."

"And me?" the man whose name Ian couldn't pronounce asked, feeling incredibly left out.

Blaken seemed to have forgotten he was there again and said, "Oh, I'm sure we can find something for you too."

"Sounds great," Margaret squealed, which made Blaken give another toothy smile.

"Well, let me say, for all of us in this fair town, welcome to Gult Gulch," Blaken said.

Blaken led Margaret to a lovely complex that rose high in the air. Seemingly every apartment was lined with a balcony covered in desert flowers. "Yes, I live on the top floor. You'll start on the lower levels, of course. But in time, I'm sure we can find ways to move you up," Blaken said, eyeing the wonder in Margaret's eyes. It was the most beautiful place she had ever seen, and it wasn't even close. "Well, get settled in. I'll be taking, uh, this guy to his living area."

"Uh, Margaret," the man whose name Ian couldn't pronounce said to his glazed-looking companion. "Can we have a word in private for a moment?"

She came back to reality for a moment and followed him to a secluded spot away from Blaken, who was checking one of his watches.

"What exactly are you doing?" asked the man whose name Ian couldn't pronounce.

"What? Look at this place. It's fabulous," Margaret said.

"How can you trust that man? I mean, look at him. He looks like he's a Bond villain."

"Jealous much?" she said, rolling her eyes. "Don't be mad just because you're threatened by a man who actually made a name for himself."

"That has nothing to do with it," he said, biting his bottom lip. "We are scouting for locations for Ian. Not ourselves."

"Come on, young man, let's get you situated," Blaken said after slinking back over to them. "I'll see you later, Margaret."

As Blaken led the man whose name Ian couldn't pronounce to the other side of town, balconies with flowers quickly turned to broken decks with mold. "Since this is all we have available, I'm afraid you'll have to stay here," Blaken said.

"I could just stay with Margaret," said the man whose name Ian couldn't pronounce, causing Blaken to chuckle in his face.

"No, I think she will be a little too busy for you," Blaken said before leaving the man whose name Ian couldn't pronounce stewing in his run-down room, which made a motel look like a five-star resort. He stomped on some cockroaches and folded the mangled, hole-ridden sheets on his crumbling bed, wondering how this had escalated so quickly.

Margaret, meanwhile, was admiring her giant apartment, which had all the necessary but unnecessary touches one would expect in this type of situation. She ran the sink and the water flowed out smoothly, a major change from Rondithmuth, where it usually slopped out in a hunk and then barely gave a steady drip. She went onto her balcony, admiring the colorful flowers no doubt acquired from a foreign land that she knew nothing of. Looking down at the city, she admired the diversity of the booths and the bustling business happening all around. She smiled, bewildered by the turn of fate.

The next day, she was offered a role as the personal secretary for Blaken at Free-Flowing Industries, whose headquarters was stationed right inside the dam that overlooked the town. The man whose name Ian couldn't pronounce was struggling to find work, which made it hard to afford—or, in this case, bargain for—food.

"These cost 43 Peders," a grocer told him the first day he was there.

"I have these," said the man whose name Ian couldn't pronounce, showing some coins. The grocer carefully observed them and then shook his head.

"No, these are Jos. I only accept Peders," the grocer said.

"Well, I don't have any of those," said the man whose name Ian couldn't pronounce, and he shoved his worthless coins back in his pocket.

"You can exchange your Jos over there," the grocer said, pointing to a stand nearby. "He'll give you Olies for Jos, which can be exchanged across town for Peders."

"I just want some beans," he cried. "I found a leech on my steak yesterday."

"Yeah, Verm's always getting complaints like that. Doesn't wash his hands," the grocer said. "Not much you can do about it, though, other than don't shop there."

"But he owns all the cows in the area," he said.

"Best start your own cow farm, then," the grocer said, shrugging.

The man whose name Ian couldn't pronounce gave up and headed back down the road, only to remember the traffic jams that hit at that hour. Everyone who had forgotten their road passes—or never had them to begin with—were sorting through their pockets, looking for the necessary form of currency.

"Yeah, freedom for whom?" he said, walking away.

He decided to head up to Margaret's place. He hadn't seen her since he had last left her. He was still slightly annoyed at her for throwing him and Ian under the bus but decided a traitorous friend was better than no friend.

"We can have dinner tonight," Margaret had said to him.

"Are you sure? It seems like you're avoiding me."

"No, I've just been busy. I'll see you this evening," she had reassured him.

Margaret, meanwhile, was finishing signing some forms for Blaken in her office. It was cooler in the dam, which was definitely a nice change of pace from the town and, for that matter, Rondithmuth, which was always blistering hot with no shade as King Ron wanted as much sun as possible for the solar panels.

Near the end of her shift, Blaken came in, seemingly out of nowhere. "Good evening, Marge," he said.

"It's Margaret, Mr. Blaken," she said.

"Oh, please, call me Blaken," Blaken said. "Anyway, I need you to stay late and finish this work." He threw a stack of papers on her desk.

"Well, I sort of had plans," she said.

"Oh, Margaret, when I hired you here, I thought you were loyal to your company," he said, sounding hurt.

"I am," she said quickly. "I guess I can stay. It wasn't very important."

"Good," he said, satisfied. "Have a good night, then." He left her to her work.

After three hours, she finally finished her work and left her office. As she walked down the hallway, past a room that was still lit, she heard voices talking.

"Trust me, something is going to happen; it's inevitable," a high-pitched male said.

"The boss said we need to cut our costs. This is the only way to do it," a female voice responded. Listening intensely, Margaret pressed her ear to the door.

"We have to tell someone. We're all in danger," the male voice said.

"No," the female responded, raising her voice. "No one can know anything. This city is a powder keg just waiting to go off."

Margaret's hand slipped off the wall and smacked into the door, causing it to creak.

"What was that?" the male asked, and Margaret secured her belongings and ran down the hallway and outside.

"Must have been the wind," the female said.

"What? There are no windows in here," the male replied. "Just get back to work."

Margaret got home, taking a while since she kept looking over her shoulder the whole way back and fumbling the road pass quite a few times at the road stops. She went to get her keys, fumbling them as well, when something in the bushes moved, and she hit it with a nearby shovel. The bush cried out in pain, and the man whose name Ian couldn't pronounce came out.

"Why did you do that?" he asked, rubbing his head.

"What are you doing hiding in my bushes?" she questioned him after catching her breath.

"Waiting for you," he said, still rubbing his sore head. "We had plans, remember? Or did Blaken talk you out of that too?"

"No, Blaken didn't talk me out of anything. My thoughts are my own," she said, red-faced. "Unlike you, I have a stable job that I need to focus on. So pardon me for forgetting about some dinner reservation."

It was now the man whose name Ian couldn't pronounce who was red in the face. "Well, it must be nice hanging out at the top. Clinking glasses and sharing stories about what new rugs are the talk of the town," he said. "I just thought maybe since we came from the same place, and follow the same people, that we…we …"

"What?"

"Nothing. It doesn't matter. I won't bother you anymore," he said. He brushed off the thistles that were poking at his butt and marched away, fondling his pockets for his toll money. Shaking her head from this unpleasant interaction, Margaret went inside and grabbed some dinner for herself.

Later that night, she went to the balcony with some wine that Blaken had given her as a housewarming gift. She uncorked the bottle and lay back on the cushioned chair on the balcony, with vast, rocky plains on one side and the looming dam on the other. She stretched back, trying to relax.

"Tough night?" a voice said, and she spilled the wine all over herself. She looked across the balcony to the one next door and saw Blaken standing in his robe, smiling his usual smile.

"What? No," she said, wiping herself off.

"Oh, because I couldn't help but hear earlier the, uh, incident between you and your friend," he said.

"Oh, he's not my friend," she said quickly. "He was just a former coworker. Don't you live on the top floor?"

"Oh, this is just my vacation apartment," he said. "But anyway, you're far beyond him, just between you and me. You belong here. Some thrive. Others don't. And the ones who don't … only drag the rest of us down."

After pondering these words, she thought about everything the two of them had been through before they had gotten to this town. How he never seemed to be weak. He was one of Ian's disciples, after all. On the other hand, maybe he was just leaning on Ian, and without him, he would simply flop around like a flounder. "Yeah," she eventually said. "You're right."

"Oh, of course I am," he said, going back to his door before turning around again. "See you around, Margaret."

"Yeah, see you," she said, and he was gone, leaving her to her thoughts.

For the next few weeks, the man whose name Ian couldn't pronounce continued on his quest for a job so he could pay the rent on his shack, to which the landlord was now threatening to send collection goons.

"Please, I can be a sewage cleaner. I'm perfectly qualified," he said during one of his interviews.

"I'm sorry, son, but I can't help you unless you have a recommendation from someone I know or you have a connection to someone in the company," the man interviewing him said.

Knowing this information on hiring practices, he thought about applying for a position as a janitor at Free-Flowing Industries. Still, he couldn't bring himself to ask Margaret or Blaken for a recommendation. For all he knew, they might have refused anyway.

Margaret, meanwhile, was busy with work, though it was getting harder and harder to work when the wall in her office kept buckling. Blaken assured her that they were on it, but that was weeks ago.

One day, she was reviewing and signing off on a report for one of the sections of the dam when she came across something troubling. She went out of her office and knocked on Blaken's door.

"Mr. Blaken, can I have a word?" she asked, and the door opened.

Blaken stood there and smiled, smelling like a weird blend of plastic and bourbon. "Margaret, come on in, have a drink," he said, and Margaret gingerly stepped into his office. He poured black coffee, extra black, into a Styrofoam cup. He handed it to her gently, since the cup felt fragile, then grabbed one himself. He toasted, "To freedom," then took a gulp.

"Mr. Blaken, I looked over those reports you sent me," she said.

"Such a good worker you are, Margaret," he interrupted. "What would I do without you?"

"Thank you. But I was looking over these safety reports."

"Safety reports?" asked Blaken blankly. "That's odd. We aren't supposed to have those."

Margaret didn't know how to respond to that, but she continued, "I see that there are numerous cracks and leaks coming out of the far-right side of the dam. I wanted to know if that's been addressed yet."

Blaken laughed in her face. "Oh, that report," he replied. "Don't worry about that, hun. That turned out to be just some prankster drawing black lines on the walls, which looked like cracks, then dripping some toilet water down the sides."

"Oh, are you sure?"

"Am I sure?" Blaken repeated as if he had never heard of the word "sure" before. "You don't trust me?"

"No, I didn't say that," she said, trying to walk it back.

"I'm not some government, Margaret. We get things done—no red tape. No regulations to hamper our growth."

"That's great and all. But that has nothing to do with cracks and leaks," she said. "This whole town could be at risk if that dam breaks."

"If, Margaret, *if*," he retorted. "And even if that happens, those who are prepared will be fine. And for those who aren't, well, that is the stubborn fallacy of life."

"I see," Margaret said skeptically. "Well, thank you, Mr. Blaken."

"No problem. Happy to clear things up," he said, and she left his office.

She went to use the restroom. When she came out, she accidentally bumped into one of the doors next to her. The door, obviously broken, cracked open. Peeking inside, she saw piles of buckets and paper towels in a makeshift closet. The buckets were labeled "Leak Buckets" in black marker. Hearing footsteps behind her, she quickly shut the door.

She headed down the hallway, which had blank metal walls and doors on either side. She reached the far-right side of the dam. Over in the corner, she saw a row of the same buckets from the closet lined against the wall. She could hear the *drip, drip* of water hitting the bottom of the buckets.

When she moved toward them, she looked at the walls. There were cracks everywhere. The concrete was chipped, with zigzags all over it. One crack ran nearly from top to bottom. She stepped away slowly and ran off, heading out of the building, and looked up. The sound of gushing water crashed against the dam's side. "Oh, Backwards Dog," she said.

She ran to her place, quickly holding up her passes the whole way. When she got in, she went to her phone and dialed a number. The line picked up.

"Hello?" the man whose name Ian couldn't pronounce said on the other line.

"Hey, it's Margaret. We need to talk," she said.

"I don't want to talk. Why don't you go and talk to Blaken since he's so special?"

"I can't. It concerns him," she replied. "Please, both of our lives could be at stake."

"Margaret, have you ever heard of clear stew?"

"No."

"Well, it's a bowl of boiled water with salt in it," he said. "It's all I could afford. Pepper costs extra. So don't talk to me about danger."

"Look, I'm sorry, but you're the only one I can trust right now."

"Really?" he asked, surprised.

"Yes, don't gloat."

"Fine, should I come over?" he asked, trying to hide the smugness now present in his voice.

"No, it's too close to Blaken. Let's meet at your place. Where are you?"

"Well, let's just say if there were tracks in this town, I'd be on the other side of them."

"Okay, I'll see you there," she said, hanging up.

If one listened carefully, another sound could be heard from the side of the dam, amidst the crashing water. It was the sound of cracking.

Chapter 26:

The Story of the Catastrophe of Gult Gulch

Margaret headed down to the shack of the man whose name Ian couldn't pronounce. On her way, she passed by a booth with an old man who looked like he probably belonged more in a fishing novel than in the middle of a libertarian utopia.

"Hey, young lady. I hear you're looking for information on a certain dam," he said, showing his missing front tooth with a chiseled smile.

"Oh, I think I'm fine on my own," Margaret said, a little uneasy.

"Nonsense. I happen to be in the business of selling information," he replied. "If you want to know what stocks are going up, I'm your man. If you want a dossier on what is in that pudding that tastes a little off, I'm your man."

"That's okay. I think I'll just buy a newspaper," she said, and she tried to walk away.

"Newspaper? Hah," he laughed. "There hasn't been a free press here for ten years at least. Blaken and his friends run them all. I'm your only option if you want the truth. And my prices are reasonable, as long as you're discreet."

She hesitated, then finally handed over some Wats. "Thank you. Now, Blaken has run this town for years. Not legally or officially. But he effectively runs all essential operations here, including a private military," he whispered, getting close enough to her that she could smell what she thought was cod, or something, both on his breath and on his clothes. "So, be careful, because he is definitely not going to go away quietly."

"Thank you for the information," she said, flustered at this ominous news.

"Anytime," he said. "Come back, and I'll tell you which firefighters wear boxers and which wear briefs."

With that, she went on her way, thinking about how Blaken was looking worse and worse the more she thought about him. Maybe the old man was just spreading disinformation, but the more she thought about it, the more she considered it unlikely.

"I'm not sure what exactly you're getting at," the man whose name Ian couldn't pronounce said after she had finally reached the shack. It was missing some floorboards, and the sound of something flying around in the attic served as white noise.

"I told you," Margaret said, sounding exasperated. "This place isn't what it seems. Blaken is hiding something."

"Really? The man in the suit and voice straight out of a car salesman's ad, hiding something?" he said, voice dripping with sarcasm. "Color me shocked."

"Are you going to help me or not?" she asked, annoyed that he was rubbing salt in her wound.

"I have a very important job interview," he said, and he grabbed a can of garden chemicals that seemed to be glowing. "So, if you'll excuse me ..."

He opened the door, but she stopped him. "Wait," she said before he could go, and he turned around more quickly than he meant to. "Please, trust me."

He stared at her for a moment, then sighed, becoming yet another victim of doe eyes. "What are we going to do?" he asked.

"We go into the dam tonight and find out the truth."

That night, under the cool Worselands chill, Margaret let the man whose name Ian couldn't pronounce into a side door in the dam building. To her knowledge, everyone had left for the night except for a few guards who patrolled the top of the dam and some of the hallways inside. When the man whose name Ian couldn't pronounce came in, he looked around at the dark, deserted corridors. The sound of dripping water echoed through, and he could smell fresh paint coating the concrete, giving it a glossy look.

"So, where in this definitely not haunted dam are we going?" he asked her.

"In his office—that's where he keeps his files. I need you to keep a lookout," she said as she started leading him down the empty corridor.

"Oh, yes, someone will get one look at me and be scared out of their mind," he said, noticing that he barely made it up to the shelf on the wall they were passing.

"In here," she said when they finally reached a door with a gold-plated sign with Blaken's name. Margaret crept in while he stood guard.

While waiting outside, the man whose name Ian couldn't pronounce wondered what he had done to deserve this. Was this really that one time he threw that stick at that hedgehog when he was young catching up with him? Or that time he and Moof threw ultra-biodegradable toilet paper all over one of the oligarch's mansions? Although, to be fair, it had already disintegrated by morning, so they never ended up noticing.

Interrupting his melodramatic reminiscing, though, he thought he heard footsteps in the distance, and he knocked on the door. "Margaret, hurry up in there," he said.

"I'm almost done," she replied. The footsteps were getting louder.

"Margaret," he said, sweating now.

"Hold on."

The footsteps were right around the corner.

"Now," he said. A light blinded his face. When his eyes adjusted, he saw a guard standing in front of him.

"Who are you? What are you doing here?" the guard ordered.

"Hey, can you get in here and help me finish?" Margaret said from inside, and the guard raised his eyebrows.

"Oh, I see," the guard said, smiling. "Don't worry, I was young once. You kids have fun."

The guard swept past him, and the light disappeared in the distance. Seconds later, Margaret came out with a folder under her arm.

"I got it. Look at this," she said, holding her light to the papers. "There are orders here in the inspection reports in which Blaken said to ignore the suggestions for fixing the cracks in the dam. It says that there is a high probability of the dam breaking."

"We have to warn everybody," he said.

"Warn everybody of what?"

They turned around to see Blaken with a couple of his guards, including the one who had run into the man whose name Ian couldn't pronounce. Blaken smiled, then glanced at the papers in Margaret's hand and shook his head in disappointment.

"Oh, Margaret, you have no idea how much you've hurt me," he said.

"This dam is about to burst," Margaret said angrily, but Blaken only laughed in her face.

"You don't have any proof," he said.

"We have the papers right here," said the man whose name Ian couldn't pronounce, pointing to the papers in Margaret's hand.

"Purely circumstantial," Blaken said dismissively.

"I trusted you, and you took advantage of my need for a better life," she said, a tear forming in her eye. "You're no different than the rest of the dictators."

Her words seemed to hurt Blaken visibly, but he tried to hide it behind another smug smile. "And what are you going to do? Tell the police? I have a premium membership that will have you arrested for trespassing," he said.

"We'll tell the public," Margaret said.

"Please don't use words like that," Blaken said. "We prefer to call them the mass of privates."

The man whose name Ian couldn't pronounce giggled for a moment, but Margaret stared at Blaken, clutching the folder under her arm.

"We'll take our chances with the people," Margaret said, and she grabbed the man whose name Ian couldn't pronounce by the arm and led him out of the building. They headed to Margaret's building and went into her room. "Well, that was a fun night out," the man whose name Ian couldn't pronounce said after they had relaxed. "So, your boyfriend isn't being very nice, is he?"

"We have to warn everyone," she said, ignoring his remarks.

"Oh, and how are we going to do that?" he asked. "You think Blaken will just let us talk our heads off without consequences?"

"Have faith in the people. Our voices will be stronger and louder," she said. He didn't answer, but Margaret could see in his eyes that he was on board.

The next day, when Margaret went to work, Blaken seemed to be avoiding her as much as possible. Every time she passed the dam wall, the cracks seemed to grow an inch, but whenever she mentioned it to Blaken, he said it was just normal wear and tear and the typical look of dams.

Having failed his job interview to be a private firefighter because he needed to have one reference from each of the five wealthiest families in the town, the man whose name Ian couldn't pronounce went out to start getting ready to campaign with Margaret. He bartered for a megaphone by giving up his bedsheets.

The following day, Margaret didn't go to work, and the man whose name Ian couldn't pronounce met her in one of the town's commercial hubs. Margaret was handing out fliers to anybody who would take them. Many were wary but willing to listen. Others not so much, but all had the same question.

"And what can we do about it? We can't stop him. We'd have to buy the dam," one of the merchants selling police subscriptions at his booth said to them. Margaret didn't have a good answer for this.

"They're right," the man whose name Ian couldn't pronounce said after they had stopped to take a break. "It's not like we can shut Blaken down. He has the money to hire a judge who would support him."

Margaret pondered this for a moment. Her thoughts were interrupted, though, by an odd sound.

It sounded like the pop of a tree snapping, though no trees were in the area. Then there was a deep, low crackle, like wood in a fire. Margaret's eyes darted up to the dam—a roar of water burst over the town like a sonic boom. Then she saw it.

A flood of water poured through the now crumbling dam. She could hear the cries of the people around her. She saw that the man whose name Ian couldn't pronounce was looking up, mouth agape.

"Everyone get out of this gulch. Get to higher ground," she yelled, and the chaos began. She grabbed the hand of the man whose name Ian couldn't pronounce, and they tried to avoid the panicking crowd.

"Follow us," she called to the people nearby, and many began fleeing behind them. She could hear waves following them.

"Ah, survival of the fittest is in full effect, huh?" the man whose name Ian couldn't pronounce asked sarcastically.

"Can we not do this while fleeing a flood?" she asked him.

"Oh, the flood your utopia created? How convenient."

They passed a booth where a man was trying to sell off life rafts that Margaret thought looked suspiciously like pool noodles.

"The price of this has quadrupled. I can't afford this," a man said with his family huddled around him.

"These are tough times we're living in," the man at the booth said. "Supplies are scarce. Dams are breaking left and right."

A roadblock at the intersection stopped them as they ran. A group of officers was huddled in a line, blocking their path. "Let us through," said the man whose name Ian couldn't pronounce, trying to squeeze his way through, without success.

One of the officers said, "There is no entrance through this gate unless you are a member of the Blaken Flood Disaster Prevention Society," and he pushed them back. "Find another way."

"Come on," Margaret said, leading the group away. They headed down a small alleyway. "Here, climb the fence, hurry." They helped the people climb over and then followed behind them.

They slipped past the roadblocks, where individuals continued to be denied entry as the hospital refused patients without the Super Pack premium subscription. Eventually, they made it to solid high ground via the path that Margaret and the man whose name Ian couldn't pronounce had traveled just a couple of weeks earlier in wonder. Finally, they turned around to look at the damage that was being done.

The once-nice-looking Western town was now underwater, like a miniature city in a fishbowl. Margaret's balcony was a rooftop pool. The man whose name Ian couldn't pronounce saw his shack floating away, being released from its apparently shoddy foundation. Oddly enough, this didn't really anger him, as he had hated it anyway.

"So, this is what freedom looks like," he said. "I didn't think it would be so ... damp."

The rest of the dam, which was barely holding, gave up and tumbled into the lake of the floating town.

"What are we going to do?" said the bean-barterer from the market.

"We rebuild," shouted a voice from the sky. For a second, the man whose name Ian couldn't pronounce thought that Ian was coming to save him, but, as was the trend lately, he was disappointed to see Blaken dropping down in a helicopter. He jumped off the landing skid and dusted off his suit jacket.

"My friends," he said. "A terrible tragedy has taken place. But remember, with every tragedy, there is an opportunity."

Murmurs, both of interest and anger, migrated across the crowd. Blaken seemed to notice this discontent and said, "Now, I know we are experiencing heightened emotions. We've lost a lot. I myself couldn't save my good dishes that I use when I'm bored." A man next to him whispered into his ear. "Oh, never mind, we've found them."

People started yelling at him and kicking dirt at him, which caused his personal security to push them back. He stepped back, surprised at the gall of these people, but brushed the dirt off his hair and went back to his speech.

"So, I'm happy to announce that I am starting a new town that will be even better than Gult Gulch. I'm calling it Gult Gorge, and we will be offering premium insurance for future floods to our first 100 residents."

The people now seemed to be murmuring again, this time about what a deal that was. Margaret saw this and looked at the remains of the city, which was starting to become more of a lake than a town.

"No," she shouted, and the crowd went silent.

Blaken looked at her and smiled, though the man whose name Ian couldn't pronounce suspected it was not a smile of admiration. "Margaret, please, tell us what's on your mind," Blaken said. She looked at him suspiciously, but continued.

"We can't just start again and make the same mistakes as we did before. We have to have accountability," she said, and Blaken laughed so hard that he choked on himself.

"Accountability? Let me guess: Accountability with a government that oppresses the natural rights of the people in the name of security and then becomes more corrupt and oppressive than the thing that they were said to protect us against—human nature, which is always selfish. So why should we give these selfish people more power?"

The crowd nodded, and even the man whose name Ian couldn't pronounce thought he did have a point. But then Blaken smiled again, and he went back to hating him.

"A government is a necessary evil to try and protect the people's rights from being violated by others," she responded. "And we hold them accountable by getting rid of them if they become corrupt. Or at least we have to try. What *this* is leads only to chaos."

There was a silence. The crowd seemed to be thinking hard. "Well," Blaken said. "I think we'll just have to let these people decide if they want freedom or the oppression of their fellow man. Those who are in favor of freedom come over to me."

Some did—actually, a large chunk, much to Margaret's disappointment. When she looked around, only about twenty people were with her. One of them was her faithful companion.

"Well, the people have spoken, Margaret," Blaken said, quite full of himself. "I would wish you luck, but I know even that won't save you. Come on, my friends, there is a gorge to settle in. I just so happen to own a lovely housing company willing to sell our services for building your new homes."

The crowd headed out of sight, leaving Margaret, the man whose name Ian couldn't pronounce, and the remaining refugees of Gult Gulch.

"Well, shall we head back to Ian?" asked her companion.

She sighed, "Yes, we must tell him we've failed."

"I don't think so," he said, patting her hand. "We've learned something valuable. Freedom is important, and individual rights are essential, but there needs to be something that holds that all together so that all men and women can stay equal as Backwards Dog created them."

"Yeah, I guess it's true—and we have more followers," she said. "You're right, um, guy whose name um…"

"You know, I wouldn't mind actually having a name, even if it's fake," he said.

"Oh, that's good," she said. "Let's see here. What about—Nicp? Name I can't pronounce?"

He thought about it for a moment, then smiled at her. "Nicp. I like that," he said. "Let's go, Margaret."

"All right, Nicp."

They headed back southeast, across the empty, rocky Worselands, through the forest, and back to their Maud'Ian.

However, when they got there, only Mark and Moof were waiting for them.

Ian was nowhere to be found.

Chapter 27:

The Story of Ian vs. Sanity

O ff in the west, far away from the lands that four of his followers had graced with their presence, Ian, with his compatriot John and his other steed Bob, was heading down to the foot of a mountain. Now, John wasn't one to complain, but Ian was.

The journey west had been long and, at minimum, an inconvenience. West of the bony forest near what Ian assumed had once been Pennsylvania, there was just a lot more desert for thousands of miles. Ian started to suspect that whatever had happened thousands of years before was not a pleasant experience. While John walked and took everything in stride, Ian had to deal with Bob the camel, who wasn't cooperating all that much. Ian could respect that, but that didn't make it any less annoying.

Once past the desert, they were greeted with a short stretch of plains. It felt like they had stumbled into a green haven. The fields smelled great, and Bob enjoyed stopping and munching on the grass and flowers for an hour or more. However, green haven or not, they continued on their way west under Ian's direction.

"Call it holy intuition if you will, John," Ian had said after John asked why he wouldn't just settle there. "We must be sure we will be safe to grow without getting in anybody's way."

So, they left the plains and continued west, where a great line of mountains blocked their path. What happened over the mountains is quite a mystery, as Ian wouldn't speak of it and demanded it not be included in his memoir. So, as I was saying, Ian and John were descending the far side of that mysterious mountain.

"Look, Ian, flat grass." John felt the blades through his fingers. "And it's warm. We won't have to sleep in the—"

"I told you not to bring any of that up ever again," Ian snarled, and he hopped off Bob, who was looking exhausted from being a camel trekking up a mountain, and he slipped down some rocks and fell on his butt. He wiped pebbles and muck from his beard, which had grown dense in the past weeks.

"Sorry, Ian. Do you need to eat?" John searched through a fanny pack on his hip. "We still have some leftover food from that one night."

"What part of 'shut up' do you not understand?"

"Look, Ian," John said, pointing to where they had stumbled. Still annoyed at John, Ian was reluctant to look up, but was glad he did.

He saw large, chunky trees that rose high into the air, with fresh blue rivers flowing past them. In the distance, he saw a bay that connected two strips of land.

"It's okay," Ian said.

"Oh, you're never happy," John said.

"John, I thought I told you …" he began, but his voice trailed off when he and John were suddenly thrown up into the air and trapped in a brown net that hung in the air.

"What were you saying?" John asked Ian, whose legs were stuck in one of the loops.

"I thought I told you to shut up, and that point still stands," Ian barked. Suddenly he felt something sharp poking him in the butt. "Oh great, now what?"

He looked down and saw an armored man poking him with a pencil.

"Who goes there?" said the man, who Ian noticed wore a scrunched look on his face through his armored helmet. "Why are you here?"

"We are seeking a place to found a civilization," John said in a muffled voice.

"We're just passing by," Ian contradicted. "We won't bother you. Let us be on our way, and we won't hurt you."

"Oh, hurt me?" the man mocked. "Big talk from a man who apparently farts when he's scared."

"Actually, that was me. Ian's farts are scentless."

"Yes. Yes they are," Ian said proudly.

One of the men behind the one poking Ian leaned in and asked, "Sir, do you reckon these are more of them?" The man paused and thought for a moment. He would've scratched at his scrunched beard if he could reach it.

"Possibly, and we can't take the chance. Cut them down, bag them up, and tie their hands," he said, and Ian and John were cut down, flying to the ground. Brown bags were thrown over them, and their hands were tied behind their backs. A leash was thrown over Bob, who promptly kicked the captor trying to control him.

"You're going to regret this," Ian said sharply as they marched along, though his threat was directed at a big rock.

"Silence, and you will address me as Guardian Richard," said the man who had poked Ian earlier, and he pushed John.

"Hey, what did I do?"

"I heard you smiling," he said, and they marched on.

"Okay, my apologies, Guardian Dick." Ian smirked in his bag.

"Richard, you disrespectful twerp," he snapped.

"I think I touched a nerve," Ian muttered to the rock to his right.

They went down to the shore of the bay, where Ian was temporarily unbagged, and saw in the distance a hill that reached toward the clouds, but not quite touching them. On the top of the hill appeared to be a palace of some sort, though it also reminded Ian of a temple. On the shore, Ian saw a long line of ten-foot canoes.

"Get them in. We sail across Cicero Cove, then we will take them to see the Wise Ones."

"Ooh, the Wise Ones," Ian mocked. "Do you hear that, John? We're about to be lectured."

"As you ought to if you are to be our prisoners at San Filoarchos," he said.

"On what charge?" John demanded.

"That will be determined at your hearing. Move it."

"Filoarchos," Ian repeated. "Sounds like some kind of condition."

"Bag him again," Guardian Dick demanded, and Ian's sight went dark once more.

They sailed slowly across the cove. Ian could smell what he assumed was sewage all around him, though he could not plug his nose. John had passed out from the smell. When they finally landed on the other side, they marched along again. When no one was looking, Ian burned small holes in the bag so he could see, though barely.

He saw that they were headed down a freshly paved road. On either side, he could see fields and people working in them. Most were either dressed in rags or confusingly worded T-shirts. He also saw many people dressed similarly to Dick, who loomed over many of the workers, barking orders or dragging them away.

"I'm starting to feel at home, John," Ian said to his still-passed-out companion.

As they approached the city, instead of farms littering the view, tiny buildings appeared, and Ian could hear the banging of metal and the sound of military exercises.

"All right, I think we can let them see our little slice of justice," Guardian Dick said, and he pulled the bags off them. Ian could now look up and see the hill he had seen earlier, topped by a large, sprawling temple that presided majestically above all else.

As they climbed up, Ian saw great stone columns holding up the temple, which was also made from stone, with gold plates wrapping around various corners and crevices.

They were led through a heavy concrete doorway that creaked open. Inside was dark, with only some torches lining the walls. Ian saw shadows bouncing off the wall, almost like they were dancing, but he couldn't quite make them out. They were in a great hall with marble floors that echoed with each step that the men took toward the room's main attraction.

At the far end of the room stood a large black marble dais. Sitting above them all, on the platform, were seven figures dressed in black, with hoods covering much of their faces.

Ian and John were stopped just in front of them, and one of the Guardians from the temple, dressed much more nicely than the ones who had brought them, began to frisk them.

"We're checking for any weapons," he said, and began rummaging around. Ian lost many of his things, including his belt, paper airplane, and glasses, which made the shadows on the wall, and everything else for that matter, even more confusing.

"Do you mind? My glasses are not dangerous, and if nothing else, they are necessary," Ian said.

"Oh yes, so we'll let you run at the Wise Ones with glass," said the guard, shoving Ian to his knees. "Now sit down and listen. The Wise Ones will now speak."

It took Ian all his might not to respond or turn this joker into a tissue box so he could weep on himself, but he held his tongue. John was just sitting next to Ian and looking beside himself. The man in the center of the clump looking down at them rose, and everything else stopped, all eyes upon him.

"Welcome, young men, to our fair and just city, San Filoarchos," he said in a booming, carrying voice. "What brings you here among this city's great, wise kings?"

"They were found trespassing in our city's outer lands, my Wise One," Guardian Dick proclaimed, and the Wise One smiled at them.

"You there, one who looks constipated, is this true?" he said, staring at John, who indeed looked like he must have had one too many burritos last night.

John simply stuttered without an answer, and the Wise One smiled again and turned his gaze to Ian, who couldn't figure out if this man was just full of himself or completely insane. His bet was on both. "Very well, you there, the one who fails to see the truth without glass, what say you?"

Ian bit his lip, thinking before answering, "We are simple travelers who accidentally crossed into your area."

"Wise One, we have a strong belief that these men are associated with a similar trespassing from that group of rebels from a few weeks ago," Guardian Dick said, living up to his name.

"Do you have proof?" another one from the platform asked.

Guardian Dick opened his mouth, then closed it again without speaking.

"Guardian Richard, do you remember the law that makes this city what it is?" the center one asked.

"The form of the good, Wise One, and justice," Guardian Dick answered.

"Yes, and that means doing what is right and good for the safety of this city," he said.

"Yes, Wise One, that is what I was doing," Guardian Dick argued, but the man in the center was not having it.

"Silence. It is not your job to determine what is good and what isn't. That is our job and ours alone. You are just a Guardian, raised and determined to be strong. But not wise. You are to use force at our discretion, not your own," he bellowed, and the Guardian from the temple smacked Guardian Dick with a staff, buckling him to the ground.

"I'm sorry, Wise One. It won't happen again," Guardian Dick said, still on the ground.

"You are a good defender of our city, Guardian Richard, so banishing you would be unwise and unjust. So, take this as a warning. None more shall come," he said, and he turned back to Ian, who was now very glad he had not said anything earlier.

"Now, you, uh, what is your name?" he asked.

"Ian, son of, uh," Ian said before pausing. "Ron."

"A son of Ron?" he asked, perplexed. "This wouldn't be a King Ron, would it be?"

Ian hesitated. "Uh, yes, do you know him?"

The Wise One laughed, which was very unsettling. "Of course, we are on good terms with King Ron. A good man. Takes our vegetable shipments all the time. And we gave one of our best for his royal court doctor. Do you know a Dr. Fakeci?"

Ian's brain jolted, and his heart followed. "Yes, he's quite a doctor," Ian said as nicely as he could.

"Of course he is, he's a Filoarchosian. We only breed the best," he said. "But enough chitchat. Tell me, Ian, son of Ron, what is justice?"

"Justice?" Ian repeated. "Um, well, I guess justice is a fair treatment that fits one action."

The man smiled through his hood. "Close, but not quite," he said.

"Well, it's more of an opinion than a fact, isn't it?" Ian countered.

"Justice is indeed about fairness. But what about a just society? Justice is about someone's role in society and how they fit," he said.

"I see. And by fitting in, I assume you mean how *you* think people fit in."

"We are the Wise Ones, Ian, son of Ron. We know what is just for society. We are simply concerned with the welfare of the state," he answered.

"And these people that are born into these classes, are they able to jump up and … upgrade?" Ian questioned.

"Well, we are all born to fill our roles," he said.

"How convenient, you just happen to fill the role of king," Ian said, this time failing to hide his snark. The Wise One didn't like this.

"It appears that Guardian Richard was correct in his assessment after all," he said. "I'm sorry, Ian, but you and your friend are unsuitable for this city."

"Oh, poor me," Ian said.

"You will be held in our cells until we decide what shall become of you," he said. "Take them away."

The Guardians grabbed Ian and John and dragged them away.

"You have no idea who you are dealing with," Ian yelled.

"The Philosopher Kings will not be intimidated by simple-minded fools, my friend," the Wise One said, and he sat down. "Enjoy your stay at San Filoarchos."

They were taken out of the temple and blinded by the sunlight. As Ian's eyes adjusted, he saw they were going to a stone structure that again looked dark inside. When they entered, Ian saw cells and makeshift beds in each. They were both placed in the same cell, and its rusty door was slammed behind them. It smelled like a mob had been all hungover at the same time.

"Well, Ian, I would just like to congratulate you on a job well done," John said, throwing a piece of junk from the disgusting ground across the room. "We went off to escape oppression, and you landed us in the exact same situation."

"Do you think I'm not aware of that, John?" Ian replied. "I didn't see you talking your way out of that situation. You just stood there wetting yourself."

"I knew you were looking," John said.

"John, is that you?" a voice from across the room said. Ian and John looked up and saw a rugged man in a dirty tunic full of holes. He had a shaved head that was beginning to grow back, which drew more attention to his eyes, which stuck out.

"Who are you? Your voice sounds familiar," Ian said, looking at the man carefully.

"You probably don't know me, Maud'Ian. I am Tyler, the son of Simon, former leader of the Coffee Party," he said.

"Ah yes, your father was, uh, something," Ian said, struggling to find a word other than douche, scoundrel, or hooligan.

Tyler nodded. "Yes, I am sorry he was so trapped in his own image and went against you," he said. "I have sworn full loyalty to you, Maud'Ian, and that has not waned."

"What are you doing here?" John asked.

"When we were sent out to scout, by Margaret, we went far into the west. Eventually, we made it here, where we were all taken in and thrown in prison for trespassing and 'disturbing the good,'" he said.

"That checks out," John said.

"What are we going to do, Maud'Ian?" Tyler asked.

"I'm thinking. I need time to think."

Ian sat on the ground and began scratching the floor with his nails, filling the room with screeching music. The others apparently did not approve.

"Ian, do you mind?" John asked, trying to cover his ears with his hands, to no avail.

"We all have ways of dealing with our thinking process, John," Ian said, continuing to grind. "I don't criticize your habits."

"What habits?" John asked, genuinely confused. Ian put his hands on his knees as if he'd just been asked to solve a riddle in Morse code.

"Okay, John. How about when you were cooking that, um, stuff in the mountains, you kept humming," he said.

"I hummed because you kept talking about how you—" John said, but Ian cut him off.

"I told you never to mention that," Ian said.

"You brought it up," John replied.

"Just let me think," Ian said finally. He stood up, went to the corner, and stared at the wall.

At that moment, the guards had swapped shifts. Guardian Dick came in and stood by the cell door, trying to avoid eye contact. Ian turned around from whatever he was doing and gave him a stink eye.

"Ah, Guardian Dickmeister, I see you've come to gloat. About what, I'm not sure. You looked like a two-year-old crying on the ground earlier," Ian said, taking great pleasure in belittling him.

"Hey, I didn't ask for this," Guardian Dick said. "I just did what I had to for the city. Though, apparently, they don't care about me." He slid down the bars of the cell, put his hands on his knees, and placed his head on top of them. Ian rolled his eyes and went back to his wall.

John, however, slid over to Guardian Dick. "You're right. You did what you thought was right and good," he said softly. "But I think that's the problem with this place. At the end of the day, you don't matter. Whatever is determined to be for the benefit of everyone else is the only thing that matters."

Guardian Dick shook his head in agreement. "They decide what your fate is when you are only a boy or girl," he said. "You don't get to do what you want. Live how you please. None of that matters, especially to people who call themselves wise and then lock themselves away from the real troubles of everyone else. I wanted to make crosswords for a living."

"Well, it's not too late," John said. "They can't control you if you don't let them."

"The punishment for stepping out of line is the penalty of death. Do you know what they do?" he asked no one. "They just throw you down a giant hole in the middle of town. Who does that to someone?"

Ian turned around from his wall, annoyed at where that conversation was heading. "All right, I've heard enough," he said. "If you want to be useful, fine. But don't waste our time or give us false hope." He went back to his wall again.

"Think about it," John said.

With that, the cell was quiet.

The next day, Ian and John were awoken rudely by a couple of Guardians dragging them out of their cell. "The Wise Ones have requested your presence," one of them said.

"Requested? So, I have a choice in the matter?" Ian asked.

"No, now move along."

"Fine, but know your definitions," Ian said, and once again, they were bagged, and ropes were tied around their hands behind their backs.

The familiar smell of clams and entitlement entered Ian's nostrils as he felt the cold air of the temple. Ian saw Guardian Dick among the crowd of other Guardians, looking uncomfortable. They stopped, and the bags were pulled off, revealing the familiar faces of the Wise Ones, more hooded and off-putting than ever.

The one in the middle of the group stood. "Ian and John, after much reflection and discussion, we have decided that you are to be found guilty of trespassing and endangering the harmony of the city," he announced. "The punishment of these crimes is execution by *Big Deep Hole in the Ground*. Do either of you have anything to say to this?"

Ian frowned. "No," he said. "I don't feel like wasting my breath."

"I'd like you to reconsider," John said.

"Request denied," the Wise One said, smiling smugly. "Very well, Ian. You will now be sent to the hole. Take them."

Guardian Dick stepped forward and bagged them again, but Ian felt the grip of the rope tied around his hands loosen. "Hey, what are you doing?" Ian asked.

"Shh," Guardian Dick hushed. "Wait for my signal. I'm getting you out of here."

Ian smiled in his bag. "Guardian Dick, are we becoming best friends?"

"Don't change my mind," he said, and Ian kept quiet.

They were led out of the temple and walked a few steps before they stopped. Ian heard paper being unrolled and then the Wise One's voice. "Welcome, citizens. Today, we show what happens to people who don't want justice or harmony in this world—people who only think about themselves instead of the good of everybody else."

"Oh, will you just shut up and quit lecturing us," Ian said, not able to take it anymore. He heard nothing and assumed that he had the floor. He turned toward what he believed was a crowd, but it was actually the hole. "You all don't have to listen to them. They may act like they are smart or they have all the answers. But they are putting bags over all your heads. Everything they do lets them have all the power. A farmer's opinion is just as good as a stuck-up guy who just thinks all day."

Ian could feel the tension in the air but continued, "You ask what justice is, you hooded snake oil salesman. Here it is—justice is the fair treatment of others, regardless of where they are placed or held. It is their choices, not their roles that define them. You all can become what you want to be on your own terms."

Just then, a yell erupted, followed by the clashing of pencils, and then screaming. He made his move and, with his freed hands, pulled off the bag that was over his head. He saw the Wise Ones on the ground, knocked out. He saw Guardian Dick, pencil in hand, surrounded by other Guardians.

Guardian Dick looked at Ian and John. "Go," he said, and he tossed John a set of keys. "I'll hold them off."

Both Ian and John stared at him briefly, John smiling, before they ran out of the crowd. They streaked to the Guardian prison. No one was guarding it when they entered. The people of the Coffee Party stood up when they saw them.

"The Maud'Ian has come through again," Tyler said.

John unlocked the cell door. "Actually, it was some guy named Dick," Ian said, and he led them out. They all hurried out of the prison and to the path. Ian knew they had to hurry, as Guardian Dick wouldn't be able to hold all of them off for long. He quickly went to the stable, where he found Bob. Ian untied the rope and tried to hop on, but Bob resisted.

"Come on, Bob. I know we have to talk, but that needs to happen later," Ian said, and he managed to climb on awkwardly.

They got out of the city and made it to the shore of the cove. Ian desperately looked around for a boat, a log, or anything to cross with, but he saw nothing. He heard the Guardians getting closer to them. He looked across the waterway to the land on the other side. The water was deep, and he wasn't about to test whether camels or John could swim. He then held out his hand like he was doing some calculations in his head. He squinted his eyes and rotated his hands in front of him.

"Ian, they're coming," John said, next to him. Ian took a deep breath.

"All right, Backwards Dog. I hope this works," he said, holding up his arms to the cove. Monstrous waves rose in the air and, in front of

Ian, drifted to the left and right. A huge wall of water held on either side, creating a soggy but dry path to the other side. Ian's followers looked up in awe. One man grabbed at his own privates, clearly having peed himself, and his face turned scarlet. John's face, however, seemed to be locked in place.

"Quit drooling and let's go," Ian said. "Move it."

They all gingerly placed their feet on the squishy floor of the cove. Hearing thundering water from either side, they began walking across.

"Oh, this smells like dead fish, Ian," John said, covering his nose.

"Quit complaining," Ian said, riding alongside them, hands still raised in the air as Bob struggled across the squishy ground. A fish from the wall of water fell into a woman's hair and flopped around on her head. She screamed and ran across to the other side.

"My shoes are soaked," Tyler said from up front.

"Apparently, I have a bunch of babies for followers," Ian said to them. "I didn't raise you all to be babies."

"You didn't raise us, Ian," John said, nose still plugged.

Ian ground his teeth. "Cross—the—cove." Seaweed fell in his hair. "Next time, I'm building a bridge."

They finally made it across the cove. Ian turned around and saw the wall beginning to close. He saw a figure in the distance running toward them. He recognized that it was Guardian Dick. Ian tried to hold the wall, but it was almost closed. He saw him on the far shore.

"It's all right, Ian, I'll hold them off," he called out.

"But they'll capture you," Ian yelled back.

"It's all right. It's my own decision. My own choice," he said.

Ian bit his bottom lip. "Thank you," Ian called out. "Guardian … Richard."

"Call me Guardian Dick!" He turned around and held up his pencil. The water had finally given way and was as calm as ever. After taking one last look at Guardian Dick holding his ground, Ian ran after his followers, back into the tall red trees.

They traveled for weeks, crossing the woods and heading back over the mountains, where more acts Ian refused to allow to be talked about apparently occurred. Finally, they made it to the fields of green that Ian and John had discovered earlier. Around ten of the followers, including Tyler, took a liking to it and decided they would settle there, leaving Ian. Ian was gracious, though, after a day. They promised to follow his teachings and be friends and allies whenever they needed each other. Thus, the Ianfee State was founded, with Tyler becoming the democratic leader. Ian and his remaining followers headed back to the woods where he had asked to meet his close companions again. There, he would find a surprise waiting for him.

Meanwhile, back in San Filoarchos, protests and riots were crippling the city. The Wise Ones had called an emergency meeting.

"These ungrateful, uh, ingrates," one of them said. "They have no respect for everything we've done for them."

"We kept them safe," another said. "And now they say they want to be who they choose to be. Like they'd know where to even begin."

The leader of the Wise Ones just took all this in, stewing. "This is all that Ian's doing, rotting our citizens with dangerous notions," he said. "He will pay for what he has done."

"Is that smart, though?" one of them asked him. "When we executed Guardian Dick, that only seemed to make things worse."

He thought for a moment before his eyes widened, and he smiled for the first time in weeks. "Get me a messenger. I need a message sent," he said.

"Where to, Wise One?" one of them asked.

"To King Ron of Rondithmuth," he said. "It's time he knows what his son has been up to."

Chapter 28:

The Story of Ron's Revelation

O n an average dry Wednesday, in the halls of the palace of Rondithmuth, King Ron was holding morning court, which lately consisted of people complaining about things like the lack of diversity in food choices.

"It's about quality, not quantity," he would say to them, but the swine would just say the quality was not good either, which would cause an execution, which was always a terrible thing. There was always so much paperwork. Gretchen sat next to him, looking as irritable as ever. She had somehow managed to shorten her hair to the point of being mistaken for a young boy with prematurely graying hair.

Ron dismissed the court after having had enough of the complaining, and the room emptied like an anthill after a boot, or something.

Gretchen stood and walked up to him. "Ron, I need to speak to you," she said as if she was being asked to jump off a mountain.

"What is it? I have much to do," Ron sighed. "Since Ian left, I have had uprising after uprising. I only have so much pepper spray to spare."

"How is the rescue effort going to get Kimmith out of the well?" she asked.

"It's on the agenda," he replied.

"It's been almost a decade, Ron."

"Why do you suddenly care so much?"

"Because if I have to sit at the table alone, except for you chewing like a cow, I might commit murder," Gretchen said.

"Well, I'm sorry that my healthy diet, which is recommended by five out of ninety doctors, is such an inconvenience for you," he spat back.

"You hired those five doctors, Ron," she said through her teeth.

At this moment of unbelievable marital tension, the palace door creaked open. They both stopped their bickering and looked up. "I really need to oil that," Ron said.

"I'm sure that's ahead of Kimmith on the agenda," Gretchen snarked.

"Just because it's true doesn't mean you've made a point," Ron snapped, trying desperately to ignore her, though it was very difficult with the hot breath on his neck. A man wearing a bronze breastplate entered, riding a horse dressed in bronze as well. He rode up to Ron and hopped off.

"I have a message for King Ron," he said, taking out a rolled-up piece of parchment. "It's a message from San Filoarchos."

"Ah, probably about those delayed beet shipments." Ron took the parchment. He skimmed it, then read it again, eyes flying over the page. He then looked up.

"What is the meaning of this?" Ron asked through gritted teeth.

"Um, don't shoot the messenger," the messenger said worriedly.

"I'll do what I want," Ron said. "Guards, seize him." The guards around Ron began to grab the messenger.

"Wait, it's true, King Ron, what they say," the messenger said, pleading.

"It says that they detained a man who was found trespassing, and they claim it was my son, Ian," Ron said, skimming the message again just to be sure. "He was found to be disturbing the peace before escaping."

"That sounds about right," Gretchen said from the side, and she grabbed some tea and began to sip casually.

"Not only that, Gretchen," Ron said, getting redder in the face. "They claim it is my responsibility, since he is my son, and that if I don't find him and bring him to justice, all trade agreements between us will be nullified."

The messenger frantically shook his head in agreement.

"This is blackmail," Ron said, getting right in his face. "Just because he's my son doesn't make him my problem."

"The Wise Ones feel differently," the messenger said.

"Oh, The Wise Ones said it. That changes things," Ron replied mockingly. "Those pompous, so-called philosophers have looked down on me ever since we came into contact."

Gretchen cleared her throat. "Well, Ron, what if he wasn't, uh, your son?" Gretchen asked, though her voice seemed to be struggling to get the words out. Ron slowly turned to look at her.

"What did you say?" Ron asked, with terrifying calmness.

"Um, Ian may not be your ... son," Gretchen said softly. Ron shook his head as if a bee was in his ear. "Well, remember how, kind of, a surprise it was when Ian was born?"

"Yes, you said it was a fluke," Ron said, trying to remain calm.

"Well, that's true," she said. "He's the son of someone else. And it hasn't happened since, right?"

Ron looked like he had just been told that air was an illusion. "What did you do?" he said.

The messenger looked very uncomfortably at the other guards, who looked just as uncomfortable and had taken an interest in the floor.

Gretchen finally just said it. "He's the son of Backwards Dog. To restore sanity and freedom to the land," she said sheepishly. "His words, not mine."

Ron stared blankly at her for a moment, then began to laugh hysterically. He laughed, and laughed some more. Then, just when you thought he would be done, he laughed again.

"Oh, Gretch," he finally said, though his eyes reminded Gretchen of the maniac who had been running naked through the town earlier that year. "You really got me this time."

"So, you believe me?" she asked uncertainly.

"Sure, Gretchen. Why not? It makes sense. Heh, beans," Ron said. He began thinking of all the times Ian had done something that, indeed, wasn't what someone would call ordinary.

"It's not like it matters, though," he said. "Those Philosopher Kings won't believe us. They'll think we're just making excuses, right?" He looked at the messenger, who furiously shook his head in agreement.

"Good. So, it doesn't matter. We still need to fetch your son and make him answer for what he's done," Ron said, and Gretchen looked down and nodded. "Excellent. Guards, send out some scouts to look for Ian and his little posse. Bring them all in alive."

"Yes, Your Grace," one of the guards replied, and he sped out of the room. Ron turned to the messenger, who looked like he had fallen into a giant spider's web.

"You tell your kings we'll have their criminal as soon as possible and that King Ron sends his regards," he said to him. The messenger himself ran out of the room, clinking away in his armor.

Ron sat in his throne chair, grabbed some carrot juice, and sipped it. He then grabbed a bowl of Caesar's salad and silently ate, not making eye contact with Gretchen, who was staring at her husband, very uneasy. She silently left the room, leaving Ron to enjoy his salad in peace.

Back in the woods, where Ian had arranged the meeting place, Ian led John and the rest of his new followers through the thick branches and twigs. He reached a small clearing that looked familiar.

He recognized the face sitting on a rock across the way. It was the man whose name Ian couldn't pronounce. Ian ran up and hugged him after his friend yelped in surprise, alerting Mark, Moof, and Margaret to Ian's presence. Ian smiled at them all.

"You're late," Margaret said.

"Well, good to see you too," Ian said. "Glad to see you all safe and not dead."

"It wasn't for lack of trying," Mark said, and he shook Ian's hand. They all gathered around Ian to greet him.

"Well, we have a lot to talk about." He sat on a rock that proved uncomfortable, though he was too prideful to stand and change his seat. "So, Mark and Moof, tell me what happened."

Mark told the tale of them visiting Demockcrata, while Moof made gestures next to him. After they were done, Ian rested his chin on his fist, thinking.

"Interesting," he said. "So, you're saying that even though everyone had a say, their direct votes kept them from actually functioning properly?"

"Yes, and that they tended to function on the tyranny of the majority," Mark said, and Moof made some hand motion that ... well, Ian couldn't really tell what he was doing. "But it was productive, and we learned a lot together."

Ian nodded and turned to Margaret and the man whose name he couldn't pronounce. "All right, tell me what you guys found," he said.

"By the way, my name is Nicp now," Nicp said to Ian, who stared at him blankly.

"Nicp? Why does it sound like you're trying to spit at me?" Ian asked bluntly.

"It's my identity," he replied.

"Well, I liked it better the other way, but whatever. Go on."

Margaret and Nicp told them the tragic tale of Gult Gulch. "And so, I took in all the refugees that wanted to come," Margaret said. "I just wish I had figured out that something was wrong from the start."

Nicp patted her on the back. "It's not your fault. Blaken was very convincing and had excellent teeth," he said.

"Yes, he's right," Ian said. "When one hasn't seen it before, unabashed freedom looks so appealing. But it is no longer freedom when one's rights are attacked by someone else."

Ian sat up, his butt very sore. "All right, we may not have found a place to settle, but I think we've figured out something just as important," Ian said. "We have figured out what kind of society we all want to live in."

They all nodded in agreement. "So, first off, we obviously prefer maximizing individual rights as much as possible and having the government only as big as necessary."

"What does that look like?" Nicp asked.

"Likely a separation-of-powers deal, with a legislative branch and an executive with limited powers, and a court to check both branches."

"How much say should the people have in specific decisions?" Margaret asked.

"They shouldn't vote on everything. That takes too much time," Mark answered.

"Correct, they should vote for their legislators and the president. The court can be decided by the other two," Ian concurred.

"What about rights?" Moof asked. "How much should they have?"

"Well, if we take lessons from that Gult Gulch, then we should give people enough to where they are not stepping on the rights of others. We can get into specifics later," Ian said.

They talked long into the night, coming up with ideas from everyone, forming the government they had always dreamed of. After collapsing to sleep during the discussion of filibusters, Ian awoke to a sharp pain in his hip. He rolled over and saw a gaggle of men standing over him, one sticking a spear in Ian's side. He rolled up quickly and raised his hands, ready to turn someone into a peanut butter sandwich.

"Easy now, easy," warned one of the guards, who looked like the commander. "Don't want anything happening to your little ducklings."

Ian looked around and saw all his followers held and restrained, spears pointing around them. He also saw Bob, his camel, making whining noises as he openly resisted being tied up and pulled back. Ian put his arms down slowly. Hanging by one of the carriages was a red flag with the hammer and tongs of Rondithmuth.

"That's better," the commander said. "Now, here's what's going to happen. You're going to come with us peacefully, along with your pathetic posse, or you'll be starting your little rebellion from scratch."

"What does he want?" Ian asked coldly. "I was told by King Ron that I could leave in peace. I took my father for a fool, but not a liar."

"You'll just have to talk to Daddy yourself," the commander said. "Now move it. Hands on your head. I know what you're capable of."

Ian reluctantly followed his instructions and was slowly escorted into a carriage with a cage on the back. His followers were piled in with him. "Not a sound," the commander said. "All right, they're all in. Let's get this cargo back by sundown."

With a crack of the whip, they were rolling through the forest. After much time of waiting and seeing the nothing of the arid desert, Ian looked up to an oh-so-familiar sight. The sandstone building and walls now seemed to mock him openly.

Home sweet home. They rolled up to the gates and were let in. They halted and the commander came to the back of the carriage and opened it.

"Ian only," he said. "Take the rest to the jail cells. They'll be used as collateral. Just in case our holy man gets any funny notions."

Ian was led into the city, the stench of which had somehow gotten worse. There seemed to be more people on the street and fewer shops. Most shops that were still there had makeshift plywood nailed to the front doors. He passed by the well, where he could hear the distinct sound of scraping off the bottom of a metal can. The well was now graffitied with murals of King Ron. Most were not exactly of the positive variety. One that caught Ian's eye showed King Ron playing Ring Around the Rosie with a bunch of stick figures that Ian recognized, from their facelifts, as the ruling oligarchs.

He was led across the town, where the palace finally came into sight. Interestingly, this was about the only place that had not changed in the last month or so. The same dull sandstone, creaky door, and worn windows were plastered around the outside of the palace. He was led to the door to the throne room.

"The king awaits," the guard said, shoving Ian forward. Ian took a mental note of what he wanted to do to the guard when he was done with this charade. He took a deep breath and pushed open the door.

Chapter 29:

The Story of Ian's Trials

Ian entered the palace, where a row of guards lined the path to the throne. King Ron hunched over wearily beneath a long red robe, while Ian's mother looked on from the side of the room, visibly uncomfortable.

"Hey, Mom," Ian said. "Like every other young person, I've come back home." Not to Ian's surprise, he received no response. Ian continued down the row of guards.

"Ah, welcome back, Ian, my son," Ron called out to him. "Or should I call you the Holy Ian?"

"That does have a nice ring to it. Thanks, Dad," Ian said, refusing to let Ron have the last quip. He continued down the row.

"Oh, haven't you heard, Ian?" Ron asked sarcastically. "Apparently, your mother has been a very busy girl behind my back."

"Ron, you have a fireworks show and a circus running behind your back."

"I banned circuses, and you know it," Ron snapped back. "How long, though, have you been working to undermine me? Three years? Ten? Since you were born?"

"Does it matter?" Ian asked.

"No, I suppose not," Ron said. "Let's get down to business. You have been a bad boy, Ian. Causing chaos across the continent. You have caused a beautiful city to riot and rebel in the great state of San Filoarchos. And I just received word of protests and chaos from some other states down south."

"I guess I have been busy," Ian said, smiling a little.

"I thought I made myself clear that you were to settle and leave my city alone. But like the cockroaches you all are, I just can't seem to get rid of you," Ron said. "You are crippling my economy and my fridge."

"It's not my fault you have terrible choices in friends," Ian replied.

"Ian, will you just shut up," Gretchen cried from the corner of the room.

Ian turned around and glared at her. She glared back. He then saw her subtly mouth some words to him. Ron didn't seem to notice.

"Listen to your mother, Ian," Ron warned.

Ian looked at her, then Ron, then back to his mother. He then shook his head at her and turned to his stepfather. "You've known me my whole life, Ron. Do you really think I'm going to back down?" he said. Ron sat up in his chair. "You did teach me one thing. Never back down, no matter how many people say you're being stupid or stubborn."

Ron looked around his room as many people avoided his gaze. "As touched as I am, Ian, I have no choice but to arrest you and send you back to San Filoarchos," Ron said.

Ian's eyes flickered. "I am the son of Backwards Dog, and I will not be leaving here without my freedom," he said, raising his voice.

"And what exactly are you going to do to stop it?" Ron smirked. Ian took one final look at his mother, who nodded to him silently.

"I don't know," Ian said as if he were reading from a dinner menu. "Maybe I'll blow up this city."

Through the audible gasps around the room, he saw his mother fighting to hold in a smile. The guards held their weapons to Ian. Ron gripped his throne hard, his knuckles very white.

"Oh, that got your attention, didn't it?" Ian boasted. The crowd was now in a frenzy. Men were bumping into each other, and the women accidentally knocked off one another's absurdly tall white wigs.

Ron stood up and yelled to Ian, "You wouldn't dare, you pugnacious excuse for a son."

Ian was actually taken aback at Ron's decent comeback but hid it behind a wide smile. "Come on, Ron, you know I would." He saw Ron think about this for a moment, weighing the evidence. He saw him then seem to conclude that Ian was indeed correct.

"You would be killing yourself and all your followers," Ron said, still slightly puzzled and unsure if Ian was serious or not.

"That's the sacrifice I'm willing to make to send a message that the world no longer accepts your way of thinking," Ian replied darkly.

"You're bluffing," Ron said, still unsure.

"Try me," Ian said, eyes narrowed. He raised his arms into the air slowly. The room was in full panic. Ron stepped down from the steps to his throne, sweating heavily. Gretchen's face was as red as an infected strawberry, and her mouth was puffing wildly.

Ron went up to Ian with a big, sadistic smile across his face. Ian, his hands still raised, locked eyes with him. Ron locked back, seeing his reflection in Ian's glasses.

"Ian, be reasonable," he said into Ian's ear, his voice trembling like a lawn mower that wouldn't start.

"Let's talk in private, my king," Ian replied, eyes still locked.

Ron looked around his palace. "Everybody out," he yelled, though the still panicky crowd didn't seem to hear or care.

A guard nearby said to him, "My liege, I think that—"

"Now!" Ron yelled again, even louder, and the room finally began to clear quite quickly.

"Even you, Mother," Ian said to Gretchen, still sitting in her chair, desperately shifting around uncomfortably. She finally seemed to fall back to Earth and glanced up at Ian and Ron, who were looking down at her. She looked around at the now almost empty room, stood up, and slowly walked out behind the rest. Once the final person in the wheelchair had left, the door closed, and the deafening silence hovered around Ian and Ron. Ian's arms had grown tired from having his hands raised in the air, so he let them down.

Ron nodded approvingly. "Now, let's discuss this like adults." He glided over to a table in the corner. Ian followed, smelling the scent of ranch dressing next to a wooden salad bowl.

Ron sat down and helped himself to a plate. "Have a plate, Ian."

"No, I don't think so, Ron." Ian sat across from him, and Ron frowned.

"Don't be rude." Ron scooted the plate over to him, but Ian pushed it back.

"No, Ron, let's just talk business."

Ron stared at Ian blankly for a moment, surprised but also annoyed. "Fine. Now, what do you want?" he asked, his pride hurt.

"The same as before," Ian said simply. "I want a place for my people."

"What do you want me to do, Ian?" Ron asked, beside himself. "I have a major military power, and our leading food exporter, blackmailing me to turn you in. How is that fair to me? To the city you were born in?"

Ian thought for a moment, without a good response. "Ron, I don't know what to tell you. It's not fair. But I promise if you let me go, I'll be more than willing to trade with you."

Ron pondered Ian's proposal. "That sounds all right for the trade part of this problem," he said. "But we still have the matter of the military strength of San Filoarchos, which is not one to take lightly."

"We sign a military pact, then," Ian replied. "One wouldn't want to mess with the son of Backwards Dog and his stepfather."

Ron smiled a little. "True, true," he said. "But what should I tell them?"

Ian leaned back in his chair a little too much and almost fell backward. After he regained his balance and the chair smacked back on the floor, he said, "The kings of San Filoarchos are not as powerful as they make themselves out to be. You said it yourself, they have their own problems to worry about."

"And why should I trust you?" Ron asked. "We don't exactly share viewpoints except that your mother can be a pain."

"The people of Rondithmuth are my people, too," Ian said. "I wouldn't do anything that would put them in direct danger, and I think deep down you feel the same way."

Ron sat there a moment, chewing the lettuce in his mouth, first on his right side, then migrating it to the left. Finally, he gulped it down as Ian looked at him intently. "Very well, Ian," Ron finally said. "I will arrange the release of your followers and reject the kings out west."

"Thank you," Ian said.

"Also," Ron continued. "So you don't stick your toes where you could cause trouble, I'm going to tell you a place you could settle."

"Really?" Ian said, eyebrows raised in disbelief.

"There is a place way down south in the swamps we call Flodia," Ron said. "Whoever came up with a name like that has some sort of learning disability, probably acquired at a private school. But it's out of the way, and people should leave you alone and let you frolic as you please."

Ian sat in his chair, thinking, which usually made him slink. When he was done, his eyes were creeping just above the table, and he said, "All right, Ron, I think we have ourselves a deal." He scooted back up to his chair and reached halfway across the table. Ron reluctantly stretched across to meet him and shook his hand.

Just then, the door behind Ian burst open, and he turned around to see his mother coming in, looking furious and desperate. "Now you listen here, mister," she screeched, sticking her finger at Ian. "You are going to stand down and negotiate with your stepfather, or so help me Backwards Dog."

Ron raised his hand calmly and said, "It's all right, Gretchen, we've already agreed to an arrangement. It's all over."

Gretchen looked like she had encountered a squirrel that had learned to juggle. She just stood glaring at the both of them in disbelief. "Well, uh, okay then," she finally mustered, annoyed that her character development was being cut short.

Ron stood up from his chair and again looked at Ian. "Ian, your party will be waiting at the gate," he said. "I wish you luck and look forward to hearing from you."

"Thanks, Ron," Ian said, passing by Gretchen, who continued to glare at him. He looked at her, nodded, and then went toward the door.

As Ian left the palace behind him, he was escorted to the gate. He went past the well, where he stopped and looked down. He saw Kimmith banging a can of coconuts back and forth off the wall like she was playing racquetball. He closed his eyes and held out his arm. A long wooden ladder appeared next to the well. He grabbed it and slid it down the hole. He heard Kimmith jump in surprise, and he walked away.

He made it to the gate, where John, Margaret, Mark, Moof, Nicp, and Bob, his camel, were waiting for him. "Well, Ian, I'm getting a little sick of prison. Can I take a break from that?" John asked, patting Ian on the back.

"Yes, John, I think this is the start of a wonderful, uh, something or other," Ian said, trailing off as his group looked at him with confusion.

"Any news?" Margaret asked.

"We have a place we could potentially settle," Ian finally said, giving up on sounding wise.

"Well, that's good. We should check it out," Mark said.

"Where is it?" Margaret asked.

"In the deep southy swamp," Ian said. "King Ron recommended it."

"That sounds about right," Nicp said.

"Yep, but it's the best we got. So, lady and gentlemen …" Ian attempted to climb smoothly onto Bob, who backed up and almost caused him to slide off. "Let's ride, or in your case, walk."

With a loud grunt from Bob and Ian, they were off into the vast emptiness of the desert again, restless and ready to finally settle.

The journey south was not very notable. Ian let Mark and Moof lead the way since they had gone south earlier, but Mark and Moof had different directions for where to go, and they got lost several times after Ian had decided that Mark was likely the best one to follow. After they finally got back on track, they realized Moof had been right about where to go. Moof got to eat the last can of bologna that night.

As they traveled further south, the trees became greener, and the dirt became wetter. The group became closer than ever, and Ian declared that they would all be known as his Iapostles. John took exception to it, but that didn't really matter. The trees were becoming denser, and the path was beginning to fade and become incoherent. Ian realized when he looked around that they had reached their destination.

"Well, this is a bit of a fixer-upper," John said. Ian was struggling to maintain his balance as Bob angrily stomped around and splashed everyone with the swamp water they were standing in. Mark looked around, disgusted, and Moof looked around, confused. Margaret's face was making wrinkly movements, which meant she was thinking hard, likely trying to find a bright side, though she was obviously having some trouble finding any. Nicp seemed to be the only one who didn't look disappointed, likely because he hadn't had high expectations anyway.

Ron hadn't been lying about the area being a swamp. The trees were overgrown in the muddy water, with the branches seeming to do weird knots into each other. It smelled terrible, like when Moof had overeaten the bologna. When they weren't standing on water, they were slushing in wet, sticky mud. The swamp seemed to be trying to hold them hostage, as Ian had gotten them turned around. It certainly was not a desert, though, and they were all thankful for that.

"Well, get used to it, guys and gal. It's going to be your home," Ian said, hopping off Bob and splashing in the dirty water before immediately climbing back on. "This spot right here, to be exact."

"Something moved over there in the water," Nicp cried, pointing to a bubbling trickle in the water a few yards away.

"Moof, go see what that was," Ian ordered, and Moof went white in the face.

"But Ian, it could be dangerous," Moof protested.

"Hence me not going. Now, hurry up before it disappears," Ian replied, and Moof slowly scooted his way to the area where the water was doing maneuvers.

"Ian, do we have any gallons of bug spray?" Mark asked, swatting at his arm, hand, neck, face, elbow, belly button, leg, other leg, knee, and toe. "These bugs are ridiculous."

"No, John used it up," Ian said.

"Why?" Mark asked him, annoyed.

"Ian told me he likes the scent while he's sleeping," John replied.

Ian glared at him. "Don't make me regret making you my chief of staff and personal assistant," Ian said, and John backed away and kept quiet.

Ian's glasses fogged up due to the humidity, but he managed to order them to set up a temporary camp. "All right, we should wake up early tomorrow," Margaret said while putting up her tent. "We need to start building some structures, including homes and a central place for the government."

"Define 'early,'" Ian said, yawning. "Tell you what, you can be the city's secretary of development since you are so keen on it."

"I'd be happy to," Margaret replied.

"Yeah, I bet you are," Ian said.

"Yes, I am," Margaret reassured him.

"Uh huh," Ian said.

"Ugh, this place is so ugly," Mark said, continuing to swat at his body.

"You know, for being my secretary of science and technology, you don't seem to love nature very much," Ian said.

"I don't like nature when it's actively trying to kill me," Mark replied.

"When is it not trying to kill us?" Nicp asked irritably.

"Objectively, though, it is an ugly place," Margaret said, looking around.

It was an ugly place; no doubt Ron had done this intentionally, but it did seem oddly fitting. Ian thought there was potential and a sturdy foundation under the surface. John then pointed out that the ground under the swamp was very unstable and would be hard to build on, so

Ian sent John to hunt for a blueberry-strawberry hybrid that he had said he was hankering for.

"Ian, your grass sandwich is ready," Margaret said an hour later to Ian, who was sitting on a lawn chair he had stolen from Ron's rooftop. He looked at the thing that had no right calling itself food, and laughed.

"Yeah, I'm not eating that. I got these instead," he said, holding up some chicken wings. "Conjured them myself."

"Can we have some?" she asked.

"No," Ian said after faking thinking about it. "It builds character. I'm not holding favorites here."

Moof suddenly ran in from the low shrubs surrounding their camp, panting, hands on his knees, lacking bottoms. "Scared the thing that was in there away," Moof said. "Then it scared me."

"But it's gone?" Ian asked.

"For now, it thinks my pants were me, so it took off," Moof replied.

John then came out from another stash of shrubs. "Sorry, Ian, I couldn't find any of the hybrids you were looking for," he said. "Will you settle for these Pond-Apples?" Ian looked at what he thought looked like an apple with chicken pox.

"No, I do not," Ian replied. "Now, if you all don't mind, I have a powerful moment I need to tend to."

Ian firmly pushed a stick into the ground and tied a piece of brown cloth from John's pants to it. Ian stood proudly beside the stick, almost posing, as it began sinking into the mud.

"I hereby declare this place to be Orlandoish. The beacon of hope and freedom throughout the land," he proclaimed. His followers cheered and clapped their hands.

"Backwards Dog bless this land," Margaret said. "And Backwards Dog bless our Holy Ian."

"Hear, hear," Ian said. He conjured some beer into all his followers' hands, and they toasted. Ian looked at them all proudly. He did have a pretty good group of Iapostles.

As he surveyed the untouched slog that would be his new home, he couldn't help but smile. He looked up at the sky, where he knew Backwards Dog was watching down on him, hopefully proudly. That was enough reminiscing, though. There was work to be done. After bed, of course though, and after breakfast, and not before eleven in the morning.

www.ingramcontent.com/pod-product-compliance
Lightning Source LLC
Chambersburg PA
CBHW020606110726
47899CB00002B/399